On the Way
to a
Wedding

Also by Suzanne Stengl

*~ ghosts, angels, and
more than simple coincidence ~*

The Ghost and Christie McFee

Angel Wings

The Thurston Heirloom

~ sweet contemporary romance series ~

Something Old
Something New

A Wedding and a White Christmas

On the Way to a Wedding

Wedding Bell Blues

On the Way to a Wedding

Something Old, Something New
Book 2

Suzanne Stengl

ISBN 978-0-9880365-6-7

This is a work of fiction. All of the characters, organizations, and events portrayed in this novel are either products of the author's imagination or are used fictitiously.

Publisher: Mya & Angus
Cover Design: Tammy Seidick

Second Edition

www.suzannestengl.com

MYA & ANGUS

To my dad,

Ted Carron

Chapter One

A poodle.

He could hardly believe it. She wanted a poodle—a *toy* poodle. Something cute to go with the executive floor plan, the European wall-mounted oven and the cork floors.

Ryder Michael O'Callaghan stared out the windshield, blindly following the road. Their last argument had been about a dog.

He heard the static on the radio and tapped the button, silencing the noise. The music had slowly died out, and he hadn't noticed. An hour ago, he'd left the highway and turned south onto the secondary road, which had gradually changed from tar cover to dusty gravel.

Gravel with a lot of potholes, still not repaired after the spring thaw, but in reasonably good condition, considering where he was. And, so far, he was lucky. The weather held. The storm had not come.

The road wound up into the foothills, with the spruce and the aspen shading what little was left of the ebbing twilight. He'd caught a glimpse of the moon as he'd left the highway. A pale thin crescent slipping behind the mountains. The sun had set half an hour ago. The days were growing longer. Almost a week into June and the partnership agreement still sat on his desk.

Annoyance pushed into his thoughts and he tried to forget about it. The engine rumbled as he shifted into a lower gear. Rounding the next sharp corner, he saw a car. In the ditch.

It was an old Honda Prelude, probably the last year they made them. Dust-covered . . . red, maybe. Hard to tell in the failing light. Faded red. He pulled off the road, hit the flashers and then turned off the ignition.

The Prelude's engine was still running and, judging by the noise, the muffler had broken off. A tinge of adrenaline, and irritation, flashed through him. He didn't need any more problems. He had enough of his own.

The accident must have just happened. He scanned the area and saw someone sitting on the ground by the side of the road, about ten feet beyond the loudly idling car.

A woman. Long dark hair fell over her face as she bent forward, both hands pressed to the ground beside her, like she was holding herself up. Her arms were bare, her right knee drawn up, left leg stretched out in front of her. She might be hurt but at least she was sitting up.

He got out of his truck and stepped into the cool air. It still smelled thick, and heavy, the way it had in Calgary, as the world hovered on the verge of rain.

She didn't notice him because the sputter of her car's engine and the roar of the broken muffler masked all other sound. Her head rested on her knee and her hair still shielded her face. She wore jeans and running shoes and a sleeveless pink top.

Not warm enough. He shook his head. Some people didn't know how to dress for the backcountry.

When he reached her car, he smelled the exhaust and a whiff of gas. The Prelude's door was open and the air bag drooped over the steering wheel. The front tire tilted out. The bead on the tire was broken and the tire sagged over the rim.

She must have hit hard.

He looked ahead to where she sat, still unaware of him.

Watching her, he reached inside the car and turned off the engine.

Silence echoed over the forest. She lifted her head and looked at him. Her mouth dropped open as she stared at him like he was a ghost who'd materialized out of the trees. In the background, a low rumble of thunder mumbled.

"You all right?"

She didn't answer. Instead, she waited two seconds, then twisted to her right side and stood. She took a step with her left leg—away from him—and fell down.

Terrific.

A moment later, she was trying to sit up again. He knelt beside her, taking hold of her icy shoulders, hoping he could get her to lie down. But she tensed, grabbed his forearms, and tried to push him away.

He hadn't expected that. "Lie still," he said, holding tighter. "You're hurt. You shouldn't move."

She bit his hand.

A sharp pain registered on his knuckle and he jerked his hands away. So much for this approach. Apparently, she didn't want to lie still.

She was twisting onto her side again, trying to sit up. He took hold of her face with both hands so she couldn't bite him again, but she gripped his wrists. Her hands were freezing.

"It's okay. It's okay." He tried to make his voice sound calm. He could do calm. "I won't hurt you," he said. "Let me check if anything's broken."

She looked dazed, but she must have decided to listen to him. Letting go of his wrists, she sank back on the grass. A light breeze stirred in the trees.

He was still holding her head. She didn't look like she'd bite him again, so he moved his fingers over her skull. No lumps or bumps there. No cuts on her face.

She shivered. Her right elbow was scraped, probably

from falling a minute ago.

He ran his hand over her other arm. Not injured. He pressed over her ribs, avoiding her breasts. Nothing broken there. Then he skimmed his hands down her left leg to her ankle—which was sprained, or broken—and swelling up in her running shoe. Her other leg was all right. But her ankle was a problem.

He could wrap it with a tensor, then get her to the ER in Canmore. Except Canmore was two hours away. Longer, driving in the dark down this road. Even longer if it started to rain.

He'd better check her head again, to be certain. As he reached for her, she raised her hand, palm out. She sure was spooky. "Just checking for bumps," he said.

She held her hand up a second longer, then slowly dropped it to her side.

Letting his fingers slip into her hair again, he noticed how soft it was. Thick, and long, and soft. *Right.* He took his hands away. "I think it's just your ankle."

"I'll be okay," she said, in a quiet voice.

"I'm sure you will." She was shaking. She needed a coat.

"I'm late," she said, sitting up. "Thank you for stopping. I've got to be going."

The incongruence of her polite *thank you* clanged in his mind. He sat back on his heels. "Where were you going?"

She'd say the Kananaskis Lodge. This tourist had decided to take a shortcut through the forestry reserve and had somehow made a wrong turn.

"Kalispell."

Kalispell? Across the border? Into Montana? "You're taking the long way around, aren't you?"

She didn't answer.

Did she have *any* idea where she was? Detouring through here on the way to Kalispell proved she was lost.

"Don't move," he said. "I'll get my first aid kit."

"I—I'm all right." She was trying to get to her knees again.

Maybe she was in shock, but he hoped not. He didn't need to deal with a shocky female. He could tensor her ankle. Hysteria, he wasn't so good at. The breeze picked up and a blast of cooler air shot out of the trees.

He left her sitting on the ground and walked to his truck. As he pulled the red box out from under the front seat, he noticed his jacket, crumpled next to the passenger door. He grabbed it and turned around.

She was standing on her good foot, wobbling slightly, and looking weak. The breeze rippled over her, blowing her hair across her face.

"I've got to be going," she said. And then, "They're expecting me."

Somehow, he doubted that. "Who?"

"My—my friends. My family," she said. A slight pause, and then, "My father."

He didn't think so. Probably no one was expecting her. She was saying that, hoping she could make him think she'd be missed. On top of everything else, she was worried about *him*.

Did he look that scary? He rubbed a hand over his chin, feeling the coarse stubble. He hadn't shaved in three days. He should have shaved before he'd left town.

"So, I'll get going now." She hopped on her right foot in the direction of her car.

He gave her points for stamina, if not brains. She hadn't seen the front tire yet. All she had to do was look.

He walked closer and she stopped moving. She stood straight—perfectly straight—like she was trying to make herself taller.

He sighed. She *was* afraid of him, no surprise there. She was alone in the backcountry with a rough-looking stranger and she was injured.

Concerned, he set the box on the ground, then wrapped his jacket around her shoulders. He could feel her trembling, but was that from the cold? Or from fear?

Probably some of both. He released her shoulders. Maybe he should have held her for a moment to steady her, but that would make her more scared.

"Before you try to drive off, how about you let me bandage that with a tensor?"

She looked pale in the dying light. She was probably pale anyway, and very fair for a brunette.

A quick glance at her foot, then at her car, and then at him. Lifting her hand, she hesitated. Then she wrapped her cold fingers around his wrist and lowered herself to the ground.

He knelt in front of her and started to undo the lace of her running shoe. Gray Adidas with pink stripes. She sucked in a breath and pressed her hands on the ground, bracing.

Better get it over with. He slipped off the shoe as gently as possible. Her eyes were tearing up. Hard to tell what color her eyes were in the twilight. Green, maybe.

He peeled off her sock and got a good look at her foot.

It was sprained. Possibly broken. Already a purple tint spread over her skin. He shifted himself onto the ground, sitting cross-legged in front of her. Resting her foot on his ankle, he reached in the first aid box for the tensor bandage. He wrapped and secured her ankle, and in a few minutes at least that problem was dealt with.

"Thanks," she said. "That feels better."

Anything would feel better. She was hugging his coat around herself and still shaking. The breeze had washed the mugginess out of the air, making it cold.

"I'd better be going," she repeated, as she let go of his coat, picked up her sock and stuffed it inside her shoe.

Was she having trouble seeing? It wasn't that dark yet. "Can you see your car?"

"Oh. Of course. But—" She looked at the car, then back at him. "You could help me get it out of the ditch?"

He almost laughed, but stopped himself. It'd been a long time since he'd met someone so clueless. "Uh . . . that car isn't going anywhere."

She stared at him like she didn't believe him, and set her running shoe back on the ground.

"Look at the front tire."

She did. "Oh," she said. "Is that very bad?"

Very bad? Was he really having this conversation? "Looks like you've got some major damage to your suspension." Probably snapped an upper control arm.

She bit her lip and squeezed her eyes shut. Then she clutched the edges of his jacket and pulled it tighter. "I've got a cell," she said, looking at the ground. "I'll call a tow truck." She started to get up.

He put his hands on her shoulders, stilling her. "Not out here."

She met his eyes then. Yes, her eyes were green.

"No coverage out here."

She looked away from him, staring at the grass and the budding fireweed, and probably trying to figure out what options she had.

He'd better get her in his truck. "Don't move." He got up off the ground, retrieved the first aid box and walked over to her car.

"What are you doing?"

Reaching inside her car, he pulled the keys from the ignition. Her purse—a sensible navy blue canvas bag—rested on the floor. The bag tilted on edge, recovering from its slam into the dash.

He turned back to her. "You've got stuff in your trunk?"

"Why?" she asked.

"Because I'm transferring your luggage—and you—to my truck."

A few thin drops of rain sprayed through the tense air. He slipped her keys into his pocket and then reached for her purse. Better move her first, and then her luggage.

He opened the passenger door of the truck, dropped her purse and the first aid box on the floor, and walked back to where she was sitting. Then he picked up her running shoe, set it in her lap, and scooped her up in his arms.

She immediately shuddered and tried to squirm out of his hold. "What are you—"

"Look, will you loosen up? I'm getting you out of the rain. Don't make this any harder than it needs to be."

She stopped struggling, but she didn't relax. She was squeezing her hands around her running shoe, gripping it like a lifeline.

He deposited her on the passenger seat and then went back to her trunk. Two red suitcases—one larger, one smaller. He stowed them on the backseat floor with his duffel bag. Then he returned to her car. There was something in her backseat. Something big and white. And fluffy.

A dress? He touched the fabric, felt its silkiness, and then swung it out of the car.

A wedding dress? Was she on her way to her wedding? Was that the hurry?

The wind puffed up the dress, furling it like a flag. Didn't women put these things in protective packaging? He carried the dress over to her open door.

"Is this a wedding dress?" He held it up by its bodice, holding out the full skirt with his other hand. The wind rippled the soft material.

"I'm getting married," she said, raising her chin.

"I'm getting married, too," he answered, folding the dress in half. He tossed it on the backseat just as the dark sky started dumping its rain.

I really am getting married, she thought. She hadn't lied about that. She just wasn't getting married anytime soon. But, someday, she would marry.

She shivered and hugged the jacket around herself. A navy blue jacket, with a nylon shell and a fleece lining. It didn't feel right taking his jacket. *He* needed his jacket.

Except—she watched him getting into the driver's seat—he was tall, with dark hair, and he didn't seem like he was cold. She felt a moment of dizziness, and then it went away.

He was wearing a denim shirt with the sleeves rolled up to his elbows. And jeans. And heavy work boots—dark brown leather, with laces. The rain pinged on the windshield.

His truck was . . . nice. Fairly new, and clean. The heater was blowing hot air. He'd turned the heater on as soon as he'd started the motor.

"Do up your seat belt."

Yes. Seat belt. The buckle was wedged into the seat, shiny new, reflecting the weak light. Where was the rest of the seat belt? As she turned to look for it, she felt him reach over her, felt his arm brush her shoulder. He smelled like the trees at the side of the road. The spruce trees. Then she felt the seat belt pull across her chest and heard it click securely.

He didn't need to do that. She would have found it.

Now he was turning the truck around on the narrow road. Spinning it in a neat circle, dipping into the ditch on the other side and pulling back onto the road, all in one motion. The wipers swung back and forth, back and forth.

A steady beat accompanying the tap of rain on the roof.

"Where are we going?"

"I'm taking you to the ER. In Canmore."

"Canmore?"

"It's two—"

"I know where it is. I don't need to go to the ER."

"You're going."

"No. I'm not. You can take me to a gas station. I'll get a tow truck to—"

A long flash of lightning rippled and the trees appeared, silhouetted, swinging limbs. Thunder boomed, closer this time, a giant hand clap. Rain sloshed over the windshield.

She glanced across at him. Who was he? And why was he here?

She didn't need to go to the ER. It was a sprain. It didn't even hurt very much. Now.

Now that he'd wrapped her ankle with the tensor bandage. She squeezed the running shoe in her lap and closed her eyes. And she saw Isabelle, standing by the chalkboard, pulling down a map.

Just go this way, dear. Not many people know about this route.

And neither, it seemed, did Isabelle. Isabelle may have lived out here for a hundred years—well, maybe not that long, she wasn't that old, but—

The truck lurched. She grabbed the armrest and braced, but it was only a pothole. Another pothole. She let go of her breath, forcing herself to breathe. She was all right. Nothing had happened.

"You can drop me at a gas station," she said, again.

He didn't answer, didn't seem to hear her. He was watching the road, squinting through the windshield, steering with one hand and shifting gears with the other. And ignoring her, like everyone else ignored her.

She couldn't go back, not to that. There had to be a way out of this. And oh God, what if Greg was following her?

Her chest tightened. The truck bounced over another pothole and she gripped the armrest.

No, she thought, trying to reassure herself. He wouldn't come down this road. He'd take the main route. But—

What if he was worried? What if he started phoning hospitals? Emergency rooms?

A wave of dizziness washed over her. She pressed her fingers to her temples and closed her eyes.

And saw herself whirling down a twisting out-of-control roller coaster ride. When she opened her eyes, the spinning stopped. Had she hit her head?

She couldn't remember. It had happened so fast.

The heater blasted warmth into the truck, but she was cold. To be warmer, she put her arms in the sleeves of the jacket. The fleece lining smelled like wood, or spice.

Like him. The sleeves covered her hands. Her fingers were cold. Her toes were cold. Her head hurt. Her ears were ringing.

Even if she got him to leave her at a gas station, then what? She didn't have a car anymore. And the gas station would report the accident. That wouldn't be good.

Another wave of dizziness. That woozy feeling.

They were bumping back the way she'd come. Rain pounded over the truck, banging on the roof, flooding over the windshield. The drought is over, she thought, remembering the long dusty days of spring.

He slowed down, and switched the wipers to high speed. But even on high, they had trouble keeping up. He slowed down, even more. And then he came to a full stop.

"What's wrong?"

"We're not going to get through this."

Suddenly he was turning the truck around. This time it slipped on the side of the road, like the wheels were spinning. He moved the gear shift, the wheels caught and they were back on the road, turned around.

Wouldn't it be worse? Going farther along this road? And how come this road was so bad? Isabelle had said to take the first turnoff after Spray Trail.

But what if she'd missed that turnoff and taken a different one? What if she wasn't even on the right road? Where did this road go?

Nowhere, she thought. *I'm going nowhere.*

"We're moving to higher ground," he said, reading her mind. "Lower down, it could wash out. It's not a great road—they close it in the winter. And it doesn't get much traffic anyway." He paused. "Most people don't come down here."

In other words, he was wondering what she was doing here, in the middle of . . . nowhere.

"What are you doing here?"

A good question. "I may have been on the wrong road."

This, he thought, as he shifted to a lower gear, *is a royal mess.*

This was not the way Ryder Michael O'Callaghan ran things. This was supposed to be a break. A time to sort out the new partnership deal. A time to sort out the confusion of the wedding. A time to put the whole poodle thing into perspective.

And now he was stuck with this bimbo who couldn't even tell her tire was flat. He sighed. Never mind flat. It was snapped off the axle.

The headlights gleamed over the wet gravel. Rain pelted the truck. And the temperature had dropped. The way his luck was going, this would turn to hail. A chunk of gravel loosened from the edge of the road and dropped into the stream of water flowing through the ditch. At least they were moving to higher ground.

The cabin was supposed to be at the end of this road. But how much farther? And why did it have to rain now? Sure, they needed rain. But why now, for *Chrissake?*

He gripped the steering wheel and downshifted, scanning the roadside, looking for the lane. They had to be close. Pro had told him—

Good. There it was. The headlights lit up the crooked sign, nailed to a tree. *Road's Inn*, it said. This road's end. The sign was flapping in the wind.

He drove into a short lane and reached a narrow parking area sprinkled with gravel. According to Pro, the cabin was about a hundred feet ahead at the end of a curving dirt path.

Rain hammered over the truck, like it was trying to get inside.

They could just stay put. Stay in the truck. Because if they tried to make it to the cabin, they were going to get wet. Never mind wet. They were going to get soaked.

But—he turned to look at her—she wasn't getting any warmer. Even with the heater on full, her teeth were still chattering. If they could get to the cabin, he could build a fire. And there would be food in the cabin. He could make her something hot to drink.

"Why are we stopped?"

"We're here."

"Where is here?"

"There's a cabin here."

"There is?" She stared out the windshield, trying to see.

So they'd get wet, and cold. But they couldn't stay in the truck all night. He turned off the ignition, darkness closed over them, and he reached under his seat.

For his flashlight.

Except it wasn't *his* flashlight. One of his framers had borrowed his mag light, again, and left this piece of crap. He pulled out the small replacement light and clicked it on.

A pale orange glow.

"*Christ.*"

"What's the matter?"

Everything. The rain. The road. This unexpected passenger. The wedding, his business. His life.

"Slide over here."

"What?"

He took her running shoe out of her hands and set it on the dash.

"You can't c-carry me. Not far."

"You can't walk."

She picked up her shoe. "I c-can sort of w-walk," she said, teeth chattering. She reached in her shoe, pulled the sock out and shoved it into the pocket of his jacket. Then she started to ease the running shoe over her bandaged foot.

With eyes squeezed shut, she tugged the shoe on. Then she loosely tied the lace. Her hands were shaking and her fingers looked stiff.

"Okay, I—I'm ready."

Stamina, if nothing else. No brains, but stamina. He felt for the key in his pocket. Pro had given him the key. This was one of Pro's stupider ideas.

"Do you want your c-coat?"

"No. I'll get wet anyway."

"But—"

"Come on." He opened the door and stepped into the cold dark rain. The icy wet stung his face and neck. In a few seconds his clothes were drenched.

She slid down next to him, standing on her right foot. Her arm, tentative at first, slipped around his waist. Her hair blew over his throat and her body trembled against his.

He shoved the truck door and heard it latch. Then he put his right arm around her and aimed the dying flashlight at the cabin. He could barely see the path.

With the rain and the wind slamming into his skin, the mud sucked at his boots. She kept her arm around his waist, trying to put weight on her damaged foot.

At least she tried for about three steps. With each step, her whole body tensed. She let herself lean on him more and hopped with her good foot. The mud was slippery. She'd have fallen if he hadn't been holding her.

They were halfway up the path, when he noticed the mud wasn't sucking him down anymore. He pointed the flashlight onto the path where the dim light showed interlocking bricks, covered in puddles. Rain peppered the bricks and the wind blasted waves over the water.

And then the flashlight oozed out.

"This way," she said.

They stumbled forward, in the direction of the cabin. At least he could tell he was walking on bricks. All he had to do was follow the bricks, because he couldn't see a damn thing.

He could hear though. The wind, the trees swinging and creaking, and . . . water flowing, like they were near a stream?

The eavestroughs. He could hear them, overflowing, splashing down.

"Here," she said, pausing.

He felt with his boot until he touched the first step of the porch directly in front of him.

He pulled her tighter against his side and lifted her up the step, and then up a second step. And then they were on the porch and out of the rain.

A loud clap of thunder boomed overhead at the same time as a wavering flash of lightning illuminated the door in front of him. Then all was dark again.

Holding the dead flashlight in his hand, he reached for the door and touched it, tapping, metal against wood. Then, still holding the useless light, he felt with the backs of his fingers for the door knob, and the key hole.

There.

She had both her arms around him, like she was trying to press against his warmth. She was shivering, a lot, and she wasn't letting go.

"I have to get the key," he said.

She seemed to realize what she was doing, let go of him and moved away. He heard her, hopping toward the door.

Carefully, he took the key out of his jeans pocket and found the lock again. This key had better work.

It did. The wind swung the door open, crashing it inside. He reached out to find her, touched her shoulder, and waited for her to hop into the entrance. Then he followed her inside and closed the door, pushing against the wind. The latch snicked shut and they were out of the storm, standing in complete darkness. His clothes were soaked, and he was cold, and tired, and hungry.

He could hear her, close by, her teeth chattering. Outside, the wind howled and the trees shrieked, but in here, the cabin was quiet and still. Except for the sound of her teeth chattering, and his heart pounding in his ears.

He leaned his forehead against the door, took a deep breath and slowly let it out.

She must have found a chair near the door. He could hear it scraping over the floor as she moved it.

"Is there a table beside you?" Maybe she could feel it. She couldn't see any better than he could.

She didn't say anything. Then he heard the rasp of a match and saw the sudden flare of its light. She'd found the matches that Pro had said would be on the table by the door. There was a lantern too. But her hand was shaking so badly the match flickered out.

Maybe he should have left her in the truck until he'd got the fire started.

"I'll do it," he said. He felt her ice cold hand take his as she pressed the match box into his palm.

"This way," she said, setting the box so it was right side up. He felt for a match, lit it, and saw her taking the globe off the lantern. She slid the lantern toward him, he lit the wick, and then took the globe out of her hands and replaced it.

Soft light filled the cold room. Outside, the storm raged, emphasizing the quiet of the cabin. But the lantern's light made it seem—somehow—warmer.

And maybe if he'd left her in the truck, she wouldn't have stayed.

She was sitting on the chair beside the table. Her hair was dripping and the jacket she was wearing, his jacket, was plastered to her shivering body. She bent down, and with fumbling fingers she started untying her running shoe. The one on her injured foot. She carefully pulled off the muddy shoe and dropped it on the floor. Then she started plucking at the laces on her other shoe.

Good idea. He got out of his own boots. They were covered in mud but his feet were dry—the only part of him that *was* dry.

He picked up the matches from the table and walked across the room to the stove, a pot-bellied black stove with a glass door. Next to it, a brass bin held wood and kindling and old, yellowed newspapers. Kneeling in front of the stove, he clinked the door open and—*thank you Pro*—wood and kindling were laid inside. He lit a match, held it to the kindling, and watched as the fire caught and leapt and spread over the logs. Then he creaked the stove door shut, stood up, and turned around.

She was still sitting on the chair by the door. Her teeth were still chattering and her hair was still dripping.

"Take off your clothes."

He pulled one of the four wooden chairs from the table toward the stove and turned it backward to the heat. Then he unbuttoned his shirt and hung it on the back of the chair. After retrieving a second chair from the table, he unzipped his soaking jeans, hung them up and considered his boxers. They were wet too.

Better leave his boxers on. For her. She was still just sitting there. Hugging the wet jacket around herself.

He picked up the lantern, walked into the bathroom and lifted a towel from the stack on the shelf. He had a feeling she was going to make a fuss about getting out of her clothes. When he returned to the main room with the towel, he dropped it on her head.

"At least dry your hair," he said. And he left her. He'd light the hot water tank.

Five minutes later, that was done. And the stove was already heating the main room of the cabin.

"I've lit the hot water tank," he said, putting the lantern back on the table, "but it'll take a while to heat up. You'd better get out of . . ."

She was quiet. Her teeth weren't chattering anymore. She wasn't shivering either. She was holding the towel in her lap, looking at it. Her fingers were white.

Christ.

He grabbed the lantern again, rushed to the bedroom and snatched a blanket off the bed. Returning to the main room, he set the lantern on the table, tossed the blanket on the couch and pushed the couch close to the fire. Then he headed back to her chair.

He lifted the towel out of her limp hands and rubbed it over her head, scrunching her thick, wet hair. That helped a little. He tossed the towel on the table.

"Come on." He pulled her up, so she was standing on her good foot.

"What?"

After removing the jacket, he unbuttoned her shirt— the useless pink sleeveless shirt—and he had it off her shoulders before she figured out he was undressing her.

"You can't—"

She reached for her wet shirt, but he whipped it off her in the next second.

"You're hypothermic," he said, hoping she would understand. She was wearing a white bra. A lacy white bra. Crossing her arms in front of herself, she started to sit again.

"It'll be all right," he said. He pulled her up, unzipped her jeans and tugged them down just as she sat back on the chair. She tried to grab hold of the wet jeans but she didn't have any strength left in her, so it wasn't much of a contest.

He peeled off her one wet sock, left the tensor, and thought about her underwear. Her underwear was wet too, but it was thin. It wouldn't hold much water. And he didn't feel like wrestling her out of any more clothing. For the second time this night, he picked her up in his arms, and then carried her across the room. He dropped down on the couch with her on his lap, wrapped the blanket over both of them and held her.

"I—I'm—"

He leaned his head down, putting his ear near her mouth.

"What?"

"I'm cold."

He smiled. "I know." The stove was throwing lots of heat. He was already feeling warmer.

But she wasn't. Her bra—wet and cold—pressed against his chest like a band of ice. He reached behind her and undid the clasp. She didn't seem to notice. Wisping the wet fabric away from her, he tossed it on the back of the couch.

That was better. They both were wearing damp underwear, but it didn't feel right being *completely* naked under the blanket. The tensor was still on her foot. Wet.

And cold. That was probably good for her foot.

The fire crackled, dancing patterns behind the glass of the stove door. The thunder boomed again, ricocheting through the woods, farther away now. The rain was settling down to a steady pitter patter.

After a few minutes, she started to shiver again. Good. She needed to shiver. She moved tighter against him, instinctively seeking warmth. That was good, too.

He inhaled deeply, the worry leaving him. She would be all right.

Chapter Two

She must have fallen asleep. Somewhere. Had she made it to a motel?

She'd left last night, Monday night, because of Greg. Because of what he'd said. About the china.

That was when she knew she had to leave. And it wasn't like it was the real reason. It was just something she could put into words. Something she could *say* to him.

She smiled to herself. It was the china. How silly was that? But, that was when she'd made the decision. To leave. To follow Isabelle's advice and drive to Kalispell. By the back roads. But—

The road.

Something about the road. The winding road, the wrong road. The accident—

She opened her eyes.

A fire burned in front of her, glowing coals behind glass panes. She'd been cold before, she remembered that. And her head had hurt. She remembered that, too.

Her head felt better now. Still not right, but better. Her head was spinning, but it wasn't as bad. Firelight flickered behind the sooty panes of glass in the stove, and she realized she felt warm. She had been so cold before. But now she was warm.

Warm and safe. Greg would never find her here. Wherever *here* was . . .

She drifted, floating on the edges of sleep. But she needed to wake up. She didn't have time to rest.

What had happened? After the accident? The car—

She remembered now. Her car was in a ditch. And someone had stopped. She'd thought it was Greg at first, but it wasn't. It had been someone else.

Her stomach tightened. Maybe she was hungry. She'd eat first and then figure it out. Somehow she'd fallen asleep sitting up. And now she was stiff, and aching, and—

Someone was holding her?

Someone with strong, solid arms. He smelled like the spruce trees, and his head rested on top of hers. She could feel his chin.

"Don't move," he said.

"Why?" She yawned.

"You're naked."

Naked? The word dinged through her mind, meaningless.

Images tumbled back into memory. Of the rain. Of him moving her luggage. And carrying her to his truck. And more rain. The road, getting worse. Turning around. Walking to this cabin. And being so cold.

She slipped her hand to her chest. He was right. She really didn't have any clothes on. No, she still wore panties.

She touched his chest. He was warm, and his chest was hairy. Brushing her hand over his skin, she caressed the soft hair on his chest. And stopped.

"Sorry," she said, taking her hand away. She had to wake up, but it was hard, because she only wanted to sleep. And forget.

"You're warmer now," he said.

"Yes, thank you. I feel fine." She always felt *fine*. "Except my foot . . ." Something was wrong with her foot. Her left foot.

"Hurts?"

"A little." It was starting to throb, now that she was waking up.

"Hold on," he said, shifting her off his lap and onto the couch. He pulled the blanket away from himself, and suddenly she was looking at his bare chest. She switched her gaze to his face, his eyes. His eyes were blue. Deep blue, warm in the firelight.

And he was watching her like she was watching him. Like they recognized each other. Like they had known each other, always.

The moment passed, he looked away and she closed her eyes. She felt him tucking the blanket around her, felt him moving off the couch. Then she heard the stove's door creak open.

Pressing the blanket against her eyes, she waited. *Oh God, this couldn't be happening.* Was he wearing anything? She had to look, and so . . .

She peeked. And saw that he was wearing a pair of black boxers. Relief washed over her.

He knelt in front of the stove, loading more wood into the fire. He was a big man. Tall. She remembered that. A lot taller than Greg. And unlike Greg, this man was dark. Dark hair, sort of long, trailing on his neck. He had several days of beard stubble and his skin was tanned, like he worked outside.

"You sprained your foot," he said, as he stacked the wood. "Or you broke it."

It didn't *feel* broken. But how would she know? She'd never broken anything before.

"And I think you may have bumped your head." He closed the stove's door, creaking it on its hinges. Sitting back on his heels, he looked at her. His thighs were big, strong looking. His chest was broad, covered in fine dark hair, and his stomach muscles were ridged.

"I was worried about letting you sleep," he said, "but I

fell asleep, and—" He checked his watch. A heavy sports watch. "We slept about two hours." And then, "Are you hungry?"

It seemed unreal, talking to this man in the black boxers, while she huddled almost naked under her blanket. But it felt safe.

He dipped his head and said, again, "Are you hungry?"

Her stomach felt tight, but not hungry. "I don't know."

"Did you hit your head?" He was still kneeling by the stove.

"I don't remember. Hitting my head, I mean." She pulled the blanket tighter and watched him.

"When is the wedding?"

The words jarred, out of place. "The wedding?"

"The one you're rushing off to. *Your* wedding."

"It's . . ." *It's not happening anymore.* But he'd seen the wedding dress. He thought she was getting married.

"I think you hit your head," he said, as he looked back at her, his gaze never leaving her.

"No," she answered, finally. He might as well think she was still getting married. That would be simpler . . . than explaining. "The wedding is the end of this month. The last Saturday of June."

"I still think you hit your head."

"No. I didn't," she said. *I just made a bad decision.*

The last Saturday of June?

That's when *he* was getting married. At least, that's when he was supposed to be getting married. It wasn't even a coincidence. Everybody got married on the last Saturday of June. It's when people got married.

When did they get divorced?

"When's *your* wedding?" she asked.

Right. My wedding. How had this happened, he

wondered. That he'd become so involved with someone that he'd simply slid into an inevitable marriage.

"You said you were getting married, too?" She was waiting for his answer.

He watched her for a beat. This was good. She was making conversation. Maybe she wasn't disoriented.

"It's the same day as yours," he said, as he stood up.

The rain made a soft pattering sound on the roof. She was looking at the fire. Or maybe not, because her eyes were tearing up, like she was thinking about something. Her eyes were green. Funny color. Very green. More green with the tears.

Never mind her goddamn eyes.

"We'd better eat something."

He lifted his shirt from the chair by the stove. The fabric was stiff as a board. "This is dry," he said, as he tossed the shirt on top of her blanket. "Put it on."

"Where are my clothes?"

"On the table." He tilted his head in that direction. "In a heap. Not dry. We'll have something to eat and then I'll hang them up." He started toward the kitchen and saw her bra dangling off the back of the couch.

"But what about you?"

"What about me?"

"Don't you want your shirt?"

He smiled, and sighed. "I think you need it more than I do." Grabbing the lantern off the table, he headed into the kitchen.

The cabin was around 600 square feet, probably a 25 foot square, with pine floors made of wide varnished boards. Half the floor space was taken by the main room along the front. A three-foot hallway divided the back half. The bedroom was on the left, an archway, no door. To the right was the kitchen, and farther down the hallway, behind the kitchen was the bathroom. The propane water heater was in the bathroom, along with a small sink, a tiny mirror, a toilet and a shower. And a stack of royal blue towels on the single shelf.

The long, narrow kitchen had a counter on the left that ran the length of the room. The counter was clear except for a two-burner propane stove. Nothing was under the counter except for an empty cardboard box that said *Magic Mixers*, and an old-fashioned ice chest.

No counter on the right side. The wall displayed an assortment of decorative plates mounted about five feet from the floor in a long row—sunflowers, daisies, different colored roses. There was also a plate with a picture of Niagara Falls and another of the Calgary Tower. Not something Pro would have put there.

At the end of the kitchen, under the window, a large porcelain sink took up most of the counter space. The window looked ancient with its leaded panes of glass. And, he shook his head, yellow checked curtains with white lace along the bottom. The curtains were open, showing the black night. Trickles of rain zigzagged down the window panes.

He opened the ice chest. Empty, of course. There was a block of ice waiting in the cooler in his truck, and it could wait.

He positioned the lantern on the counter next to the stove.

Two open shelves hung on the wall above. One by sixes, painted white. The top shelf contained dishes, and the bottom, food. One can of Puritan beef stew, four cans of Spam, a small can of evaporated milk, a can of Tim Hortons coffee, and twelve jars of peaches. No label.

The peaches must have come from Pro's oddball aunt. Canning peaches would be something she'd do. The curtains would be hers. So would the decorative plates.

Along with the dishes on the top shelf, there was an

assortment of pots and pans, and a blue plastic box of cutlery. He found a can opener, opened the can of beef stew and considered the pots.

He chose a small one and dumped the stew into it. Then he set it on the propane burner, flicked the knob, and adjusted the flame.

A tarnished silver tray leaned against the back of the dish shelf. He set it on the counter and brushed his fingers over the ornate swirls. And smiled. He was preparing a meal for someone. He hardly ever prepared a meal for himself.

So. They'd need some bowls. And spoons.

The dish collection consisted of—two egg cups made of a delicate white china, a wide red plastic funnel, a black mug with *Canadian Bar Association* in gold letters on one side and a pair of legal scales on the other, a six-cup coffee pot with a purple Melitta cone, a stack of yellow plastic measuring cups, three tin plates, two clear mugs with snowflakes embossed on the glass, and seven china bowls in different shapes and sizes.

He turned over a white, gold-rimmed dish. Royal Doulton. Another bowl was Wedgwood. A third was Royal Albert.

Leftover pieces of someone's china collection?

Must have come from crazy Aunt Dizzy. No, not Dizzy. Something like that. He couldn't remember what Pro called her.

The stew boiled over.

He turned off the burner, found spoons and a pot holder, scraped the stew into two bowls, and set them on the silver tray. Not exactly the way Catherine would do it, but it would work. He added one of Aunt Dizzy's jars of peaches and . . .

"Do you have your shirt on?" *Please let her have the shirt on.*

She hesitated. And then, "Yes."

He carried out the tray and the lantern.

She was sitting where he'd left her, snuggled into his Levi's shirt, with the blanket over her lap. Her lacy white bra still dangled from the back of the couch.

With her hair curling around her face, she looked messy, but cute. She'd buttoned the shirt right up to her neck and rolled up the sleeves. Her left foot was up on the couch, poking out from under the blanket. He'd have to rewrap that tensor.

After setting the lantern on the floor, he kicked the chair in front of the couch, and arranged the tray on the chair. Then he sat beside her, on her right side.

"Some of it burnt a little," he said. "Got stuck to the pot." He handed her a bowl and a spoon.

"I'm not hungry."

"You are. Eat."

She reluctantly accepted the bowl. Then she scooped up half a spoonful, blew on it, and tasted.

"It's good," she said. She sipped another spoonful, and then another, her appetite taking over. She ate like she hadn't eaten in a long time.

What was she doing out here? All alone. And who was she?

"I'm Ryder." He reached out his hand, without thinking. "Ryder O'Callaghan."

She dropped her spoon in the half-finished bowl and shook his hand. "Toria Whitney," she said.

"You're still cold."

"I'm better." She released his hand.

He let go, too. He'd just shaken hands with her. Strange. Considering he'd been holding this almost naked woman on his lap for two hours. Some things were just automatic.

He took a bite of the stew. Hot, and salty, and satisfying. *Toria . . .*

"Vic-toria?"

"Yes. It's short for Victoria. My mother doesn't like it shortened."

Neither does Catherine. Like it shortened. "What else doesn't your mother like?"

Toria had just about finished eating. She was scraping some last bits of stew from the edges of the china bowl. "What's that supposed to mean?"

"Nothing," he said, wondering why he'd said it. But he'd bet her mother didn't like a lot of things if she didn't like her daughter's name. "It's not supposed to mean anything." He took another bite of the stew. And then, "Where is your mother?"

"In Calgary."

"Planning your wedding?"

"No," she said. "I mean, yes."

"Which?"

She paused and licked her spoon. "My fiancé's mother is planning the wedding."

Her fiancé's mother? "That's unusual."

"It's what she does. She's an events planner."

Events planner . . . like a wedding planner. His mind sorted the information and it still seemed odd. He couldn't imagine Catherine turning the planning over to *his* mother.

"That's convenient," he said, trying to say something positive.

She waited a moment, considering. "Is *your* mother planning *your* wedding?"

"I don't know. She probably has something to say about it. My fiancée is running most of it. I think."

A flash of lightning illuminated the dark windows. Three seconds later, the crash of thunder followed. The trees shook off some water and the rain swept over the roof. The wind had picked up again.

Make it stop raining, he wished. Make the partnership

hassle go away. Make the wedding go away.

The wedding?

At least, make the poodle go away.

Maybe he had jitters. Grooms were supposed to get jitters, weren't they? "Do you ever get the jitters? About getting married?"

"All the time." Not a second's hesitation.

"You do?"

She laughed, a musical sound. "I can't believe I said that. Can we eat these peaches?" She reached for the jar.

An image of her wedding dress blowing in the wind played in his memory. "You're running away, aren't you?"

"No," she said, simply. Not arguing. She gripped the jar, twisting the lid. Not budging it. Then she handed it to him.

He took the jar from her and with a light twist, the seal popped.

"I think you *may* have been getting married," he said, giving her the jar. "You've got the dress—it's a nice dress, but—"

"Thank you."

"—I think you called off the wedding."

She scooped several peach wedges into her empty bowl.

"So?" he asked.

"What?"

"Are you calling it off?"

"Why would you say that?"

"Postponing it then?" Why was he questioning her? Did he *want* her to be a runaway bride?

"These are good," she said, tasting her first peach.

"You could postpone, I suppose." He felt like he was talking to himself. "You can't very well hobble down the aisle with a broken foot."

"Why not?" She ate another peach slice. "And it's a sprain. It's not broken."

"My fiancée wouldn't hobble down the aisle with a broken foot."

"She probably wouldn't break her foot three weeks before the wedding."

"I thought you said it was just a sprain."

"You should try these. They're great." She scooped several more slices into her bowl and poured in some of the juice. A lot of the juice.

A log shifted in the little stove. Sparks flashed and the fire burned brighter for a second. The strangeness of their conversation hit him.

What did it matter? If she was getting married, or not? It was none of his business.

He set his empty bowl on the silver tray. He didn't like peaches. At least, not canned. He liked them fresh. But, he needed to eat something else, and it looked like peaches were the something else. He'd rewrap her tensor first.

"Give me your foot."

"Why?"

He closed his eyes. Why did she have to be so difficult? "The tensor is loose. Your ankle needs some pressure on it."

"The bandage is fine," she said.

"No, it's not. It will fall off while you're sleeping. I'd better rewrap it."

"It's all right."

"No, it isn't. Give me your foot. I'm going to rewrap the tensor, then I'm going to eat some of those peaches and then I'm going back to sleep."

She shrugged, turned on the couch, and plopped her foot onto his lap.

"It doesn't hurt at all now," she said, yawning.

She looked like she was fighting sleep. Or more likely, she *had* hit her head. She ate her last peach slice and then drank the rest of the juice out of the bowl.

Her foot was purple but the swelling seemed less. He rewrapped the tensor, still damp from being in the rain. Then he poured the rest of the peaches into his own bowl.

"I have to go to the bathroom," she said, pushing aside the blanket.

"I'll help you."

"I can do it myself." She was on her feet, swaying.

He plunked his bowl on the tray and stood, catching her just before she fell.

"I can do—"

"—it myself." He picked her up in his arms, bent his knees to catch the handle of the lantern, and carried her down the hall and right into the bathroom.

After he set her on the floor, she said, "Are you going to stay?"

"You can only hop so far." He set the lantern on the floor. "I'll be outside." He left her, closed the door, and waited in the dark hallway.

There wasn't any sound for a few minutes and then she turned on the tap. Running water, so he couldn't hear her pee. Cute. It was like taking one of his sister's toddlers to the bathroom.

Then he heard the toilet flush. And then she must have been washing her hands. And judging by how long she was taking, her face too.

She opened the door, holding the lantern, and looking very sleepy. He would have said drunk, except she hadn't been drinking.

"You hit your head back there."

"No. I didn't."

He picked her up again. This time she held the lantern.

Once he had her settled on the couch, he loaded more wood into the stove. And then he went to the bathroom himself.

When he got back, she was curled on her side at the

end of the couch, and she was sleeping. Snoring lightly.

He sat on the other end of the couch, picked up the bowl of peaches, and tasted one. The rich mellow flavor melted in his mouth. They *were* good—just as Toria had said. And they should be, considering how much brandy was in them.

Terrific. Another of Aunt Dizzy's magic recipes.

He looked over at Toria. Her hair had fallen over her face, and her hands were folded together and tucked under her cheek.

He looked down at the peaches and sighed. She wasn't making a lot of sense, she probably had a concussion, and he'd just fed her a lot of brandy.

Chapter Three

Catherine Margaret Forsythe ordered her usual double-double and a low-fat apple muffin, scanned the early morning Tim Hortons for an empty table—and didn't find one.

But she did see Jimmy Bondeau.

He sat at a table at the back, in the corner, hunched over a Calgary Sun newspaper and eating a bagel. His stylishly cut hair and his green striped polo shirt made him look out of place among the crunch of construction workers grabbing a quick breakfast.

It was about time she introduced herself.

Maneuvering her way through the close set chairs, she reached him just as he was turning a page. She set her tray on his table and smiled at him. One of her best PR smiles. He smiled back, looking like he couldn't believe his good luck.

"Hi," she said, extending her hand.

He eagerly took her hand and started to stand up. A real gentleman.

"I'm Catherine Forsythe," she announced. "I'm Ryder's fiancée."

His smile faltered. She'd been right. He'd thought she was *interested*. In him. As if that could happen.

He quickly recovered his smile, sat again and folded the newspaper, making room for her tray. "So," he said, "we finally meet."

"It's about time, since you're going to be—"

"Ryder's partner. Yes, I'm Ryder's partner." He was smiling more now and nodding his head up and down.

It was done? "You mean he finally signed the papers?"

"Well, actually, no. He hasn't signed the agreement yet. His lawyer wants to go over a few more things."

One more time. She didn't like Prometheus Jones. Normally Ryder listened to *her* opinion, but apparently only on house details or wedding details. He wasn't taking her advice about his business. She said, "I guess you're in charge today."

"On the site, you mean?"

"Yes. Ryder won't be there."

"He won't?"

"Doesn't he tell you anything?"

"Not unless it's really important."

She laughed, happy to hear Jimmy admit that. "Then I'm not the only one. He never tells me anything, either. Unless I force it out of him."

Jimmy grinned.

And then she made her proposal. "We should keep each other updated."

"We should," he agreed. "So where is he today? Going shopping with you?"

"Hardly." Ryder shopping? The notion was laughable. "He left last night."

Jimmy stared at her for a second. "Left?"

Not left, you idiot. As if Ryder could ever leave her. "His jerk lawyer has a cabin in the Kananaskis," she explained. "Loaned it to him for a few days. Said he needed some time to think."

Jimmy tipped his head and looked at the table, as if considering what she'd said. "That's good." He nodded. "Ryder needs a break. He did say he might take a day off this week." He lifted his coffee mug and took a drink.

"How long will he be gone?"

She shrugged. "I don't know. I can't see Ryder staying away from a job site for more than twenty-four hours."

Jimmy took a bite of his bagel, chewed and swallowed. "Why didn't you go to the cabin with him?"

"A cabin? In the wilderness? I don't think so." She started to cut her muffin into pieces. "I'm not sure it even has a flush toilet." She laughed then, realizing she felt relieved. She hadn't wanted to go. "You can't take a Cadillac into Jeep country, I always say."

"No," Jimmy agreed, "you certainly can't."

And besides—she inhaled deeply, as her last conversation with Ryder replayed in her head—she hadn't been invited.

The trees dripped water on the cabin's roof, but the rain had stopped. The sun was shining through the leaded windows.

Ryder smiled to himself, remembering. And realizing that it felt good to put the world on hold. To have the world gone.

And for some reason it also felt good to be crowded on this sagging couch, sleeping with this stranded bimbo waif. Who ate too many peaches and got drunk.

During the night, he'd roused her every couple of hours. And she'd woken up—enough to assure him she wasn't drifting into unconsciousness. She'd told him to go away the first time, and then she'd called him "Isabelle" the next time, and the last time, she'd said, "Not *now*, Mom."

He'd got up twice to load wood into the stove, and each time he'd returned to lie beside her on the edge of the couch, she'd snuggled into him, like she belonged there.

Maybe Pro had been right. About getting away for a few days. Nothing could be done, for now, about Jim redesigning the partnership agreement. And nothing could be done, for the moment, about the house plans. And nothing could be done about Catherine, and the wedding, and the poodle.

The poodle.

Dread shuddered through his chest. Maybe—just maybe—he could do something about the poodle.

The cabin was cold. The fire needed more wood. Toria wiggled in closer to him, mewing in her sleep.

So much for getting away for a few days. He'd have to get her to a hospital. Her ankle was probably okay, but it should be looked at. And she might have hit her head. They should check her head.

She'd object. But as soon as they had something to eat, he was driving her to Canmore, assuming the road was passable.

He heard a sound in the distance, lifted his head and looked over the back of the couch at the door. And listened . . .

A vehicle had driven up. He could hear the engine cut, hear someone running up the path, hear footsteps on the porch. And then the door swung open and Pro burst into the cabin.

They stared at each other for a beat. And then Ryder watched as Pro took in the scene—two pairs of jeans, her pink shirt, his blue jacket, and two pairs of socks draped over the chairs by the stove.

And a lacy white bra dangling off the back of the couch.

He should have moved that, but he hadn't wanted to. He'd wanted *her* to notice it. Stupid of him, but there it was.

Anyway, it didn't look good. To be found here, sleeping with a woman other than Catherine.

But it didn't matter. This was Pro. Pro would understand. But . . . Why—

"What are you doing here?"

"I was worried about you," Pro said, closing the door behind him.

"Me?"

"Why are you sleeping on the couch?"

"You were worried about *me?*"

"There's a car back there, in the ditch, with the air bag—"

"She's okay. She's right here." He glanced down at her. She was stretching, starting to wake up, and inadvertently rubbing against him in a way that was—not good. He looked back at Pro.

The guy seemed a little more relaxed now. His shoulders had dropped and he seemed to be exhaling, letting go of a tense breath.

Very odd. For Pro to worry about him.

Pro took a step forward. "So you were . . ."

"She was cold. It's not what you think."

Pro lifted his eyebrows. "What do I think?"

"Nothing." Why was he feeling guilty? "She was freezing." He *wasn't* feeling guilty. "And I think she hit her head."

"I didn't hit my head," Toria mumbled. Her eyes were squeezed shut and she was frowning. "Why does my head hurt?"

"That could be from the peaches," Ryder told her, trying to move his arm out from under her neck.

Pro walked around the couch to stand between the couch and the stove. "You found Aunt Tizzy's peaches," he said, looking at last night's leftover supper.

"Right. Tizzy. I thought it was Dizzy."

"Tizzy. Dizzy. Same thing. She has her moments, and she makes great peaches." He paused. "You guys sure ate a lot of them."

"I didn't eat any."

"No?"

"Yeah, she ate half the jar."

"Oh." That was all.

"Why does my head hurt?" Toria lifted her hands to her head, but her hands were tangled in the sleeves of his shirt.

"Because you're hung over." And then he noticed—the buttons of the shirt had come undone.

"I'm not hung over. I don't drink." She blinked, trying to wake up. "Why does my foot hurt?"

"Her foot?" Pro was somewhere behind him.

"Yeah. I think she broke it."

"It's a sprain," Toria said, trying to wiggle away from him. "What are you doing? How come you're on my couch?"

"So now it's *your* couch?"

"Get off me." She tried to push him away.

He held her tighter. "Why don't you get the cooler from my truck? I've got breakfast."

"Of course," Pro said, as he moved toward the door.

"And we need more wood," Ryder called over the top of the couch. "Then we'll get her to a hospital."

"I'm *not* going to a hospital." She'd stopped pushing. Now she was pressing her sleeve-covered hands to her forehead.

Pro made his exit, closing the door behind him. And, knowing Pro, he'd give them a little time before he carried in the cooler.

"Who is that guy?"

"My lawyer."

"Your lawyer?"

"Well, he's my friend. And he does some work for me."

"What are you doing?" She tried to push him away again. "Let go of me."

"Take it easy, tiger. You've been sleeping with me all night."

She quit struggling. "I have?"

"Yeah," he said, still not releasing her. "I'll carry you to the bathroom. You can have the shower first."

"I can walk."

"No. You can't."

"Yes, I can."

"All right. Have it your way." He kept holding her, watching her green eyes. "Hop to the bathroom. But give me my shirt first."

She looked down at her shirt. His shirt. And she noticed the buttons.

"I didn't want Pro seeing you . . . like that."

She closed her eyes and slowly shook her head. "Could this get any worse?"

"Probably." He let go of her and sat up. He could hear her moving behind him, rearranging the shirt, fumbling with the buttons. Then she was sitting next to him. After a moment, she stood up, then sat down again, holding her head in her hands.

"Did those peaches have . . ."

"Brandy," he said. "Apparently, Aunt Tizzy makes a lot of interesting recipes."

Toria pressed her fingers to her forehead and groaned. Soft and wavy, her hair fell forward, covering her face.

He leaned over and picked up her foot. She flopped back on the couch. Cradling her ankle, he unwound the loose tensor and set it aside. Her ankle was solid purple, but not too swollen.

"What's wrong with going to a hospital?"

"I—I don't . . ." She was pressing her hands over her eyes.

"Let's deal with one thing at a time. Would you like a shower? Can you stand up?"

"Yes." She sat up, carefully, then stood. Not so wobbly this time. Then she hopped and squeezed her eyes shut. "It hurts my head."

"I thought so. Come on."

He lifted her easily, brought her to the bathroom, and set her down. It was light in there now, with the light from the small window.

"Stand still. I'll get your clothes."

He did. Her shirt, and her jeans, and her bra. The lovely lacy white bra. He set her clothes on the shelf beside the stack of towels.

"My shirt?" He waited.

"You want your shirt?"

He turned around, facing the door.

With a brush of soft cotton, he felt the shirt land on his shoulder and felt her give him a little push out the door. Then the door closed behind him. He pulled the shirt off his shoulder and brought it to his face.

Warm. From her sleeping in it. And a scent like . . . spring. Fresh and real.

Pro cleared his throat. He was at the door with the cooler in his hands, looking over at the stove. Looking like he hadn't seen what Ryder was doing.

Slipping the shirt on, he decided his mind was playing tricks on him. Why else would he be smelling his shirt? He needed to focus, and to make breakfast.

Half an hour later they were sitting at the table in the cabin's main room. Ryder had made bacon and eggs and fried toast. Pro had rebuilt the fire and made coffee. And Toria had been a big help and poured the orange juice. Her purple foot was propped up on the chair across from her. Ryder sat beside her and Pro sat across from him.

"I don't need to go to a hospital." Her hair was drying in cute little ringlets and she looked worried.

Pro looked unconcerned. Like he was at a normal Tuesday morning business meeting.

"Then what am I supposed to do with you?" Ryder asked her.

"I'll get a ride back to Calgary with your friend. He can bring me to my apartment."

"Not good enough."

"Not good enough?"

"I'll bring you to your parents' house," Ryder said. He scooped up the rest of his eggs with a piece of toast. "Except your father's not there. Right?"

She stared at him.

"Last night, you told me he was expecting you. In Kalispell."

Closing her eyes for a moment, she took a deep breath, and held it. She must have remembered telling him that. "Yes."

"How come he's in Kalispell?"

"He's . . ." She was looking at her lap.

"He's not with your mother."

"No."

For some reason, she didn't want to talk about her father. "Are they divorced?" Why would she not want to tell him that?

"No." And then she looked up at him. "Are you sure *you're* not the lawyer. I'm feeling interrogated."

Pro laughed and, speaking to Ryder, he said, "You don't have to come back to Calgary."

"I'm not. I'm taking her to Canmore."

"She might as well go to Calgary. She's got to get back there anyway."

"All right. Then I'll take her to Calgary."

"I can do that," Pro said.

"Can you make her go to the hospital?"

"I can't make anybody do anything."

"Then I'll take her."

"Good," Pro said.

"*Good?*"

"Yes," Toria said. "What do you mean—*good?*"

"You're not expected back at work," Pro explained, not explaining at all. "We'll have time to look at this." He picked up a manila envelope from beside the frying pan and set it next to Ryder's plate.

"The partnership agreement?" He didn't want to face it.

"No. Your prenup."

"Pre— I don't need a prenup."

"Everyone needs a prenup."

Ryder turned to Toria. "Do you have a prenup?"

"I don't think so."

Naturally. She wouldn't know if she had one or not. He couldn't stand ditzy women. Catherine, at least, was logical.

He pushed the envelope back to Pro. "Catherine won't go for it."

"I know."

"You do?"

Pro set his fork down, lining it up parallel to the knife balanced on the plate's edge. He took a sip of coffee. "I've already given her a copy."

"*You what?*"

"She wasn't impressed."

Resignation pounded into Ryder's brain. Maybe he needed more caffeine. He reached for the pot. What he didn't need was another argument with Catherine. "I doubt she'll sign it."

"No, of course not. She can't. She'll need her own lawyer to look at it."

Terrific. He hadn't even dealt with the poodle, and now this. "Pro, I know you mean well, but—"

"I'm your lawyer. I'd be remiss if I didn't do this."

"Pro?" Toria asked. "Why do I need a prenup?"

• • • • •

Toria waited on the porch beside Pro, watching as Ryder carried the cooler down the path to his truck. The sun was shining and a few tentative clouds flitted across the sky.

A sense of safety enveloped her and she relaxed her guard, for just a moment. But then she tensed, making her foot hurt again.

Last night the thought of going to a hospital had scared her. But now, in the clear light of morning, going to the hospital didn't seem like such a bad thing. It seemed like a practical thing. She needed to get her foot checked, to be sure it was only a sprain. And it wasn't like Greg . . . would . . . like he would . . .

Her body tensed again, firing a blast of pain to her foot.

Ryder had rewrapped the tensor after breakfast. And he'd shaved. He was on his way back to the cabin now, looking so tall and strong and competent. And handsome.

No. She wouldn't go there. Who cared about handsome? Best not to think about Ryder. So she thought about Pro, who was standing beside her.

Pro. What a funny name . . .

He was tall, like Ryder, though not as tall as Ryder. And, like Ryder, he had dark hair, though not as dark as Ryder. And where Ryder's eyes were blue, this man's eyes were brown. A warm, kind brown.

His navy polo shirt, navy pants with the tightly pressed creases, and dark leather shoes with laces seemed out of place. For a cabin. At least he wasn't wearing a suit—although, now that she thought about it, he carried himself like he was dressed for his lawyer office. And for some reason, he seemed content with himself. Like he'd just won a round of negotiations.

Ryder had returned. As he stepped up on the porch, his heavy work boots dropped pieces of mud. He reached for her arm, ready to pick her up like a caveman and haul her to his truck.

She hopped back. "As long as we're here, can I see what the rest of this place looks like?"

"Certainly," Pro said.

Ryder let go of an annoyed-sounding breath. "It's not like she can move around, Pro. Let's get out of here."

"I can hop," she said, touching Pro's elbow. A second later, she felt Ryder lift her into his arms and she had a moment of dizziness. She clutched her hands around his neck. "Put me down. I can walk."

"Yeah. Sure you can. With a broken foot."

"It's a sprain. Why do you have to keep making it worse than it is?"

Pro seemed to ignore them as he walked off the porch and headed along the brick walk that edged the cabin. Ryder followed, carrying her.

One of his arms lifted around her back, his fingers pressing over her ribs. His other arm pulled under her knees, pinning her snug against his chest.

She had a horrible urge to put her head on his shoulder.

They came around the cabin to a bricked patio, puddled with rain. Beyond the patio, natural grasses and early wildflowers bordered the area. A dirt path led away, about thirty feet, to a fire ring.

Six wooden benches surrounded the fire ring in a hexagon. The wet benches steamed in the sun. The fire pit waited, ready, neatly stacked with wet wood.

Beyond the fire ring, the path continued down a slope to a small turquoise-colored lake. Ryder set her down, keeping his arm around her waist.

His arm felt . . . reassuring?

"We used to come out here every summer," Pro was saying. "There's a great fishing spot down there. Can you see?"

She could see it. She could see it all. And she wished she could stay. For a long time.

But she needed to go back to Calgary. Leaving had been a silly impulse and she never acted on impulse. Except—she sighed heavily, shoulders slumping—except for last night. And now, even though she didn't want to go back, it was the only decision that made sense.

"You're cold again," Ryder said. "You should have taken my jacket."

"I'm fine." She tried to keep from shivering.

Ryder studied her a moment. Then he turned to Pro. "Can we go now? I'll have time to check on the site after the hospital."

Her breath caught as she thought about the hospital. That was second on the list of things she had to do. First she had to face her mother, who would not understand. And then her mother could drive her to the ER. She couldn't take any more of Ryder's time.

"You can bring me to my mother's house. She'll take me to the Nose Hill."

"You mean you do what she tells you?"

Her heart stuttered. Knowing he was right, she straightened her shoulders. She *did* do what her mother told her. At least . . . she always had. She was the perfect daughter, and look where it had got her.

"We're here," Ryder said.

So far he'd seen minimal damage from last night's storm. Calgary seemed to have been on the edges. A few fallen poplar limbs littered front yards. Debris settled at the storm sewer openings. The light fluctuated and dark patches of clouds rushed across the sky, but the sun still fought its way through the gray.

He'd had to insist that she take his jacket. And then after she'd given him her mother's Varsity Estates address, she'd snuggled under his jacket and fallen asleep. The poor thing was worn out.

Whoa. Not *a poor thing*. A ditzy female who didn't know how to take care of herself. She was worse than his mother.

But . . . he had to admit, he kind of liked watching her sleep. Her dark hair curled all around her face. Her lashes were impossibly long, covering those strange green eyes.

Right.

He touched her arm and shook her.

She awoke with a start and looked around, like she didn't know where she was. Or, like she did know, and she didn't want to be here?

"Sit still. I'll be back in a minute."

He got out of the truck, jogged up the walk and rang the bell. Almost immediately, the door opened and a woman, about his mother's age, stared out at him. Her dark hair poked out of a clip on top of her head.

"Mrs. Whitney?"

"Yes?" She smiled at him, her eyes wide.

"I've got your daughter here."

Mrs. Whitney frowned.

"She had an accident."

Mrs. Whitney's hand went to her heart.

Christ. This was coming out all wrong. "She's all right," he said, reaching out to touch Mrs. Whitney's arm. "Her car is totaled, but she's all right." He let go of her arm. "I'll bring her in."

Turning around, he saw Toria getting out of the truck. He ran down the walk and reached her just as her good foot touched the ground. "Take it easy, tiger."

"Oh—my—God. Victoria, what have you done?" Mrs. Whitney stared at Toria's tensored foot.

"It'll be all right, Mom. Don't worry." Toria handed her mother the running shoe.

"But your foot? What happened? Can you walk?"

Ryder slipped his arm around Toria's waist, ready to lift

her. He would have picked her up right away, except—

She was shaking, and she looked pale.

"Can you walk, Victoria?" her mother repeated as she fluttered around them.

Toria didn't answer.

So he said, "It's a sprain. She says, it's just a sprain."

"Oh thank goodness," her mother said, wringing her hands. "She's getting married in three weeks. Did she tell you? She has to be able to walk down the aisle and—"

"Mom, I don't know if I—"

"Of course you can, Victoria. It's only a sprain. You'll be all right in three weeks. You have to be. We can't postpone now. The hall. The caterers." She paused for a breath and then, speaking to Ryder, she added, "We've got the Red & White Club at McMahon."

"Mom, he doesn't need to know th—"

Mrs. Whitney ignored her. "Greg's mother has hired the band. Did she tell you? We've got a four-piece band. Two guitars, drums, and an accordion player who sings. And the—"

Toria gripped his arm. "Mom. I think it's broken."

"That's her mother?"

Pro had driven up just as Mrs. Whitney had backed out a white Cadillac SUV from the triple car garage, and driven away with Toria. The gray sky was threatening more rain.

"That's her mother," Ryder confirmed.

"Taking her to the ER?"

"Yeah. Nose Hill."

"What about her luggage?"

Pro must have noticed the extra suitcases in the back of the truck. "I didn't think Mrs. Whitney wanted to take time to move luggage," Ryder said.

Never mind the time. He didn't think—in fact, he was

sure—Mrs. Whitney didn't know her daughter had taken off for Kalispell last night. Bringing out the luggage would have meant a lot of questions that Toria probably didn't want to answer. And she probably wouldn't have been able to explain the wedding dress either.

Why would someone who was having a reception at the Red & White Club be taking her wedding dress to Kalispell?

He shrugged. None of his business.

Maybe her father lived down there and she wanted to show him the dress? Maybe he hadn't seen it yet?

Maybe he wasn't invited to the wedding.

Pro stood next to him, with his arms folded. "So, what are you going to do now?"

Ryder stared at the empty driveway. "Damned if I know." The construction site would be solid mud.

"You could try to stay away from work. At least, give it a try," Pro said. "One day won't kill you."

"Okay," Ryder said. "I'll stay away." He didn't like mud anyway. And then he looked at Pro. "I can help Toria get her car back to Calgary."

"A tow truck can do that."

"Wait a minute." He remembered. "I've got her purse." It was on the front seat of the truck. "I'd better bring it to her." He started walking back to the street.

"Yes," Pro said, falling in beside him, "you could do that."

"She'll need it. For the ER." And then—yes— "I'll get her address," he said, as he reached for the door latch on the truck. "So I can take her luggage to her apartment."

Chapter Four

Why had he come into her life now? Would she ever see him again?

Toria shivered in the car, wishing she'd taken time to get a sweater, wishing her mother didn't need to have the air conditioning on.

Did she *want* to see him again?

No. He was a blip on her radar, something out of sync in her life.

She smiled to herself, rubbing her hands over her bare arms. What a silly thought. *Out of sync*. Like her life wasn't already horribly out of sync.

Silence permeated the car as thoughts raced in her head. Doubt was right up there, taking the lead, still asking the question. What if Greg was right? What if her mother was right? What if she simply had cold feet? What if she was afraid of commitment?

She crossed her arms over her chest and tucked her hands in her armpits, and she thought about all the mistakes she was in danger of making. She thought about how her mother and Greg's mother were trying to decide everything about her future. And she knew they meant well, but what was the right thing to do? Fear sucked at her. The wedding date advanced, the invitations summoned. The hall waited. Everything was in place.

Except for her.

Among all the feelings tumbling through her mind,

Loneliness stood out. Always Loneliness, sitting in the back of her mind. She missed her dad so much. And then Responsibility came charging in, demanding, who will take care of your mother? It's your job.

And it was. Her job. To take care of Mom, now that Dad was gone.

And then another voice, from somewhere far away, echoing. No. No. No! I don't *want* to take care of her!

And now Guilt pounded into her thoughts. *What a horrible daughter you are.*

If only she could think. That's why she was driving to Kalispell, to Aunt Glenda. To think. If only she could get some time alone and then—

"I tried to call you last night." Her mother clenched the steering wheel.

"Oh?"

"You weren't home."

"No." *I was on the road, running to Aunt Glenda.* Her answering machine would be full of her mother's calls.

"Geraldine wanted to check with you. To be sure you liked the accordion player."

Toria closed her eyes. An accordion player to sing at the wedding. *The* wedding. Not *her* wedding. It had never been her wedding.

"You'll like him," her mother said, in her cheerful voice. Her fake cheerful voice. And then, "Geraldine told me about the china."

"The china," Toria said, feeling her throat tighten. The traffic was thick near the construction, as they closed in on the hospital.

"It's a beautiful pattern."

Black and white, clashing angles. She couldn't do it. Not the china. Not the accordion player. Not any of it. She didn't want to marry Greg.

It had been a mistake. All of it. Saying yes on

Valentine's Day, after all that wine. How could she be so stupid?

But she *had* said yes. To Valentine's Day, to happy memories, to trying to change everything back to the way it was when her father was still there.

"We had to get the pattern in to the bridal registry." Her mother laughed. "I know you wanted to pick out your own china but you didn't. *You* didn't have time. The school. Always that school. Never any time. Not even for your own wedding."

"Mom, I'm not getting married." She felt her voice shake.

"Of course you are. You're just overexcited."

Overexcited. Better not get excited. About anything.

"And you're not at the school now. That will help. It's too bad they could only give you three weeks."

Make it stop. "You don't understand. I'm *not* getting married." Her voice was thin and hoarse.

"And," her mother added with her fake cheerfulness, "if you *really* don't like the china, you can pick out a different pattern in a year or so. Lots of people have more than one pattern." She signaled to turn.

Don't cry. Don't cry.

"You're doing the right thing, you know."

Count. One, two, three, four—

"Greg is such a nice man. You could do a lot worse."

"Yes, I know."

"You know what?"

"That I could do a lot worse."

"Victoria, don't be like that."

Ryder pushed the button on the parking gate, and then waited. And waited.

Finally, the useless machine spit out a ticket for him. He

found a parking spot and got out of the truck. A few speckles of rain touched his face.

He'd talked to the RCMP. They would arrange for towing the Honda to Cochrane.

The automatic doors of the ER whooshed open to admit him and he stepped into the waiting room.

The air had a non-smell. Not offending, but not fresh either. The air conditioning was doing its job. The room had beige walls and beige tiled floors. Gray metal chairs with gray fabric were set in a grid. They needed Catherine in here to decorate.

Four boys in baseball uniforms sat near the door. One of them held an ice pack on his eye.

In the next row, an old man rested with his eyes closed. A bunched-up brown corduroy jacket drooped over his lap.

Two chairs down, a smartly dressed woman sat beside a little girl, maybe four years old. She wore pink overalls and held a worn teddy bear in her arms, rocking it, and crying. The woman was reading a magazine. She turned the page slowly, ignoring the child.

And then, around the post, he saw Toria sitting alone, still wearing the same clothes as last night. The pink sleeveless shirt. The jeans with the muddy hems. Her injured foot was propped on her other foot, down on the floor.

No mother, thankfully.

"How's it going?"

"You're back?"

He dropped her purse in her lap. "You forgot your purse." No use telling her he was trying to prove he could stay away from a job site.

He pulled a chair around and lifted her injured foot up onto it.

She grimaced. "I'm—"

"All right," he said. "I know." He sat in the chair next to her.

She looked cold. He should have brought his jacket in. "I called the police."

"You did?"

"They'll get your car towed back to Cochrane. Then they'll want to talk to you."

She looked at the floor, nodding her head.

"I already told them about the potholes in the road—they know about that road. They asked me if you were drunk. I told them you weren't."

"I wasn't."

"Not when you were driving. But the peaches—"

"I didn't know about the brandy."

"Do you have collision on the car?"

"Collision?"

Please tell me she knows what that means.

"Yes."

"Then your insurance company will want to get your car out of the impound lot."

"Can't the police tow it straight to a garage?"

"That's not the way it works."

"So my insurance company will get it towed to a garage?"

"No."

"Why not?"

"It's totaled."

"That means they can't fix it?"

God, she was dense. "That is what it means."

"Then why not tow it straight to a scrapyard?"

"Your adjuster will have to look at it."

"My adjuster?"

"You do have insurance, don't you?"

"Of course I do. But—"

He took her purse out of her hands and zipped it open.

"What are you doing?"

"Looking for your wallet." Because it was going to take

forever otherwise. He lifted the burgundy wallet out just as she pulled the purse away from him.

"You can't do that!"

He flipped the wallet open. "I'm taking your pink card." He found it, pulled it out. "I'll call your insurance company. They'll contact you. They'll look at the car. And then they'll tow it to a scrapyard." He folded her wallet and handed it back to her.

"Why?"

Why? "Would you like to keep it? Sentimental value?" Is that how women did things? At least women like this? Catherine didn't have a sentimental bone in her body.

"I mean, the Good Samaritan thing. Why are you doing this?" She paused. "Helping me."

Finally, a good question. "Because I don't have anything else to do today," he admitted. "My fiancée tells me I have trouble staying away from work. So I'm staying away." And then he added, "For one day."

"Oh." A pause. "Do you like your work?"

"Love it."

"Then . . ."

"Then what?"

She shrugged and smiled. A sort of smile. Kind of sad. "It's funny. I like my work. Mostly. But my fiancé says I spend too much time there."

He ran his fingers over the pink card from *Loche Monne*, reading her address. She lived in Dalhousie. Probably in the Towers.

"What do you do?"

"I'm a teacher."

A teacher? "Really?"

"What do you mean—*really?*"

"I didn't think . . . well—" What had he thought? "I put you more as a . . ."

"A what?"

"I don't know." *A bimbo.* "Just not a teacher. Where's your mother?"

"Making a phone call."

"Cancelling the wedding?"

"Not yet."

"You sound hopeful."

"Don't be stupid."

A middle-aged, overweight nurse with a big smile and an orange uniform interrupted them. "Victoria Whitney? Oh good," she said, looking at the wallet in Toria's hands. "Your fiancé brought your Alberta Health Care card."

Fiancé? Did the nurse think *he* was the fiancé?

Amused at the thought, he watched as Toria fumbled through her wallet and handed the card to the nurse.

"You got here fast," the nurse said, smiling at him.

Yeah, she thought *he* was the fiancé. A complete misunderstanding. As if he could ever be this woman's fiancé.

"I can bring you in now," the nurse said. "I'll get a wheelchair."

"That's all right." Ryder got to his feet. "Just tell me where to put her."

Another big smile, directed at him. "Hospital policy," the nurse said. "I'll get her a wheelchair. Then you can bring her in." She left.

"You?" Toria asked.

"Why not? I don't have anything else to do."

"But—"

The orange smiling nurse was back, pushing the wheelchair.

Ryder stood in front of Toria and reached for her waist. She glanced up at him for a second, then put her hands on his forearms. Cold hands. As cold as they'd been last night. He lifted her over to the wheelchair.

"Right this way. Follow me," the cheerful nurse said,

taking Toria's purse.

They entered a large room with rows of stretchers on either side and a mission-control-style desk in the center. Beige curtains hung from the ceiling and divided the area into cubicles.

Ryder pushed the wheelchair, following the orange nurse past the desk, to the last cubicle on the right, the only one without an occupant.

"You can help her up here," the nurse said, as she put Toria's purse on the nearby table and began propping up the head of the stretcher.

Ryder locked the brakes on the wheelchair, lifted Toria in his arms and set her on the stretcher.

"Oh my," the nurse said, looking like she hadn't expected him to get Toria out of the wheelchair so quickly. She lifted the rails on her side, walked around to the other side and lifted those as well. "You can have a seat," she said, as she whisked out of the curtained area. "The doctor will be right in."

Ryder pulled the beige chair away from the wall and positioned it so he could watch the central desk.

Nurses—or doctors or whatever they were—flitted back and forth from the stretchers to the desk, sometimes sitting in one of the swivel chairs and sometimes hovering near the desk for a few seconds before buzzing back out of sight.

The desk held racks of silver-colored clipboards, piles of brown envelopes, clear bags of fluid labeled with red tape, three monitors beeping out wiggly patterns, and an empty clear plastic Starbucks cup with a green straw.

"Why are you staying?"

"She told me to have a seat."

"She offered you a seat. She didn't tell you to do anything."

A short, tired-looking doctor with shaggy brown hair

and rumpled green scrubs hurried into the curtained area. The pockets of his long white lab coat bulged with two coil bound notebooks, four pens, a stethoscope, what looked like a small hammer and who knew what else. The doctor consulted his clipboard, glanced at Toria's tensored ankle and looked at Ryder. "Take off the tensor?"

Ryder stood up and took the clips off the bandage while the doctor scribbled on his clipboard. His name tag said *Dr. B. Delanghe*.

"What happened?"

"I guess I twisted my ankle getting out of the car."

"In a hurry?"

"Well, the car was in the ditch. I thought I should get out."

Dr. Delanghe stared at the notes on the chart. Probably the nurse had already asked all these questions.

"Seat belt," Dr. Delanghe mumbled. "Good." And then, "Air bag?" He lifted his eyebrows and looked at Toria. "The car must have been going fast."

"No. It just stopped quickly," Toria told him.

Ryder glanced at her. Was she toying with the doctor? She looked serious, but she always looked serious. And clued out. And kind of sad.

"Are you finished?" the doctor asked him.

Finished?

Right, he thought. He'd been holding Toria's foot in his hands. He let go and started rolling up the bandage.

Dr. Delanghe set down his clipboard and picked up Toria's ankle. Tensing, she drew a breath as he pushed and prodded. In a few minutes, he was finished.

"Just a sprain," he said. "Tell your mother not to worry. You'll be fine in three weeks. You'll be able to walk down the aisle." He scribbled some notes, spending more time with the chart than Toria's ankle. "Make sure she rests," he said, speaking to Ryder. "Ice for comfort. Keep the tensor on as long as there's swelling. And keep the extremity elevated. That should take care of it."

"What about her head?"

The doctor stared at him. "What about her head?"

"I think she hit her head."

"I *didn't* hit my head."

Dr. Delanghe retrieved a small flashlight from one of the bulging pockets and flicked it at Toria's eyes. "She's alert, awake, oriented. No deficients."

He pulled out a pad of paper and looked at Toria. "Do you have any allergies?"

She hesitated, and then, "None that I know of."

Dr. Delanghe scribbled on his pad, then handed the piece of paper to Ryder.

It was a prescription for 292s. He'd had those before. They made him fall asleep.

Then the doctor wrote something else on the chart and closed it.

"Can she go now?"

"Soon," Dr. Delanghe said. "Put the tensor back on. Physio will be in to fit her for crutches. Then you can take her home." With that, he was gone.

Ryder set the prescription on the end of the stretcher and picked up the tensor. "You live in Dalhousie? The Towers?" He wove the bandage around and around.

"Yes. But how—"

"I've got your insurance card." Almost done, just needed the clips.

He looked at her. She had another question forming somewhere in that scatterbrained head of hers. "I've got your luggage." He paused. "And a wedding dress."

She closed her eyes.

He'd guessed right. She wasn't supposed to be carting around her wedding dress.

"I could give it all to your mother," he said, making it

sound like it wouldn't make any difference. He attached the clips to the tensor and released her foot.

"Uh . . ."

"Or I could bring it by later." He rested his hands on the edge of the stretcher. "Will your mother be taking you home? Or to her place?"

"Home," Toria said, firmly. "My apartment."

He picked up the prescription again. "Six. Tonight. Don't do anything special. I'll bring dinner."

"But—"

"You like pizza?"

Her mother fluttered into the room. "Victoria, I was looking for you. What did the doctor say? Will your ankle be all right?"

Ryder looked at Toria, right into her deep green eyes. "Well?"

She looked back at him, holding his gaze. He could see the struggle going on in her mind, the weighing of options. And then she nodded.

"Victoria?" Her mother again, asking for attention. "Will it be all right?"

Toria's face showed doubt and wariness, and something he couldn't name. She seemed to brace herself. "It's a sprain," she said. "It'll be fine."

Her mother exhaled, like she'd had a close call. Finally, she looked at Ryder. "What are *you* doing here?"

Oddly, it felt like an attack. He took a step back from the stretcher, set his stance and felt the need for discretion. "Toria forgot her purse in my truck."

Her mother rolled her eyes. "She's so forgetful. And it's Vic-toria. You don't still use that nickname do you, Victoria?"

With her mouth half open, Toria stared at her mother.

"Let's go then. I have to meet Geraldine. The chef at the Red &—"

"She needs crutches first." Somebody needed to stand up for Toria, since she didn't seem to be standing up for herself. At least not with her mother.

Mrs. Whitney stared at him. "Crutches?"

"Yeah. They're these stick-like things that you lean on. They help you to walk."

Mrs. Whitney watched him for a second longer. And then she laughed. "What a funny man. Yes. Well. Where do we get the crutches?"

"Physiotherapy will bring them." He handed Mrs. Whitney the prescription. "You'll need to get this filled for her."

Mrs. Whitney glanced at the paper and then looked up at the ceiling. "Oh my. So many things to do." She stared at her daughter on the stretcher and shook her head. "Victoria, you can be so much trouble."

Toria watched him leave, saw his tall dark form turn around the corner of the nursing station and disappear from sight.

Why had she agreed to let him come over tonight?

"How long will this take?" Her mother glanced at her watch. She was probably tapping her foot.

But what was the alternative? If she hadn't agreed, he would have hauled in her luggage—and the infamous wedding dress. And—

"Geraldine and I need to meet with the caterers at the Red & White Club."

And if her mother saw the luggage, and especially the wedding dress—

Might as well face it. She was afraid of what Mrs. Samantha Whitney would think of her ungrateful daughter. Her forever ungrateful daughter.

What would her mother say if she knew Toria had

packed, taken the wedding dress her father had spent so much money on, and left?

And not only left, but gone to see Aunt Glenda. Her mother and Aunt Glenda might not be speaking to each other, but Toria liked Aunt Glenda. Aunt Glenda listened.

"This physiotherapy is taking forever."

Was she doing the right thing by ending this wedding? Maybe she should just postpone? In February, she'd said a year. They could get married next January. That might have worked.

But Greg's mother—the wedding planner—had said no one got married in January. It would have to be June. June was the month for weddings.

And so Toria had agreed to June. But to the following June, not this June. Somewhere along the line, her mother and Geraldine had advanced the date.

Behind the curtains, Toria could hear someone coughing—a young girl, trying to catch her breath.

"I should go. I've called Greg. He can take you home."

A buzz of adrenaline flashed through her body and she stiffened. "You called Greg?"

"Why, of course." Her mother lifted her eyebrows. "He's your fiancé. You've been in an accident. He'd want to—"

"He has meetings in the afternoon."

"I know. I left a message for him."

"He never interrupts a meeting."

"Yes, of course, but he'll see the message is from me. We need him to pick you up."

Why?

The word was there, on the tip of her tongue, but she couldn't let it out. Choking on words again, she had become a complication for Geraldine and Samantha as they tightened their hold on her.

If only she could think. What would her father have said to all this?

No. He would have said, no. "I can take a cab."

"Nonsense. Greg will be happy to get you. I wish these physiotherapy people would hurry up with your crutches."

"Just go. I'm fine." She always felt *fine.*

"Well, if you're sure."

"I am."

Her mother checked her watch, turned and took two hurried steps away from the stretcher—

Tell her. Say it now. Get it out in the open. "I was driving down to Kalispell," Toria said, speaking to her mother's back. "To see Aunt Glenda."

Panic threatened and Toria swallowed, dreading the next few moments. But the words were spoken, no turning back now.

Her mother stopped mid-step, slowly turned and lifted her hands to her heart. Her jaw fell open. A silent gasp.

"You were *what?* What's got into you? *Glenda.* Of all people. She just puts ideas in your head. That's why you're so distraught. What would people think if they knew you were acting like this?"

"I can't do it, Mom. I can't marry him."

"But you have to."

"Why?"

"Because . . . Because . . . he's perfect. It's the perfect solution."

"Not for me."

"How can you talk like that?"

How? *By opening my mouth, by letting the words out, letting them flow past my choking throat.*

A commotion near the entrance to the stretcher bay interrupted them. Toria could hear the nurses, several of them, speaking at once.

"Sorry. This is not—"

"Can I help you?"

"Just a moment, sir. You can't—"

And she knew Greg had arrived.

He swept past the nursing station, never pausing, wearing one of his black three-piece suits, and zeroing in on the last stretcher in the unit. Then he saw her.

He glanced at her face, and at her bandaged foot. His expression clouded with anger. "What's going on? What happened?"

"Are you a relative?" The nurse in the orange uniform stood next to Greg.

"I'm her fiancé," he said, snapping the words as if they gave him some kind of special rights.

The nurse frowned, then seemed to collect herself. A loud beeping from the nursing station summoned her and she quickly left.

Samantha Whitney arranged a smile on her face but her lipstick looked crooked. "Victoria had a little accident. She tripped."

"I had a car accident."

"Car—" He paused for a single second. "That old Honda? Are you all right?" He looked at her tensored foot again. "Your ankle?"

"It's only a sprain."

Concern flooded over his face, and it looked real. The anger—if it was anger—was gone.

"*Only?* You could have been hurt even worse than this." He brushed his hand over his hair, messing the neat strands. "I never liked that car."

"I did."

"I know, I know. It was *your* car."

"It was paid for."

"Victoria." Her mother was back by the stretcher, standing behind Greg. "You can afford a new car, for Pete's sake."

"Anything else wrong?"

"Not with me."

"How's the car?"

"It's had a lot of damage. Probably totaled."

"Good."

"What do you mean, *good?*"

"That car hasn't been dependable. Not for a long time." A slight smile touched his lips.

Her mother laughed, an almost genuine laugh. "Remember at Christmas when it wouldn't start?"

That was the day she'd met Greg at her parents' house for Christmas dinner. He drove her home because the Honda wouldn't start.

"Don't worry about the car." His voice had turned soothing. "The important thing is you're all right."

At that moment, his phone rang and he checked the readout. Torn. "I have to take this."

Toria's nurse, with the orange uniform, reappeared. "Turn off that cell. It interferes with our telemetry. Can't you read the signs?"

Greg looked at the nurse like he was ready to have her fired. But he clicked off his phone. And then he turned back to Toria, holding the phone between them. "I need to take this, darling."

"I have to go," her mother said, checking her watch. "You'll go home with Greg."

"I'll take a cab."

"Victoria," her mother said, simply, a warning in her voice.

"Greg and I are no longer engaged."

Her mother opened her mouth and gaped. Behind the curtains, Toria could hear the young girl coughing, the monitors beeping, and the sound of the PA system asking for a French interpreter.

"You don't mean that," her mother said.

"Of course she doesn't," Greg confirmed. "But we're

entitled to the occasional lovers' quarrel, aren't we, Samantha?"

The curtains fluttered and a short woman with long red hair and freckled skin moved past her mother and bumped into Greg, knocking his elbow with a pair of aluminum crutches.

"I've got your crutches, dearie," she said, without apologizing to Greg. "I need you to sign here." She placed a clipboard in Toria's hands.

"How long will this take?" Greg asked, rubbing his elbow.

"Too long," her mother said, with arms folded.

The physiotherapist handed a gold-colored pen to Toria and showed her where to sign.

Greg's phone vibrated, a familiar buzz. He hadn't turned it off. Behind the curtain, the monitor was making high-pitched squeaking sounds.

"Sit on the edge of the stretcher, dearie," the physiotherapist said, as she adjusted little wing nuts on the crutches.

Greg's phone vibrated again, that buzzing sound like a trapped hornet. "I have to take this."

"You always do."

His eyes met hers, uneasy. He glanced at her mother, put away the phone, and then looked at her hands. Finally.

"Where's your diamond?" A quiet voice now, as some of his confidence slipped.

"On my dresser. Don't worry. I'll give it back to you."

"I don't want it back. I know you were upset, and you're just reacting. Everything will be all right."

"I'm not getting married, Greg."

"She's shaken up from this accident," her mother said, explaining.

"It's the china, isn't it?" Greg nodded. "You wanted to be involved and they took over."

"We didn't take over," her mother said. "We had to—"

"My mother thought you would love inheriting her pieces." Greg ignored Samantha. "It meant a lot to her."

"She wants to run . . . everything."

"She's a wedding planner. Most brides would love to have a wedding planner." Greg was using his quiet, make-the-close voice. "She's excited about this. So is your mother."

"It doesn't matter, Greg." This was pointless.

"I'll call a cab for you. I've got a deal closing right now, but I'll see you tonight."

"No."

"We'll talk about this, and if you want, we can postpone."

"But the invitations!"

"Now, Samantha. They're only pieces of paper."

"But . . . but . . ."

The physiotherapist had been fiddling with the wing nuts on the crutches. Now she plunked them on the floor. "How tall are you, dearie?"

"Five seven."

"That's what I thought."

"We simply cannot postpone—" her mother started again. Greg took her arm and led her away.

The nurse in the orange uniform poked her head around the curtain. "I liked the other one better," she said.

"The other one?"

"The other fiancé."

"I—"

Greg returned, whooshing open the curtains and pushing past the nurse. "Don't worry, darling," he said. "Just take care of that ankle." He tried to step around the physiotherapist. "We can postpone," he said, peering around her, "if that's what you want." He moved to the left. "I'll come by tonight," he said. "We'll talk about it."

He moved closer.

Oh no. He wanted to *kiss* her.

Pressing against the pillow, she flinched back.

The physiotherapist turned and caught him in the stomach with the crutches. "Whoops," she said.

Greg's phone vibrated and the monitor in the next cubicle squealed. He yanked the phone from his jacket pocket, looked at the readout, and then at Toria.

"Tonight," he said, and he left.

Chapter Five

Catherine flipped through the work orders, checked the appointment schedule and switched the phone to the answering machine. Then she pulled out the file for her new house.

After she'd met with Jimmy at Tim Hortons, he'd agreed to pick up the carpet samples at Dale's Interiors.

Of course, it was the least he could do, considering he was going to be Ryder's partner. She should have thought of meeting Jimmy before. It had been so simple. Whereas trying to get Ryder to do anything was like . . . well, like trying to get Ryder to do *anything.*

He wasn't easy to manage.

She took out the page of paint samples. The company's designer had several recommended color schemes. She'd picked this one. Why couldn't Ryder agree?

At least he'd agreed to upgrade the flooring to cork, even though it meant they needed the humidifier for the warranty. She would have to reward that behavior. Maybe she could go for a walk with him down by the river—as long as they stayed on the path. That would make him happy.

The brass bells on the back of the door jangled and Jimmy Bondeau stumbled in, lugging four large carpet sample books in his arms. He brought them to the desk.

She felt a rush of lightness and a surge of power. She was getting something done. "Oh, thank you, Jimmy.

You're such a dear."

He plopped the books on the counter. "No problem. Happy to help." He turned to go.

"Got time for some coffee?" she asked, moving toward the BrewWell Unit.

"I need to get back to the site."

"In Royal Oak?"

"Yes."

"Good. I can go with you. We can stop by my house." She'd never be able to get Ryder to take her. "I want to see how the construction is going."

"Uh, not a good idea. They've just started framing." He stepped toward the door. "Too dangerous."

Men could be so stubborn. "That's what Ryder always says." And then, "I'll wear a hard hat." She gave him her best smile.

At least she'd *tell* him she'd wear a hard hat. Those things were horrible for your hair.

He hovered near the door. "It's really muddy with all the rain. Maybe another time. I have to get back."

He was being difficult. "You go to the sites every day?"

"That's what Ryder pays me for." Jimmy checked his watch. "They're craning a unit in Royal Oak in about an hour. I need to be there for that."

Oh no you don't. You're not leaving yet. "I'm so glad Ryder will finally have someone to help him."

Jimmy paused.

Good. She had his attention. "Assuming—" she watched him, "—assuming he signs that partnership agreement."

"Yeah," Jimmy said, touching the door knob. But then he turned back to her. "He needs to be able to take some time off."

She was right. Jimmy would do what she wanted *if* he thought she'd put in a good word for him.

"There's so much that needs to be done for the wedding." She filled one of the clear company mugs with coffee. The black liquid steamed behind the BDB logo.

"Less than three weeks," Jimmy said, still standing next to the door.

"It's getting down to the wire." She needed sugar—two packages, rip, tear. "Everything is ready, except for him. He was supposed to be fitted today, for his tux, but he's at that ridiculous cabin."

Jimmy took a step into the room, and eyed the coffee. "I doubt he'll stay long."

"You don't think so?" She poured in one creamer, watching the black mix with the white.

"No. He hates being away from work." Jimmy shuffled his feet. "Ryder said you were getting a dog."

Wonderful. Jimmy was making conversation. She added a second creamer.

"Yes, I am. I mean, *we* are." She stirred her coffee. "She's the most adorable little poodle. But I need Ryder to come to the breeders with me. He needs to meet her before we bring her home. Make sure they're compatible." Still stirring. "Though I doubt he'll be home much anyway, so it probably doesn't matter."

"What doesn't matter?"

"If he meets our poodle before I buy her."

The brass bells rattled again and Ryder walked in. So much for taking a day off. Somehow, she wasn't surprised. "You can't stay away from a job site, can you, sweetie?"

"I'm not at a job site. I'm here to see you."

He might say he was here to see *her*, but he was looking at Jimmy. The man would want a complete report of what he'd missed today.

"Aren't you—I thought Ryan was craning."

"I know. I'm on my way," Jimmy said, as he headed toward the door.

"How's that lot in Royal Oak? Get flooded?"

"Yeah, it's a mess." Jimmy had his hand on the door knob but he turned to face Ryder. "The weeping tile in the footing is keeping up but we've got the usual problems with the ground faults."

"Other than that, we're on time?"

How did Jimmy put up with this? "For heaven's sake, Ryder. You were just there yesterday."

"Right," Ryder said, looking at Jimmy. "And I'm taking today off. Did Pro tell you?"

"No," Jimmy answered. "I guess he thought you'd tell me."

"It was a last minute decision."

"Pro's cabin?"

"Yeah." And then, like he was finally paying attention to *her*, he said, "Have you two met?"

"This morning, at Tim Hortons. I asked Jimmy to bring over our carpet samples."

"Lots of rain out there? In the Kananaskis?" Jimmy asked.

"Yeah. Lots."

"You could have stayed longer." Jimmy pulled the door open, keeping his hand on the edge of it. "It's drying up now, and everything's under control here."

"I know," Ryder said. "I know you can handle it, Jim. I'm just not—"

"I know," Jimmy said, on his way outside. "Catch you later."

"I'll be back tomorrow morning. At seven."

And if she knew Ryder, he'd be there at six. The man had a problem letting go. She'd have to teach him about delegation.

He turned back to her and then noticed the pile of sample books on the counter. "Carpet samples?"

"Yes," she said, from the other side of the counter.

He approached from his side. "I thought we picked those out."

"Your colors are too light. The designer wants something more . . ."

"More what?"

"Fashionable."

"Fashions go in and out of style." Ryder drummed his fingers on the counter.

Of course, Ryder knew nothing about fashion. He needed to take her advice for those kinds of decisions. And speaking of advice—

"Pro brought over his prenup."

"Oh," Ryder said. He put his hands on the edge of the counter, pushing himself up. "That."

Yes, that. But at least he looked contrite. "You really think we need a prenup?" She smiled, making it extra sweet.

"I never thought about it," he said, watching her eyes. "It's Pro, being a lawyer."

Damn that man. "I think we know what we're doing. We don't need him interfering with the wedding, too."

Ryder raised one eyebrow. "Too?"

"The partnership agreement with Jimmy. You were ready to sign it."

Ryder's mouth opened, and closed. A quick breath, and then, "Don't worry about my partnership agreement. You worry about getting this wedding organized, all right?"

"I am." She pulled out her folder for the wedding. "We need to get you fitted."

He stood back. "I forgot about that. I'll take time from the site. Tomorrow."

"That will work." She reached for her list. "I'll put you down for ten?"

He hesitated a second. "Ten. I'll be there."

"Jimmy really will be useful," she said, adding a note to her list. "He's got a degree in Accounting, you know."

"In *business*. I know." A short pause. "He even knows something about framing."

Better change the subject from Jimmy and the contract. And the degree. For now. "Too bad about the rain."

"Yeah," he nodded, touching the carpet stack. "The job site is going to be slick with mud." Then he frowned. "It's a hazard."

"I meant the rain at the cabin." Sometimes Ryder could be so distracted. "You did get to the cabin, didn't you?"

His hand rested on the samples, but he seemed to be looking at the BrewWell Unit, or at something beyond that. At any rate, he was sidetracked, again. "Yes. I did get to the cabin."

"I knew you wouldn't stay long." She flipped through the wedding folder.

"You did?"

"You need to learn to relax." Closing her house file, she set it on the counter. "My mother says you don't know how to relax."

"Really." He nodded, his focus on the carpet pieces.

"Yes. And she wants everything finalized at the gift registry."

"I thought everything *was* finalized," he said, turning to look into her eyes.

"The china, yes. The crystal, you didn't like. And we've got to finish with the carpet and the paint chips."

"Why don't—" He cut himself off and sucked in a deep breath. "Why don't *you* decide on the crystal? I trust your judgment."

"Now you do? You didn't like it before."

"It seems . . . ornate."

"Ornate? Of course, it's ornate. It's beautiful. You'll get used to it." She checked it off, and ran her finger down the list.

The poodle.

Straightening her shoulders, she set her jaw. "I think we should go to the kennels this afternoon."

"I wanted to talk to you about that."

She was not about to argue again. "Now that you're here—"

"Don't you have work to do?" He looked around the empty office.

He was searching for excuses. "I'm the office manager. I can do what I want. And you need to meet our poodle."

He folded his arms. "I don't want a dog."

"You will once you see her."

"I hate little dogs," he said, arms tight across his chest. "They yap."

She sighed. Why did he have to be so stubborn? She gave him a little smile, and waited.

He closed his eyes, dropped his head, and let his arms fall by his sides. And right at that moment, the bells jangled again.

Wouldn't you know it? Mrs. Milton had decided to come in this afternoon. Just when she was getting Ryder to cooperate.

"Appointment?" Ryder asked.

"Yes," Catherine said. Keeping her voice low, she leaned toward him across the counter. "I didn't think she'd come in today."

Catherine stood up straight and called across the room. "Good afternoon, Mrs. Milton. I'll be right with you." Then she turned back to Ryder and lowered her voice again. "She's choosing her interiors this afternoon."

"All in one afternoon?"

"She makes all the decisions. She's divorced. No husband to consult with."

Ryder spread both his hands over the carpet samples. He was probably thinking about work. It would be a miracle if he stayed away for the whole day.

"I've got to go," he said.

"Job site. I know."

"No. Not the job site. I'll . . . I'll visit my mother."

His mother? *Almost as bad as the job site.* That woman could be so flighty.

"Good. Tell her hello from me." And who knew? Maybe Nancy O'Callaghan would encourage her son to pay some attention to his wedding.

At least he'd get measured for his tux tomorrow.

Ryder sat in his truck outside the BD Builders Show Home Office, as Catherine, his *fiancée*, went through her spiel for the divorced Mrs. Milton, helping her choose suitable flooring, painting, molding, fixtures and tiles.

Were those the things that made a home?

The weather was changing again. Bits of sunshine escaped the cloud cover. The breeze picked up, then dropped off and whipped back.

Catherine had a gift for organization and a flair for decorating. She managed the Show Home Office and the BD Builders clients. And the gift registry, the house plans, and—

His breath hitched. There it was again. Jitters.

—the wedding.

Catherine also masterminded the wedding. The hall, the caterers, the band. The march down the aisle. Where they would stand, what they would wear, and what they would say for their vows.

Vows. His mind flipped to the contract with Jim. He shook his head. Contracts and vows. And a poodle.

Everything felt rushed. Too much at once. Too many things needed decisions right now. He looked up at the clouds moving across the sky.

What if they could postpone? Would that be possible?

At least until the partnership deal was done? One crisis at a time?

Was marriage a crisis?

No. Marriage was simple. It's what he wanted. It would make his father happy. Finally. Because not only was he getting married, he was marrying Herbert Forsythe's daughter.

Well, he was marrying *Catherine*. She just happened to be Herbert Forsythe's daughter. And she was talented, competent, in charge.

He *could* compromise about the colors in the house. Then maybe she'd compromise about the poodle.

Life was about compromise, wasn't it?

He inserted the key in the ignition, and twisted. The engine flared to life. And in his mind he saw all those dark walls.

His heart sank, because he wanted light. Did that matter?

After all, he had everything he wanted. His business was doing well—so well, he needed help. He was building his own estate home and he was getting married like his father had always hoped.

Catherine Forsythe thought he was good enough to marry her. So he had to be good enough for his father, good enough for Donald O'Callaghan—who always wanted him to be more than he was.

He gripped the steering wheel. So now, what to do?

An image popped into his mind—of a sagging old couch in a cold cabin. Of being warm, and holding on to—

Wrong.

That was not part of his life. His life was organized, focused, perfect.

He glanced in the back at the fluffy wedding dress spilling off the edge of the seat. And on the floor, at the two red suitcases that didn't belong to him. At six o'clock, he'd bring them to her apartment. And the pizza. He'd said he'd bring pizza.

She'd need something to eat. And maybe he could help her since it was her first night on crutches. That was a good thing to do. It was part of the whole Good Samaritan package he'd stumbled into.

But for now, he'd visit his mother. It was Tuesday and she didn't work today. His father would be gone, so it might be a decent visit.

He put the truck in gear, shoulder checked, and then it hit him. He hadn't kissed Catherine.

But, he thought, as he backed out of the parking area, he hadn't wanted to.

Toria paid the cab driver. By the time she had her purse strap over her shoulder, he was opening the door for her. She juggled the crutches out of the cab and stood up. The air was cool, but at least the sun was shining through the clouds.

"You all right from here?" he asked.

"I'm fine." She was always *fine*.

"Thanks a lot. Have a great day."

Yes. A great day.

She followed the instructions from the redheaded physiotherapist and crutched her way up the sidewalk to Dalhousie Towers. After unlocking the main door, she maneuvered her way to the mailboxes and took out a shiny magazine wrapped around this morning's mail. With the bundle tucked under her arm, she made the unfamiliar detour to the elevator bay.

She hated elevators. Especially this one. But the alternative was three flights of stairs, and she didn't want to attempt stairs today.

The elevator behaved and deposited her with a clunk,

only slightly above the level of the floor.

In front of her apartment door, she fumbled the keys out of her purse, dropped one of the crutches, and then dropped the keys. As she was picking them up, her across-the-hall neighbor opened her door.

"What did you do to your foot?" Mrs. Toony asked. Her silver hair was tightly stretched on tiny pink rollers.

"I twisted my ankle," Toria said, retrieving the fallen crutch.

Mrs. Toony frowned. "At the school?"

"No, not at the school." She didn't elaborate, but she got the other crutch under her arm. "How are you, Mrs. Toony?"

"I'd be a lot better if I didn't get my sleep disturbed."

What?

"That boyfriend of yours. Over here at midnight last night. Pounding on your door. It's none of my business if you want to have him *visiting* that late but you should give him a key."

Toria felt her chest tighten. "Sorry about that."

To get some attention, Mrs. Toony's old gray cat wound around her legs. She prodded the tired animal with a fuzzy-slippered foot and went back inside her apartment, mumbling something about *back in my day.*

Toria aimed the key at the lock, but her hand shook.

So, Greg had come over last night. Their argument had bothered him, more than she'd expected.

She took a slow breath, tried again, and fit the key inside.

This time the lock turned, and the door opened into her little entrance with its burgundy mat. Straight ahead was the galley kitchen. To her right, a short hall led to the living room.

Her purse dropped to the floor, and her bundle of mail slipped from under her arm. Too tired to pick it up, she poked through it with the foot of one crutch and saw Chatelaine magazine, the Shaw bill for the Internet, a Royal Bank statement, a brochure from the Bay for crystal stemware and—a large white envelope with big loopy writing and little heart stickers scattered across it.

She picked it up and left the rest. Carefully, she hobbled to the love seat, propped the crutches on the coffee table and sat down to open the envelope, addressed to Miss Toria Whitney and no doubt from one of her students.

Then she looked across the room at the bookshelves, at the answering machine—with the light blinking.

Dread twisted her stomach and the card tipped out of her hands, falling to the carpet.

That would be her mother's empty messages, crowding the machine's memory. Had anyone else called? Better check the messages and delete them. She reached for the crutches, touched one, and then the phone rang.

Its jarring mechanical sound.

She jumped, and the crutch slipped out of her fingers. Staring at the insistent phone, she froze on the love seat.

Don't answer it. Not now. I can't deal with her now.

A second ring, seeming louder than the first. *What if it was Greg? Even worse.*

A third ring. Pounding against her mind. Just breathe.

And finally, the fourth blaring ring and the machine clicked on. The electronic butler, the cultured male voice, answered with the usual *You have reached two-eight* . . .

The drone of her number, the invitation to leave a message. *We are sorry no one is available to take your call* . . .

And then next would be the promise that if you left a message, we would return your call as soon as possible. *We.*

It was a silly trick. Anyone with half a brain could figure out there was only one person living here. Alone.

But she kept the message. Partly because her mother didn't like it. She knew it was juvenile but it was a small token of independence.

The recording finished. The caller came on. "Toria?"

Instant relief swept over her. A sensation so strong she hadn't known she was bracing. It was Isabelle.

Toria reached for the crutch and it toppled.

"Are you there, dear? Are you all right?"

The euphoria gave way to fear. *Don't hang up. Hold on.*

She grabbed for the other crutch, but it bounced off the coffee table, landing with a clang on its partner.

Damn. She dropped to her knees.

"I was thinking I could bring over some soup," Isabelle's voice said, and paused.

"I'm coming," Toria told the voice. "Hold on." She crawled across the floor to the bookshelves, reached for the phone—and knocked it off its cradle.

"Maybe you're at your mother's? I didn't want to bother her but I was hoping—"

She grabbed the receiver. "Isabelle?"

"Toria? Are you all right? You sound out of breath."

"I'm fi—" *No.* I'm *not* fine. "I don't know where to begin." The wedding, the accident . . . the stranger.

"You're all right? I heard about the accident."

You did? "How?"

"Someone at the Nose Hill told me."

"Who?"

"One of my friends," Isabelle explained. "Saw you in Emerg. Remember, dear, I used to work in coronary all those years."

Isabelle was a coronary care nurse. A heart nurse. She saved hearts.

"I feel so bad sending you off in the dark like that."

"Isabelle." How could she think that? "It's not your fault. Certainly. It's a bad road. And I think I may have made a wrong turn."

"It's just your ankle then? You'll be all right?"

Toria still sat on the floor in front of the bookshelves. "I—will—be all right," she said.

"But not yet."

"No. Not yet."

"Oh dear," Isabelle said, sounding distressed on her end of the line. "This is all so muddled. And they miss you at the school, dear. I was volunteering this morning. They've put Mrs. Sidorsky in charge of the grad decorations and she can't get anyone to do anything."

Oh no. Not Mrs. Sidorsky. She wouldn't let them have any input.

"They don't like her theme," Isabelle went on.

"And what theme is that?" Toria asked.

"She wants Beauty and the Beast."

No, they wouldn't like that. Toria shook her head and tightened her grip on the phone. "Tell her to let them pick their own theme."

"I did," Isabelle said. "But she won't listen to them. They want to build a waterfall."

A waterfall? "In the gym?" Probably not what they really wanted. They simply wanted to be heard.

"They're calling it a Tropical Paradise, but mostly they just want the waterfall."

An image played in Toria's mind, of the overweight Mrs. Sidorsky, with her tidy bun of dark brown hair, trying to organize a group of excited Grade Twelves.

The poor woman.

"It's a major project," Isabelle said. "And they've got less than three weeks to accomplish it. Even if Mrs. Sidorsky lets them try." And then, "Can you come back?"

A sigh of longing drifted through her and she closed her eyes. It would be so wonderful to be with her students. Those predictable teenagers. Predictable in their unpredictableness. "I'm signed off for the year," she said.

"Just for the Grad, not for classes," Isabelle was saying.

Like she could wave a magic wand and make it so.

"I—"

"Have you talked to your Aunt Glenda? She knows about the accident?"

"Uh . . . no."

"You'd better call her. She'll be worried you haven't shown up yet."

Toria waited a moment, knowing Isabelle would not like to hear this. "She doesn't know I'm coming."

"You didn't tell her?"

"I couldn't. Not over the phone. She'd just worry."

"Oh, Toria," Isabelle said, distress in her voice. Toria could imagine Isabelle wringing her hands. "And you were all alone on that road. No one knew you were out there."

"You did."

"I could have died," Isabelle said. "And no one would have known to look for you."

"I don't think you're going to die for awhile." Toria twirled the phone cord over her fingers.

"But you're okay now?"

"Yes. It will all work out. And," she paused, considering the last twenty-four hours, "it was good. The drive. As far as I got. Because . . ."

"Because?"

"I was going to postpone. That was my plan when I left."

"And now?"

"Now I'm not postponing."

"Are you sure, dear? You didn't feel right about the June date and—"

"I'm not getting married at all."

Chapter Six

Ryder walked into a kitchen filled with cookie smells.

His mother was pulling a tray of baking from the oven. Flour and cocoa powder dusted three counters. The fridge, as usual, displayed a dozen pictures of his sister's two daughters, along with a hundred stick-it notes in a rainbow of colors.

And Pro sat on a stool at the island with a glass of milk and a plate of crumbs.

"How come you're here?"

"Had some time, was in the area," Pro said, licking his index finger and dabbing it at the crumbs.

"How are you, honey?" His mother set down the cookie tray. "Pro said you took a day off?"

Why did they all make it into such a big deal? "I can take a day off whenever I like."

"Yes, of course, you can, honey," she said, half absently, as she nudged cookies from the tray to a sheet of waxed paper. "It's very busy. Your business is doing well."

His mother always said that. His father never did.

The microwave timer beeped, the doorbell ding-donged, and the phone rang. All at the same time. His mother slid another tray into the oven, set the timer and turned to Pro. "Can you take those out when the timer goes?" She picked up the phone on the third ring. "And get Ryder a glass of milk and some cookies."

Like she was giving instructions to a maid, instead of the senior partner at Jones Jamieson.

Ryder sat at the island and watched her as she hurried to the front door. "Hard to believe she's a secretary."

"Why?" Pro said, getting milk from the fridge.

Why? The sink full of dishes, the stack of unopened mail balanced next to the coffee pot, the sewing machine set up on the dining room table. Even working only three days a week, his mother could not run the house. "She's so . . . scattered."

"You should see Aunt Tizzy," Pro said. "That's scattered. Although," he added, more to himself, "she has her moments."

He carried the milk to the island. "Your mother knows what she's doing. I'd hire her if she wasn't already working for Forsythe." He poured milk for Ryder. "You do want milk, right?"

"And cookies."

Pro found a small plate in the cupboard, loaded three cookies on to it and set the plate in front of Ryder. "That's funny, you know."

"What?"

"You marrying the boss's daughter."

"He's not *my* boss."

"I know. But it's still funny." Pro helped himself to one more cookie.

It was not funny, not in any way. But, Ryder conceded, it was important. To his father. Because his father liked . . . What?

Status? *Could you marry status?*

He wasn't doing that. He was marrying Catherine. Who just happened—

His taste buds connected with the warm chocolate chip cookie, dancing a dozen emotions over his tongue. Safety, warmth, caring—and other things he couldn't quite name.

He didn't have to. Some things were just automatic. Like chocolate chip cookies and good feelings.

"Pro?" he said, picking up another cookie. "How come you're not married?"

Pro thought a moment, swirled the milk in his glass and shrugged. "I've never been in love," he said.

"You mean be a volunteer?"

"I'm a volunteer," Isabelle said, like she was defending herself. She picked up the rest of the mail by the door and set it on the coffee table.

"In my own school?" Baffled, Toria leaned her head back on the love seat and stared at the bookshelves on the other side of the room.

"Sure. Why not?" Isabelle disappeared into the kitchen with her bulging pink canvas bag. Late afternoon sunlight streamed in through the balcony windows. Since Isabelle had arrived, the clouds had disappeared, like there had never been a storm.

"And what about . . . What do I tell them about the wedding?"

Isabelle came out of the kitchen, without her bag. "The one that's not happening?"

"That's the one." Toria studied the bookshelves, where toasters and towels and teacups lined up, waiting for thank you notes. "What do I do with all these shower gifts?"

"We'll have a party and give them back." Isabelle sat beside Toria on the love seat and then lifted her feet onto the coffee table. She wore orange and purple striped stockings today.

"A party?"

"Everyone buys you what they wish they had themselves," Isabelle said. "They'll all be happy to get their gift back. We'll get a case of wine and some of those appetizers from *Magic Mixers.*"

Toria watched as her friend sat there, blithely planning a party out of the ashes of her dismal engagement.

"We'll have balloons and streamers," Isabelle said. "And I'll bring some peaches. I have this terrific recipe."

Peaches. Just what she needed. More peaches.

The intercom buzzed, announcing a visitor.

A sudden flutter ran over her skin, a ripple of anticipation. She looked at her watch. Six o'clock. Exactly. It would be Ryder.

"Do you think that's him, dear? Your Good Samaritan?"

Or was it Greg? Could it be him? Her stomach tensed. But no, she didn't think it could be him. He would be with clients until at least eight, probably nine.

"Sit still, dear. I'll get it." Isabelle hopped off the love seat and bounced over to the intercom. "Come on up," she said, without asking who it was.

Just like Isabelle. Never check. "You should ask who it is before you let them in."

"We'll find out who it is when they get here," Isabelle said. She waited by the door, bobbing her heels up and down like a small child waiting for a surprise.

"It could be Greg," Toria said, getting to her feet, lining up the crutches.

"Oh." Isabelle frowned and stopped bobbing. "I hadn't thought of that."

If it *was* Greg, at least Isabelle was here. Although, it shouldn't really matter. She was *not* afraid of Greg.

And if it was Ryder? What then?

"And if this is him, I don't want you to—"

"If this is who?"

"If this is the Good Samaritan. Ryder."

The intercom buzzed again. Toria answered it this time. "Hello?"

"It's me," Ryder's voice said. "I've got a delivery for you." A slight pause. "Is it all right to bring it up?"

Anticipation and relief collided in her brain. He was checking—to make sure it was all right to bring up the wedding dress.

A warm feeling washed over her. He knew how to be considerate. And then she remembered the pizza. "Come on up," she said to the beige box on the wall.

Isabelle was still at the door, bobbing again and she was smiling, even more than usual.

Toria adjusted the crutches. "It's my Good Samaritan," she said, confirming what Isabelle must have guessed. "And Isabelle—"

Isabelle stopped bobbing, looked at Toria, and raised one carefully plucked eyebrow.

"Don't say anything about me cancelling the wedding. All right?"

Isabelle blinked. "Why ever not?"

Yes, a little voice inside her asked. *Why ever not?* She didn't want to think about that. "I just don't want to tell him. Not right now."

"If you say so."

Having the impending wedding there was like . . . a shield. She needed a shield around a man like Ryder. He couldn't get close to her if she was getting married.

Where had that come from?

Not that he would try to. After all, he was getting married, too. It was just that she'd felt so close to—

What was she thinking?

Her ankle ached, shooting pain all the way up her leg.

"Are you all right, dear? Maybe you should take another one of those pills."

No more pain pills. She felt woozy enough. "I'm fine," she said, automatically. And then, "No, not fine." *I will quit being fine.* "It just hurts, a little."

She made herself breathe. She'd never felt this way about Greg. Never. Greg was like a fairy tale, a Prince Charming, taking her to fancy restaurants in his sleek red sports car, bringing her roses and jewelry and theater tickets.

And Ryder? Certainly not your standard Prince Charming. Ryder was full of rough edges and impatience. None of Greg's smoothness.

Or phoniness.

But what did that matter? Ryder was getting *married*. In three weeks. So why did she keep thinking about him?

Maybe it was a reaction from finally deciding to get Greg out of her life. Maybe it was a protective mechanism her brain employed to keep her from thinking about Greg?

That must be it.

But, the little voice in her head prodded, if Ryder is getting married in three weeks, why is he helping you? Why is he being so nice to you?

Because he's a nice person, another part of her argued. Can't people be nice without having ulterior motives?

Did Greg have ulterior motives?

A knock sounded on the door.

Her heart raced. She took a step closer to the door . . . then stopped . . . and breathed. And gathered her wits.

Isabelle opened the door.

He wore his navy blue jacket over the denim shirt. And the jeans, and the heavy work boots. He was pulling the suitcase on its wheels, with the smaller one piggybacked on it. In his other hand, he balanced a pizza box with a brown paper lunch bag on top of it.

The wedding dress draped over his shoulder.

He looked at Isabelle, and then over Isabelle's head at her. And he smiled, like he couldn't believe what he was seeing.

Isabelle had that effect on people.

"Hi," Isabelle said, sticking out her hand. "I'm Toria's friend, Isabelle."

And then even Isabelle seemed to realize he had his hands full. She reached for the pizza box.

"Hi," Ryder said, smiling down at her. "I'm—"

"Ryder. I know. She told me."

Toria had told Isabelle Ryder's name, his first name. Not his whole name—Ryder Michael O'Callaghan—the name she'd seen on Pro's prenup agreement at the cabin.

And she'd told Isabelle that Ryder had rescued her from the side of the road last night, taken her to his cabin, and then driven her back to Calgary this morning.

Isabelle, thankfully, had not asked for details about the overnight stay at the cabin.

Taking the pizza box and the bag into the living room, Isabelle set them on the coffee table.

"Cookies from my mother," Ryder said. "She was baking and thought you'd like some."

"I—tell her thank you. That was very kind."

Isabelle was back, snatching the dress off Ryder's shoulder and bundling it into her arms as natural as could be. Like men often showed up at the door with billowy wedding dresses over their shoulders. Isabelle dumped the wedding dress in the chair.

"Have a seat," she said, taking the suitcase handle from him, and then rolling it part way down the hall. She parked the suitcase next to the wedding dress. "And sit down, Toria. You look faint."

Ryder glanced at her.

Was he checking to see if she really did look faint? She did feel a little weak. Or was he checking to see if it was all right if he stayed?

She shrugged.

So did he, and then he bent down, loosened the laces of

his work boots and stepped out of them.

"Toria?" Isabelle said, again. "Sit down."

She didn't need to sit. But she would. And maybe she did feel a little tired. She definitely felt hungry. She crutched over to the love seat and sat.

Still wearing his jacket, Ryder sat on the other end.

Instantly his scent touched her, tempting her with something that reminded her of spruce trees and fresh air. And peace. And at the same time, something exciting, and scary.

He was so close to her on the love seat. But that was the only place to sit since the chair was full of wedding dress.

"Would you like a drink?" Isabelle asked, standing in front of them, taking on the role of hostess. "I brought over some wine."

"Wine? I thought you were bringing soup?"

"I thought wine would be better." Isabelle exited to the kitchen.

"But I don't drink," Toria said, into the space that Isabelle had left. "You know that."

Isabelle came back from the kitchen with the wine, a corkscrew and three glasses. "This will make your foot feel better, dear."

Toria had a strange mother . . . and an even stranger friend.

This Isabelle character looked like a born again teenager. The old lady wore a green sleeveless top, a green and orange and red flowery full skirt, and purple and orange striped stockings. She was about a head shorter than Toria, and she might have been anywhere from fifty to a hundred years old. Her long hair was blonde and frizzy, like Rapunzel having a bad hair day.

And right now she was pulling the cork out of the wine bottle. Both wrists had bracelets made of woven cotton. Friendship bracelets, like his sister used to weave. Isabelle had four on one wrist and three on the other. She knelt on the other side of the coffee table, oblivious to the fact that she'd just dumped what was probably a designer wedding dress in a heap on the only chair in the room. The cork came out with a loud pop.

She filled the first glass and handed it to him.

A sparkling pink wine. He tasted it. Light and sweet and slightly exotic. Not bad but, with pizza, he would have preferred beer.

Should he have brought some beer?

No. That would have been pushing it. He hadn't expected to be invited in. Not really. He was just bringing her the pizza and the cookies. And her luggage. And the wedding dress.

He looked away from the wedding dress and back at Toria, who cradled her glass of wine in both hands as she sat huddled on her side of the love seat.

She was wrapped in a long, dark brown sweater, still wearing last night's jeans and the pink blouse. The sweater sleeves were turned up so they didn't cover her hands. She glanced at him and then looked at her wine.

Awkward. They sat next to each other on the love seat, fully clothed, and last night they'd slept together on that old couch, practically naked. Nothing to feel awkward about. It had just happened. Because she'd been so cold, and they'd been—

Stop. He didn't need to replay that. He shrugged out of his jacket, dropped it on the carpet beside the love seat, and scanned the room. A meager array of furniture—this love seat in red velour, the mismatched light green chair holding the wedding dress, and a garage-sale-style coffee table facing a set of bookshelves. An improvised set of bookshelves—varnished one-by-tens and blue painted cement blocks.

To his left, floor-to-ceiling windows led to a sunny balcony with two rusty lawn chairs, a dented aluminum watering can, and a piece of tree stump acting as a table for a flower pot of pink . . . daisies? He wasn't sure what they were called.

To his right, the wall boasted two professionally framed pictures that looked out of place with the rest of the room. The hall at the end of that wall, just past the bookshelves would lead to the bedroom, or bedrooms. He had a feeling this was a one-bedroom apartment.

Taking a moment, he studied the framed prints. Giraffes, made of fabric, silk maybe. Calm, soothing scenes done in browns and greens.

But his attention was pulled to the makeshift bookshelves in front of him, crowded with what must be wedding gifts waiting to go to their proper home.

She would move in with her fiancé after the wedding. They didn't live together now. Somehow, he knew that.

But then, he didn't live with Catherine either because she hadn't wanted him to move in. She wanted them to start fresh in the new house that was still being built.

It wouldn't be ready on time. He closed his eyes and tried not to think about it.

When he opened his eyes, he saw the bookshelves again. And all those gifts competing for space. Nesting blue, green, and orange mixing bowls in hard plastic, a teapot that looked like a frog, a crystal vase, several white china teacups in some delicate pattern, one of those strainers, like his mother had, only in brass—a colander, and then a pile of sheets—beige and navy and still half-wrapped with striped yellow wrapping paper. And towels and oven mitts and a toaster oven. All tucked in between a teak-based lamp with a white shade, some pitiful pieces of stereo equipment, an old black land line and an ancient answering machine.

All of it a soothing, comfortable mess. Like at his mother's. Except this apartment was even more ramshackle than his mother's house.

He shrugged. Just now, at this frozen moment in time, he liked it. It was at least familiar. And it wasn't like he had to live with it. He would be living with Catherine and he'd say one thing for her—she knew how to organize a space.

Her own and anyone else's.

The coffee table was almost as cluttered. The pizza box, the cookie bag, the wine bottle and glasses, the corkscrew, a roll of paper towels, a prescription bottle of pills—probably the 292s, a stack of unopened mail, some woman's magazine—Chatelaine, same as his mother.

They subscribed to the same magazine.

Another piece of mail rested upside down on the light beige carpet. Little pink and red hearts cascaded over the back of the envelope, some of them were sparkly, and some of the sparkles had sifted onto the carpet, winking at him.

"So, will you come back to the school?" Isabelle asked, as she separated a paper towel from the roll. "Just for a few days? To help them with the grad decorations?"

"Grad decorations?" *What was she talking about?*

"Yes," Isabelle said. "When they finish Grade Twelve they have a special celebration—"

"You teach high school?" He tried to remember what she'd told him. She'd said a teacher. "For some reason I thought you taught kindergarten."

Wrong. He didn't mean to insult her.

She laughed, not insulted at all. "I've always wanted to teach ECS, but it's very difficult. And my father was—"

She stopped. Like talking about her father was a problem.

"Her father was a history teacher," Isabelle said.

"Before he retired."

Her father who now lived in Kalispell. But— "I thought you had a wedding to plan?" Ryder accepted the paper towel Isabelle handed to him.

"I don't," Toria said. And then, "I mean—I do. But my mother—and—"

"Your fiancé's mother," he said. "They're planning it."

"Yes." She also accepted a paper towel from Isabelle. "That's right."

"Toria is wonderful with teenagers." Isabelle opened the pizza box. "They'll do anything for her."

"No, they won't," Toria said, shaking her head and grimacing. "I just let them do what they want to do in the first place."

"And what do they want to do?"

"They want to build a waterfall," Toria said.

"A—" He paused with the wine glass halfway to his mouth. "Why?"

"For their Grad Dance," Isabelle explained, as she lifted the first piece of pepperoni, bacon and mushroom from the box, and handed it to him.

He set the wine glass down, and slipped the paper towel under the pizza slice.

"They're decorating the gym," Isabelle said. "It's happening the last Saturday of June."

The thought flashed through his head. That date kept turning up. "The same day as your wedding," he said, turning to Toria.

"And your wedding," she answered.

Another reminder. Another poke, prodding his mind. Dread. Anxiety. Inevitability. His head ached, his chest tightened and his arm stiffened as he held the pizza. Surprised by the strength of those feelings, he made himself let go of the tension. "Right," he said.

He took a bite of pizza, realizing how hungry he was.

You can't fill up on cookies.

"So," Isabelle persisted, "you can help them build their waterfall, can't you, dear?"

"I don't know." Toria accepted a piece of pizza, catching the dripping cheese on her paper towel.

"I can build a waterfall," he said, like he would say I can build a deck or a garage or your whole frigging house.

"You can?" Isabelle pressed her palms together like she was giving thanks. Ahead of time.

"I'm a framer. I've never built a waterfall but how hard can it be? A little pump. Like people put in their garden ponds."

"It doesn't have to be huge. We were thinking about eight feet with a—"

"We?" Toria interrupted. "*Eight* feet?"

"You know they talk to me," Isabelle said.

"I'll bet they do." Toria wiped some cheese from her lips.

"We'll frame it," Ryder said. "Cover it with some six mil poly and then Styrofoam—or maybe expanding foam. Then we can set up a pump and—"

"But," Toria interrupted again, "don't you have to be at work?"

Work?

Right . . . work. He'd forgotten about work. Just for those few moments. Must be the crazy company he was keeping. He glanced at Isabelle.

But wasn't that what he was supposed to do? Let go of work? Prove that it didn't own him? It was the perfect solution.

"I'm trying out a business partner," he said. "This will be an opportunity to test him. I need to get out of his way for a few days."

. . . . .

By eight o'clock, Toria and Isabelle had each eaten a slice of pizza and split one. He'd eaten three slices and discussed grad decoration plans, mostly with Isabelle, since Toria looked sleepy.

And they'd finished the first bottle of wine. Isabelle was opening a second bottle when the intercom buzzed.

Toria instantly snapped awake, fumbled her empty wine glass, and dropped it in her lap.

Isabelle, in the middle of removing the foil top, stopped and said, "Who could that be?" Then she went back to inserting the corkscrew.

The intercom buzzed again. One long buzz followed by three short stabs. Someone was in a hurry.

Isabelle set down the wine bottle, with the corkscrew poking out the top, and got to her feet. But instead of answering the intercom, she gathered the wedding dress into her arms and calmly carried it down the hall.

The buzzer sounded again. Longer, more insistent.

"Are you going to get that?" Ryder asked.

Toria didn't say anything. She was staring at the empty wine glass in her hand, twirling it by its stem. She looked groggy. Either too much wine, or . . .

The pain pills?

"I'll get it," he said. And then it stopped buzzing.

Isabelle had returned to the living room and now she was rolling the two suitcases down the hall.

Like she was hiding them?

In another moment, Isabelle was back in the room. "Let me take that, dear," she said, motioning for Toria's wine glass.

Toria reached to give her glass to Isabelle and, he saw it then, Toria's hand was trembling. Why—?

There was a knock on the door, and both Isabelle and Toria stopped moving.

Another knock.

"I'll get it," Toria said, with a lot of tiredness in her voice. Or resignation. She set her wine glass on the table and reached for her crutches.

"Sit down," Ryder said. "I'll get it." He walked to the door and pulled it open.

"Who are you?" the man in the hall asked. He wore a three-piece suit that belonged in an office like Pro's.

"Ryder O'Callaghan," Ryder said, watching the man. "Who are you?"

"I'm Greg Lorimer." A slight pause. "Victoria's fiancé."

Victoria? For no reason in particular, Ryder didn't like the man. Not one bit. Neither of them made a move to shake hands.

"What are you doing here?" Lorimer asked.

"He's with me," Isabelle said, hustling up beside him. *What the hell . . . ?*

He almost jerked his head toward Isabelle, but he forced himself to keep his eyes on Lorimer. Maybe this guy was the jealous type. Maybe Isabelle was covering for Toria?

"He's a friend of my nephew's," Isabelle said, like it was true.

"Hello, Isabelle," Lorimer said. "What are *you* doing here?" He made it sound as if Isabelle had no business spending time with *his* fiancée. Then he walked into the apartment.

"Toria hurt her foot," Isabelle explained and hurried after Lorimer into the living room.

Feeling ignored, Ryder shrugged and closed the door.

Lorimer stood on the other side of the small coffee table staring down at Toria. He picked up the empty bottle of Summer Island Cherry Blossom Rosé and read the label.

"Don't feed her this stuff, Isabelle. You know it doesn't agree with her."

Toria stayed on the couch but she held her crutches in front of herself.

Lorimer set the bottle back on the coffee table, and looked at the pizza box, two pieces left. "So you've eaten," he said. "I thought we were going out."

Toria didn't say anything. Ryder remembered her reaction to the peaches . . . with the brandy. The 292s were making her sleepy. Especially with the wine.

"How's your ankle, darling?"

Standing near the entrance, Ryder listened, the sounds jarring in his head. He frowned. The way Lorimer said *darling* didn't sound like . . . *darling*.

"Hurts a bit," she said. "It'll be all right."

"I never had time to find out what happened. Whose fault was the accident?"

"No, you didn't have time. You were in the middle of a deal."

"Which was quite successful, by the way," he answered. "So, whose fault was it? Does this mean your insurance rates will go up?"

"It was no one's fault. I drove off the road."

"Not paying attention, again, Victoria?"

Victoria? There it was again. How come he called her *Victoria?*

"It's a bad road. Full of potholes."

"Which road?"

"The one she was on," Isabelle said, intervening. "Would you like some pizza, Greg?" She offered him the box, bumping it into him.

Lorimer took the box, stared at it a moment like he didn't recognize it, and then sat next to Toria with the box in his lap. No one said anything. Lorimer watched the pizza languishing on the cardboard, Isabelle studied the label on the wine bottle with the corkscrew still sticking out of the top of it. And Toria stared at her wedding gifts on the blue cement block bookshelves.

It seemed unreal. One minute they'd been laughing about how to explain the garden hoses to the janitors, and in the next moment they were acting all guilty, as if her fiancé had caught the three of them playing strip poker. A horrible image when he looked at Isabelle.

Not a bad image when he looked at Toria. In fact . . . not bad at—

He should leave. Right away. He had no business being here. Even if he wasn't imagining a game of strip poker.

"I'd better be going," he said.

And he left.

Ryder was gone. It was just as well. Before he came back, she would somehow talk Isabelle out of this ridiculous waterfall idea, borrow Isabelle's car, and drive to Kalispell to see Aunt Glenda. And then maybe Toria could put her life back in order.

Greg finished the last piece of pizza, then tapped his fingers over his lips, brushing away imaginary pizza crumbs. Isabelle sat in the chair that had held the wedding dress, looking like she was chaperoning.

"Who is that guy?"

Someone I actually enjoy being with—

No. He's an infatuation. A reaction to the circumstances. Nothing more.

"A friend of my nephew's," Isabelle said, again.

Isabelle was trying to protect her, as if she needed protection, from Greg.

A lightness touched her, waved through her, like a window opening to freedom. She smiled, knowing she could deal with Greg.

But Ryder? What about him? Did she need protection from Ryder?

Of course not. At least, she hoped not. Just because she had enjoyed having him here, having him sitting next to her, that didn't mean anything. Did it?

"We needed him to carry up some wedding things," Isabelle explained.

Toria almost laughed, because it was true.

"I see," Greg said, dismissing Ryder as any kind of problem. Greg handled problems all day. That was his job—to make problems go away.

Now he was looking at her bookshelves. "You should start moving that stuff to your mother's house."

Feathery tentacles of fear touched the edges of her mind. But the wine, and probably the painkillers, blunted her response, and it took a moment to get out the words. "I won't be doing that."

"We've been over this, Victoria."

"I'm not living in my mother's house." The words slipped out. Of course she wasn't living there. She'd never agreed to that particular idea.

"Don't worry, darling. She'll be in a different part of the house. She'll have her own little suite and she'll be—"

"I never agreed to that." And it's irrelevant, she thought. "We aren't—"

"I've put the Eau Claire condo on the market."

What? When had he decided that?

"I thought you were just getting the condo appraised?"

"That was the first step, and now it's on the market. I want the Varsity Estates house."

Want? When had *this* happened? "That's why you want to marry me? For my father's house?"

"You shouldn't drink wine, darling."

Odd bits of conversation tumbled through her mind. Greg telling her mother not to worry about money, her mother's suddenly important renovations.

"You never intended for us to live in the condo, did you?"

Toria was aware of Isabelle in the background, sitting with ankles crossed and arms folded, leaning back in the chair. Watching.

"See what I mean?" Greg said, making it sound like an endearment. "You're drunk, darling."

"I'm not. I had two glasses." Why was she arguing about how much wine she'd had?

He lifted the pill container from the pharmacy. "What is this?" he asked, sounding so reasonable.

She hated Reasonable. She had lived with Reasonable for too long. "I told you I am *not* marrying you."

"Of course you are."

Her breath caught as a suffocating blanket of memories pressed against her. She shook her head and cleared her mind. "Isabelle, in my bedroom on the dresser, bring me that ring."

Isabelle popped out of her chair and left the room.

"Were you angry?" Greg asked.

"What?"

"Driving angry? Is that why you—what did you do?"

Don't answer the question. He's distracting you. "I made a sharp turn and hit the ditch."

Don't talk to him!

She felt the ring, the pinch of the sharp diamond as Isabelle pressed it into her hand. Toria looked at the platinum band, then with the ring on her palm, she held it out to Greg. "Take it. I'm not your fiancée."

I'm not your property to manage.

Greg stared at her for a beat, never looking at the diamond. Then his lip lifted on one side. "I'm not taking that ring. I'd just have to give it back to you."

And with that, he calmly stood, and walked out the door.

Isabelle bounced out of her chair, rushed over to the door and locked it. Then she spun around, with a twirl of her flowery full skirt and with her hands held in front of her, fingertips touching. "That went well," she said.

It did?

Toria held the ring between her thumb and index finger, twisting it in the evening sunlight coming through the balcony windows. The diamond was perfectly cut, Greg had said. Multi carat . . . she should remember the number. And expensive. The light bounced around inside the gem, trapped there.

"What do I do with this?"

"We'll courier it to his office," Isabelle said. "He'll have to sign for it."

"You're right," Toria said. "Good idea."

Isabelle took the diamond. "I'll do it first thing tomorrow morning."

Chapter Seven

Ryder watched from his truck as Greg Lorimer exited the building and got into this year's model of the BMW Z4 Coupe. A second later, boom boxes cranked up and pounded over the still night air.

As relief washed through him, he loosened his grip on the steering wheel and tipped his head down. He didn't know what he would have done if Isabelle had left first.

Lorimer was driving away, a flash of red and chrome and noise, past the restored Firebird.

Now Ryder allowed himself to look at the Firebird. The classic muscle car lined up next to the geranium-filled flower boxes along the circular drive of Dalhousie Towers. It waited, like a limousine, across from the place where Lorimer had parked his Bimmer. The Firebird glowed in the late evening sunshine.

The color looked close to the original, a brilliant orange. Headers protruded from the hood, giving the car a commanding presence. He wished he had time to take a closer look at the vehicle . . . wished he knew the owner. Probably some creative teenage genius.

Besides the Firebird, three other cars remained on the circular drive. A rusty blue Astro minivan, a relatively new Honda Accord—maybe three years old, and an ancient Oldsmobile station wagon. That would be what Isabelle was driving. Or would she take the bus? Probably the bus.

Maybe she'd spend the night with Toria? That would be

good. He could go now. He touched the key in the ignition, but his hand froze and he couldn't turn the key. He couldn't turn the engine over. So he didn't like the guy. So what? Lorimer was typical of Toria and the crazy cast of characters that populated her life. This was none of his business.

He saw a flicker of green and orange and red just past the entrance doors. Someone was coming out of the building—

Isabelle.

She squeezed her large pink canvas bag tightly to her chest, like she was carrying something important. Her long flowery skirt fluttered in the breeze over top of her purple and orange striped stockings, and her frizzy blonde hair rippled like a flag. Pausing by the entrance, she reached inside her bag and pulled something out. He couldn't see what it was, it was too small, but she was staring at it, studying it in the light of the setting sun, like she was trying to decide what to do with it. And then she seemed to—

Yes. She pushed it on her finger. A ring. Something to complete the eccentric wardrobe.

She fished in the bag again. This time she'd find her bus pass. Maybe he should offer to drive her home? But then, how would he explain still being here? He could say his truck wouldn't start or—

A flash of metal in the dimming light. Not a bus pass. She was holding a set of keys. She did have a car, but—

It couldn't be. She was getting into the Firebird. The orange Firebird with the headers and the attitude.

He touched his forehead to the steering wheel and closed his eyes for a second. When he looked up again, she was driving away, spinning the tires momentarily. She probably didn't realize how much power she had.

So, he thought, Isabelle was gone. And so was Lorimer. The entrance to the building stood empty. Inviting . . .

A sense of anticipation swirled around him, lightly touching him, like the first flakes of snow coming out of the sky. Then he remembered. He still had her pink insurance card. He pulled the keys from the ignition. And smiled.

Not only that, he needed the address for the school. It would be a lot of fun to build that waterfall.

A moment later, he buzzed her apartment.

"What!" she snapped.

Whoa. What's up with her? "It's me," he said. "I forgot to give you—"

Before he could finish what he was saying, the lock buzzed open. Just like that.

He opened the door and stepped inside, pausing as it closed behind him. She hadn't answered when Lorimer had buzzed. What was going on? Were they fighting? The thought made him happy.

Stupid, thinking that. And no, it didn't make him happy, he told himself, feeling contented. Just a—what did they call it?

A lovers' quarrel. Could be anxiety about the imminent wedding. If he was getting married in three weeks, he'd probably feel the same way.

Except . . . he *was* getting married in three weeks.

Right.

A jerk of realization stunned him. He saw the date in his head, saw it circled on his calendar, like an oil change due date.

Less than three weeks. It was Tuesday already. Both he and Toria were getting married in two and a half weeks. And now she was having some kind of argument with her fiancé.

Ryder, on the other hand, never got upset with Catherine.

Except, well, there was the poodle—

Then he had an unconnected thought, anxiety for Toria, and a feeling of protectiveness. He frowned.

How *had* Lorimer got in? Had someone else let him into the building?

Must have, he decided, looking around the small lobby. And that was not a good thing. Letting someone in who didn't belong here.

He glanced at the old elevator and remembered riding it earlier this evening. A flash of doubt, and he wondered if the elevator had passed a building inspection lately.

He ran up the three flights of stairs. As he entered the hall, the door opposite Toria's opened, and an old woman with silver hair peeked out and looked at him. Her gray cat wandered into the hall. She bent to retrieve the cat and went back inside.

Feeling uneasy, he paused, then continued down the hall to Toria's door. Her neighbor's door, across the hall, had a peep hole installed. Toria's did not.

He knocked lightly on Toria's door.

She opened it, still wearing the long dark brown sweater, and leaning on her crutches.

Again that feeling of protectiveness hit him. "Uh . . ." he said, speaking quietly and not turning around. "Can I come in? I think your neighbor is spying on us."

Toria closed her eyes and shook her head. Then she whispered, "Mrs. Toony. She probably let Greg in." She shuffled back with her crutches, allowing him to come inside.

He closed the door behind him and leaned against it. Something classical—something light, and airy—was playing on Toria's old stereo.

The gentle music ebbed around him and he let himself relax against the door.

She stood directly in front of him, close, in the small entrance area. In the kitchen, a single light glowed over the stove. The other one had burned out. The June sun, now low in the sky, still filtered through the balcony windows into the living room. But here, near the door, it was not well lit.

"I forgot to return your pink card," he said, still speaking quietly, as though the nosy neighbor could hear them through the door. And the hall, and her own door.

"Sorry." She smiled. "You shouldn't have come back for that. I can't drive anyway. Well, I can *drive* but I don't have a car," she babbled.

"And I forgot to ask you which school—"

"You don't need to do this."

"I would like to."

She looked up at him, and again he noticed her eyes.

The piece of music ended and a new one took its place. Something with the same gentle serenity.

"I—" he started to explain, but he looked into her eyes, which were several shades of green. Like the green of a quiet lake in the Kananaskis. And mixed with the green, a little gold—

He caught his breath and blinked. "I didn't go to my own Grad," he said. "This might be fun."

"You didn't go to your Grad? Why not?"

He shrugged. "Juvenile." He'd never admitted that to anyone. Not even to Pro. "I wanted to piss off my parents." *My father mostly.*

She smiled, like she understood.

"Which school?" he asked again.

She paused. A few seconds passed. "Aberton."

Aberton?

"Do you know where that is?"

"Yeah," he nodded, watching her mouth. "I do."

It was *his* school. His old high school. Eleven years ago. Light years ago.

The peaceful music eased into his mind and a sensation

of longing floated through him. He should just reach in his wallet, give her the pink card, and leave. But he didn't want to leave.

"We didn't have any of your mother's cookies," she said.

"Milk and cookies time?"

"Yes."

"You sit down," he said. "I'll get the milk."

He took off his work boots again, dropped his jacket beside them and walked into the kitchen. In the fridge, he found a jug of *skim* milk, along with a carton of eggs, a package of cream cheese and a jar of marmalade.

He could drink skim milk. He set it on the counter. Then he opened the cupboard directly above the counter.

Right the first time. It was the cupboard with the glasses. Two medium-sized A&W root beer mugs, a set of crystal bourbon glasses with heavy bases and four clear mugs with shamrocks around the rims.

The A&W root beer mugs. They'd work. He filled them with milk, walked to the other end of the kitchen, past the small table, and turned into the living room.

She had a cookie in her hand and her left foot up on the coffee table next to the empty pizza box. "Tell your mother," she said, licking her lips, "these are very good." She took another bite.

He positioned her mug of milk on the coffee table beside her tensored ankle.

"You have a lot of wedding gifts," he said, looking at the improvised bookshelves again.

"Shower gifts."

Right. Shower gifts. That came first. "You have a lot of shower gifts."

"Yes, I do." She sounded tired.

He started to walk around her to sit on his side of the love seat, and then he noticed the envelope on the floor, in the same place as before. A few sparkles flashed in the light from the setting sun. He picked up the envelope, walked around the cluttered coffee table and sat down beside her.

She handed him a cookie out of the bag. He handed her the heart-covered envelope.

"What's this?" She took it from him. "Oh, I almost forgot. It's from a student."

The envelope said *Miss Toria Whitney.* A large envelope, covered with pink and red, shiny and sparkly, heart stickers.

Her face softened, as if she was giving in to something. She tucked one slender fingertip under the flap, opened the envelope and pulled out the card. A cascade of red and pink hearts showered over them both, like confetti thrown at a wedding.

He leaned closer, to read over her shoulder. A thread of air separated them.

"You're reading my mail." She nudged him away with her elbow.

"It's just a student," he said. Several of the shiny hearts had landed in the weave of the brown sweater and on the front of her pink blouse.

"Don't say *just* a student."

"All right." And one of the red hearts had fallen on her throat, at the opening of her blouse.

He wondered what the student had to say, and he leaned close again. His denim-covered arm lightly touched her sweater-covered arm. Not a problem, he told himself. Easier to read over her shoulder.

By now she was focused on the card, and she didn't push him away.

Dear Miss Toria,

"Miss Toria?"

"I like that better than Miss Whitney. And they're not

supposed to call me Toria."

> *We know you said we would be able to handle this just fine but we can't. Mrs. Sidorsky is not playing fair. She said we could pick our own theme, and then she impositioned her theme on us.*

"Impositioned?" He turned his head, which was right next to hers.

"They like their own words," she said, without looking away from the card.

"What about spelling?" He watched her eyes, her whole expression.

"They're communicating."

"Yeah, but shouldn't—"

"Will you let me read this?" She glanced up at him. Their eyes connected for a microsecond, and then she looked back at the card.

So did he.

> *Mrs. Sidorsky wants Beauty and the Beast.*

He stopped reading, disgusted, and pulled back from the card. "Beauty and the Beast? That's a fairy tale!"

"You'd like these kids," she said, still reading the words. He leaned close again.

> *Like, we're going to decorate some fairy tale? We're not in kindergarten. For ~~Christ~~ cripes sake.*
>
> *Oh, and the results from the provincials are coming in. We scored highest in the province, even though you never followed their curriculum. But don't worry, we never told anyone.*

"I thought you taught history? That's a provincial exam?"

"No. It's not," she said. "I still teach some history, I started there, but I mostly teach mathematics. That's a provincial."

Mathematics? Toria? It didn't add up.

He laughed at his own pun. Normally it would not be funny. Must be Isabelle's wine messing with his brain. And naturally, Toria, in her scattered way, would not follow the curriculum.

Longing wove through his memories. He would have liked a teacher like this, like the one sitting next to him.

Whoa. Where had that thought come from? He didn't need a teacher. He kept reading.

> *So we were wondering if you could please please please come back? Just to help us get the gym in shape? Otherwise Mrs. S is going to embarrass us. Miss Isabelle said you might be able to fit us in.*

Toria dropped the card in her lap and frowned at the bookshelves. Could she say no to her students?

"We've got to do this," he told her.

Lost in thought, she didn't say anything for a moment. Then she looked at him. "We?"

The room had darkened. The sun was gone behind the mountains. Twilight. Yesterday, he'd met her, at twilight. He'd found her car in the ditch, almost twenty-four hours ago.

He had a sense of traveling through time, like he was reliving a memory. Sparkles of hearts twinkled before his eyes and he blinked. Maybe he should turn on the lamp on the bookshelves, assuming it worked.

His arm still touched her shoulder, and a little chocolate chip cookie crumb balanced on the edge of her lip. She had beautiful lips—soft and full.

She was staring at the bookshelves now, not seeing them. He watched her eyes, that unbelievable shade of green . . . It was the light, from the leftover sun, playing tricks with his mind.

He reached out and brushed away the crumb at the edge of her lip.

"Cookie crumb," he said.

She's getting married. Get out of here.

She smiled, and blushed.

And she's had too much to drink, for her. *And never mind that, I'm supposed to be getting married. In a huge wedding that is going to impress the socks off my father.*

He moved away from her, sat forward and drained his mug of milk. Then he got to his feet. "I'll pick you up tomorrow morning," he said, wondering at the same time why he was saying it.

But it wouldn't be a problem. In the morning. In the daylight.

"Why?" She was standing up, too, swaying a little.

"We can go out to Cochrane and talk to the RCMP. You can check the car, see if there's anything in it that you want."

She swayed a little more as she tried to get her crutches under her arms.

He wanted to touch her—a bad idea. And anyway, she was steady now. He headed for the door.

She followed him.

At the door, he pulled on his boots, picked up his jacket and turned to her. This was confusing.

But, he was never confused. He knew exactly what he was doing.

"Lorimer," he said. "Do you love him?"

Except for when he asked questions like that.

"I thought I did," she said, dreamily. "I mean, yes, of course."

Chapter Eight

Ryder rolled over and turned off the alarm before it could ring. The digital readout on his bedside table said 6:18 a.m.

Surprisingly, his head felt clear. He'd actually slept. And as far as he could remember, he hadn't thought about the partnership agreement all night. But, he'd been dreaming about something else.

Wanting to remember, he squeezed his eyes shut, hoping to catch a fragment. And he sighed. It was on the brink of recall, all jumbled like morning dreams often are—a dark, winding, rain-sloshed road, something white waving in the wind, a fire blazing in a potbellied, black stove.

And something else. Words that repeated over and over in his mind, taunting him.

I thought I did?

Why had she said that?

No use trying to figure it out. Who knew what she was thinking? Especially after the wine. She was just being her spinny, scattered self. He threw back the blanket and sat up.

But, how could she be a teacher? And—even more strange—a mathematics teacher? Weren't they supposed to be logical?

And what was *he* thinking? Why had he volunteered to drive her to Cochrane?

Because it was a good idea, his logical brain told him. Driving her to Cochrane was a distraction, something to keep his mind off work. He needed to get away from work for a while, let Jim work on his own, and let the man demonstrate what he could do. And then they could finalize the partnership agreement.

With that out of the way, Ryder could cope with this building frenzy. And, he could get on with his life—with finishing the new house in Royal Oak, marrying Catherine, and—

And proving, once and for all, to his pigheaded father that he was just as good as his father was.

A sense of futility threatened. Ryder slumped his shoulders and blew out a breath. He couldn't do anything about the partnership agreement right now. Pro would deal with it. And he couldn't do anything about the wedding—it would roll along, and happen the way Catherine wanted it to happen. And he couldn't do anything about the poodle.

He stood, headed for the shower, and cranked it on.

Maybe, just maybe, he could do something about the damn poodle.

I thought I did? Oh God, why had she said that?

Toria got out of the shower. She'd overslept, and she never overslept. Since Monday night when she'd decided to go to Kalispell to see Aunt Glenda, she'd stepped into a whirlwind. What to do first?

She needed a car. And, if she was going to help her students, she needed to talk to Mrs. Sidorsky. And Ryder—

A chill fluttered over her skin. They were going to Cochrane. Oh dear.

Fitting a crutch under one wet arm, she stood on her good foot. Then she reached for the green towel on the rack and tugged it off.

It would be all right, she told herself, as she blotted the towel over her body with one hand. He probably hadn't even noticed what she'd said.

I thought I did? What was wrong with her?

It was true, though, she *had* thought that. Way back in the beginning, she'd been swept away . . . and look where it had got her. That was not going to happen again. Not ever.

She propped the crutch against the wall, steadied herself on one foot, and then wrapped the towel around herself. Today was Wednesday. Today would be better. She would stop by the school. But first—

The car.

Water dripped from her hair over her skin and tapped on the tiles. She needed another towel for her hair. Better not hop, not on the wet floor. She reached for her crutch.

So what if he was giving her a ride? Somebody needed to give her a ride, and he seemed to want to stay away from his work to let his would-be partner have some space.

She'd better hurry. He'd be here soon. If he was really coming. He couldn't possibly want to work on grad decorations, could he? Last night, he was only being polite. She eased another towel off the shelf and felt the one around her loosening. The crutch wobbled.

At any rate, if he did come this morning and if he did drive her to Cochrane, she'd get the forms signed so they could release her poor old Honda from the police impound. So it could be towed to Calgary to the insurance company's impound. So they could write it off and pay her out.

And somehow, she'd have to make time to buy another car.

Still gripping her crutch, she shook out the other towel. After Cochrane, she'd spend an hour or so with Mrs. Sidorsky. Ryder could leave her at the school.

And then she would borrow Isabelle's car, drive to Kalispell, and talk to Aunt Glenda like she'd wanted to do in the first place.

Little drops of water still rolled off the ends of her hair, pinging down on the tiles. She propped the crutch on the wall, stood on her right foot, and bent over to wrap the towel around her head.

"How did you get in?"

He wondered that himself. Toria stood in front of him in the doorway of her apartment, her hair in a towel and her body wrapped in a frayed, pink robe.

Her nosy neighbor was probably monitoring this. Mrs. Loony Toony.

"One of your building residents let me in," he told her. "A young couple on their way out. They really shouldn't do that."

"I know."

She held up her purple foot as she moved with her crutches away from the door to let him come in. Her face was clean and shiny, without makeup. Fresh out of the shower, he guessed. It looked like she never wore makeup, because she always looked like this.

And right now, she looked flustered. She was trying to retie the belt of her robe and balance on her crutches at the same time.

"Have you had breakfast?" He took hold of the belt, brushing his hands over hers.

She jumped back, dropped one of the crutches and clutched her robe.

"I'm tying it for you," he said. And he did, as quickly as he could. While he tried not to think of her naked body under—

Wrong.

The belt secured, he bent down and retrieved the fallen crutch. "Have you?" he asked.

"Have I what?"

"Had breakfast?"

She smiled then, and she seemed to relax a little. "Just coffee." Her face and throat were flushed, a pretty pink. Was she blushing?

She probably wanted to get dressed. "Want me to make breakfast?" he asked. "I noticed some eggs in the fridge last night."

She smiled at him like he was her savior. "Don't look like that," he said.

"Like what?"

"Like it's going to be really good."

"It *is* going to be really good. I'm hungry. There's bread in the freezer if you'd like toast." She took the crutch from him. "Sorry, I'm not ready. I overslept."

"No problem. Take your time." It wasn't like he had anything else to do.

She hobbled down the hall, and he headed into the kitchen. And then he remembered the I-beams and wondered if Jim had contacted Rona. Automatically, he reached for his cell, index finger hovering over the speed dial.

He waited a moment, and realized he was interfering. Then he turned off the power button, and returned the cell to the clip on his belt.

Jim could handle it.

Half an hour later, they were finishing breakfast on the balcony, sitting on the two rusty lawn chairs in the warm sunshine. Monday's storm was forgotten.

"More coffee?" He picked up the coffee pot from the tree stump table.

"Please." She held up her mug. "You don't need to wait on me, you know."

"It's nothing." And then again, maybe it *was* something,

since he rarely cooked. Tim Hortons was breakfast central for him. For most of them.

He refilled her mug and set the coffee pot beside the pink daisies.

No, not daisies. "What are these?"

"Impatiens."

"Mmm," he said, picking up the jug of milk and adding some to her cup. Her foot still needed the tensor bandage but the rest of her was dressed. Nice fitting jeans, a white long-sleeved blouse and a navy blue cardigan with a denim collar. He set down the milk jug and picked up the tensor. "Give me your foot."

"I can do it."

"So can I."

She watched him, took a sip of her coffee and did not move her foot.

Better rephrase that. "I would like to do it," he said. "Please."

She smiled then, turned in her chair and held out her poor purple foot. He propped her ankle on his knee.

She sipped more coffee. "Did you talk to your partner this morning?"

"He's not my partner yet." He wound the bandage around her foot. "And yes, I talked to him before I came over." He finished with the tensor and secured it with the clips. "And now he's on his own."

"Does that worry you? Having him in charge?"

In charge. Jim.

"He can't do anything I can't fix."

"You wouldn't leave him, if you thought you'd have to fix things."

Right. He wouldn't. It wasn't leaving Jim in charge that was the problem.

"I've been the boss for so long." Too long, now that he thought about it. He'd never planned to have anything this big. But now . . . "I guess I'm worried about—" What? Losing control?

"You're worried about . . ." She prompted him.

"Everything," he admitted. "Sharing the responsibility. Having to make joint decisions. Everything."

"You'll be learning while he learns." Another sip of coffee.

"Yeah," he said. "I guess I will."

Having breakfast on her balcony was like finding an oasis of calm. For the first time in days, he could finally relax and forget about everything.

Someone knocked on the door.

Irritability replaced the calm. He glanced at Toria. She shrugged.

"I'll get it." He stood. "And somebody should put up a sign," he said, sliding open the balcony screen door. "Or they should have a meeting about letting people just walk in here."

A few seconds later he was at the door.

"You again," Greg Lorimer said, standing in the hallway.

"Yeah," Ryder answered. "Me."

The loony neighbor had her door slightly ajar. Lorimer held a small Bow Valley Courier package in his hands.

"You own the black Dodge Ram?" Lorimer asked.

"Yeah, it's mine. Did you want something?"

"I'm here to see Victoria. This *is* her apartment, isn't it?"

Anger flared inside Ryder's chest. His fists clenched by his sides, and with all the willpower he could muster, he took a deep breath and stepped out of the way.

As he stood by the open door, he wondered, again, what was wrong with him? This crazy, out-of-proportion response to seeing Toria's fiancé baffled him.

She was coming in from the balcony and one crutch

was across the threshold when she saw Lorimer . . . and stopped.

"How's the foot, darling? Feeling better?"

"I feel a lot better," she said, holding her chin up and making herself tall.

Yeah. They were having an argument. He was convinced of it. Not that it made him happy, or anything . . .

"Toria! Good morning!" Pro walked in.

Pro?

Surprised, Ryder checked outside the door to see if anyone *else* was out there. Loony's door remained partly open. The old lady wasn't satisfied with just the peep hole. He closed the apartment door.

"Morning, Ryder. How are you?"

I'm wondering what the hell is going on. "I'm—"

"Who are *you?*" Lorimer turned away from Toria and focused on Pro. Pick a number and come on up. This was ridiculous.

"Prometheus Jones," Pro said, extending his hand to Lorimer. "Toria wanted me to draft a prenup for her."

"A prenup? You want a prenup, darling? What for?"

"What are they usually for?" She smiled, her parent-teacher interview smile. And she would have screamed at Greg if Ryder had not been there.

"So that's what this is all about?" Greg was rocking on his heels, as if a sour deal had suddenly gone right again. "Good," he said, sounding pleased. "We can talk tonight." He turned to look at Pro and Ryder. "Should I make an appointment?"

"Why don't you call to see if I'm here?" Breathe, she told herself. And then she realized he had the Bow Valley Courier package in his hand, tapping it on his leg. Like he could slip the ring back on her finger. A noose around her neck.

"Eight," he said. "Tonight." His cell rang. He checked the readout, stuffed the courier package in his suit coat and left.

She let go of the sigh she'd been holding in. Time out. Obviously, she needed to do something more about getting rid of Greg.

But, Pro was here? She didn't actually remember asking Pro to help her with a prenup. Why would she have done that?

"You want to do a prenup now?" Ryder looked impatient as he talked to Pro. "We're on our way to Cochrane."

"Of course," Pro said. And *his* cell rang.

Although, Toria thought, having Pro show up like this, out of the blue, was a stroke of luck.

"Did you want to do Cochrane later?" Ryder asked, his impatience seeming to leave him as quickly as it had come.

"No," Pro answered for her. "Don't do that. That was Aunt Tizzy."

Toria remembered. Pro had mentioned his Aunt Tizzy when they'd been at the cabin on Tuesday morning. She was the one who made the brandy peaches.

"Aunt Tizzy," Ryder repeated, like he had his doubts about her.

"She needs me . . . for something."

"How come you're not at work?" Ryder asked. "Don't you have to be at work?"

"I do," Pro said. "But Aunt Tizzy has something important she needs me for. So," he said, looking at his watch, "I'd better be going."

After that, Ryder drove Toria to Cochrane. On the way, he spent about ten minutes telling her about the beams, and then, when she did not tell him to *not* worry, he forgot about worrying. They spent the rest of the time talking about the Grad Dance, Isabelle's involvement with the students, and the importance of hands-on learning.

"If you insist on building this waterfall, you're going to have to do it in a supervisory capacity."

"I know how to supervise. I do it all the time."

"These are students, not framers."

"We're all students of some sort."

She ignored that comment and continued. "The students will build it. You will act as a resource person."

"Wow. A resource person. Never thought I'd be a resource person."

"Don't be silly."

At the Cochrane RCMP office, no one had any real questions for Toria. The papers were quickly signed. She cleared out her glove compartment and they headed back to Calgary and the school.

Catherine waited on the couch in the dressing room, studying the guest seating, and penciling in changes while her mother paced.

"Can't he leave his work for one blessed morning?"

"He said he'd be here," Catherine told her. "He will. He's reliable." That was one thing about Ryder—he was reliable. She might not be able to get him to do much but if he said he'd do something, he would.

Now, was it a good idea to sit Aunt Anita beside Aunt Matilda? Probably not. The two sisters never got along . . . never wanted to share the limelight.

"It's ten-thirty. He was supposed to be here half an hour ago. Can't you reach him on his cell?"

As though she hadn't already thought of that. "His cell is out of service." And it was odd for Ryder to have his cell turned off. "He'll be here. Don't worry. Something must have happened at work."

Her mother continued to pace. "Maybe a roof fell on somebody. He *would* think that was more important than getting fitted for his tux."

"His work is important to him," Catherine said without looking up.

"His work is his life. He should have finished his degree."

A warning clanged inside her head and her pencil broke. "What does that have to do with anything?"

"Nothing. Nothing at all." Her mother stopped pacing and turned to face her. "But, Catherine, three *years* of an engineering degree and he walks away from it? For a summer job?"

"He . . . he liked it. And he was making too much money to go back."

Her mother returned to her pacing and said, "Anyway, he's thinking of finishing his degree once his work slows down. Once he has a partner helping him."

"How do you know that?" Ryder hadn't told her anything about going back to school.

"Remember, sweetheart, his mother works for your father. She mentioned that Ryder was thinking of finishing his degree. Not that the woman cares one way or the other." The pacing stopped, and her mother faced her. "Your sisters' husbands make a lot of money too, you know, but they're lawyers. They work in an office . . . with set hours."

Here we go again. "Lawyers who don't make nearly the kind of money Ryder does. I thought you liked it that he made a lot of money?"

"Of course I do. I mean . . . it doesn't matter. It's just that your sisters—"

"Can we talk about something else?"

"Yes. Yes, we can."

A pause. Now what?

"Catherine?" Her mother sat on the couch, smoothed her skirt and folded her hands in her lap.

Not a good sign.

"How do you feel about him?" her mother asked, making eye contact and holding it. "About Ryder?"

"What do you mean?"

"How do you *feel* about him?"

"I'm marrying him."

"Do you love him?"

"Of course I do." Why did her mother have to go emotional on her? She hated it when her mother got all sensitive and melodramatic.

Her mother's shoulders slumped. She seemed to be switching topics, again. "What did you say he was doing right now?"

"I don't know." *He never talks to me about work.* If he did, she could give him suggestions, ideas for how to be more organized—

"Don't you ever talk to him?"

At the back of her mind, another warning throbbed. "We've been too busy with the wedding."

"*You* have been too busy with the wedding. He's not showing up for any of the showers or parties. Is he even *having* a bachelor party?"

"Prometheus is supposed to organize it," Catherine told her. *But he's too busy writing prenuptial agreements.*

"Prometheus?" Her mother raised her eyebrows.

"Yes. His lawyer. Prometheus Jones."

Her mother looked up at the ceiling. "What a ridiculous name."

Chapter Nine

Ryder stood outside the principal's office. A sense of déjà vu prodded his mind, and then a flare of anxiety. And then anger. Then it was over. He was no longer a student, no longer under their thumb. No longer under anyone's control.

"And this is Mrs. Sidorsky," Toria was saying, introducing him to the fat lady.

But . . . it couldn't be.

Mrs. Sidorsky was staring at him. "I recognize you," she said. "Didn't you used to—"

"Go here? Yes," he said. "Eleven years ago. You threw me out of your English class. Several times."

"Well." She bristled, then caught herself, and pasted a smile on her pudgy face. "You've grown up," she said.

"You've grown old."

He felt Toria's hand on his elbow, squeezing. Cautioning.

To hell with caution. A satisfying pause followed. Mrs. Sid looked like she was ready to send him to the principal's office, except they were already there. He smiled.

Mrs. Sid turned her attention to Toria.

"You can't be serious?" Mrs. Sid was saying. "About letting them build a waterfall?"

"It's their choice." Toria shrugged, and let go of his arm. She looked self-assured.

"You give them too many choices." Mrs. Sid's lips made a thin line as she frowned and narrowed her eyes.

"Toria!"

Another teacher barreled toward them, dodging students. The man looked older than Mrs. Sid but fit, like a runner.

Toria smiled at the man as he approached. "This is Mr. Burrows, our principal. This is Ryder O'Callaghan. He's—"

"Helping us with some grad decoration work. I know. Isabelle told me you were coming." Mr. Burrows looked at her bandaged ankle. "How's the ankle? We heard you had an accident."

"Nothing serious. I have to stay off it for a week, then I can try to put weight on it again."

"This won't interfere with the wedding plans?"

"No." She leaned on her crutches. "A sprained ankle won't do that."

"Everything going according to schedule then? I thought when you needed the extra time off . . ."

"I think that's mostly my mother."

"She needs to have you handy," Mr. Burrows said, answering for her. "For those last minute decisions. I understand."

"We don't need you here, Toria," Mrs. Sid interrupted.

"By the by," Mr. Burrows said, ignoring Mrs. Sid, "congratulations."

Toria raised her eyebrows, like, congratulations for what?

"Your classes have the highest math marks in the provincials."

Mrs. Sid rolled her eyes.

"Don't congratulate me," Toria said. "The students wrote the exams."

Mrs. Sid tightened her jaw and did another eye roll. No wonder her face looked so weird. All that eye strain.

"Well, Mrs. Sidorsky," Mr. Burrows said, turning to her at last. "Looks like you've got the help you wanted."

Students had started to trickle into the gym when their spares began at one o'clock. By one-thirty, a steady stream flowed through the doors.

Ryder doubted that Mrs. Sid had the help she wanted. The old girl had probably been complaining about no one doing what she told them to do, but she did not want Toria here. Mr. Burrows—Budge was his name—didn't seem to notice that fact, or he ignored it. Now the gym was filled with workers, and Mrs. Sid wandered around looking for ways to be a nuisance.

Everyone was turning up when they had time. All kinds of students, not just the popular chicks who had run the show when he'd been in grade twelve. Some of them were skipping classes. And many of them stayed after classes finished for the day.

An odd sense of nostalgia touched him. *His* high school time had not been like this. Here, the students were pulling together, forgetting their differences.

At six o'clock, Ryder left the school with Toria, and an assortment of students in tow.

They didn't look like they were friends because they dressed so differently. A boy with dyed black hair and black clothes, another with a buzz cut and sloppy jeans, a girl with frizzy hair and a pierced eyebrow, and one girl with smooth hair like Catherine's and designer clothes like Catherine's. In fact, a miniature Catherine.

He treated everybody to supper at McDonald's, then synchronized watches with Toria. She led her troop of students over to the fabric store to pick up supplies for tomorrow. And then he had an hour to kill.

Might as well go home and see if he had any mail.

As he turned out of the parking lot, a feeling of satisfaction swept over him, even though he hadn't been working today. Not working, but he'd accomplished his goal of getting out of Jim's way. Of giving the man that respect.

And he'd done it by helping Toria with her projects.

He'd never been able to go on a holiday and leave his mind in a vacuum. He needed a distraction. Like getting her car, and working with the students. Working on grad decorations, of all things. And meeting Mrs. Sid again after all these years. That had been worth the price of admission.

Good old Mrs. Sid—who had predicted he'd never finish high school and never amount to anything.

But, he had. He had his own business, a good income, and he was in demand.

And then, that nagging little doubt. She'd been right about the university. *Even if you get accepted, and I seriously doubt that you will, you'll never finish. Not with your attitude.*

He pulled into his apartment parking lot at the top of the hill, jumped out of the truck, and slammed the door.

He hadn't finished the engineering degree. So what? He'd done three years, earning top marks, and then he'd let that last year go. He didn't need it. He had no debts, lots of money in the bank, and he was building his own estate home. Cash, no mortgage.

As he entered his apartment, the phone was ringing. His land line. And the light on his answering machine was flashing.

Damn. He'd forgotten about turning off his cell. Jim must have had a problem. Must have been trying to contact him.

He reached for the phone. "O'Callaghan."

"Ryder?" Catherine's voice. "Where have you been?"

"I've . . ." His mind spun, searching for the right answer, knowing he was missing something and not knowing what it was.

"You were supposed to be fitted this morning."

A blanket of cold rumbled over him.

"You forgot, didn't you."

"I . . ."

"I can't believe this," Catherine said, shouting into the phone. "My mother says you're not paying enough attention to the wedding, and I'm inclined to agree. Why was your phone off?"

To give Jim some space. "Jim—"

"Jim, Jim, Jim. You've got to learn to turn over responsibility to someone else. You're not married to your job, you know."

And I'm not married to you. Not yet. "Catherine—"

"Can't you even get your tux—"

"Can I phone you back?"

"I—"

"I'll phone you back."

He hung up before he said something he'd regret.

In one hour, her students had chosen all the materials they'd need to grow the flower gardens for a respectable Tropical Paradise. Finally, they were doing what they wanted to do.

They traipsed out of the store into the sunny evening, bundling their purchases. Silk and crepe and linen. Starchy and shiny sprays. Pipe cleaners and interfacing and thread, and three reference books. They were ready to create orange bird of paradise, pink ginger, and white and red and pink hibiscus, along with roses and carnations.

They'd also purchased the supplies for the Leis Group. A dozen students would string the garlands of plumeria and orchids and kukui nuts.

A third group headed up the Operation House Plants

division of the three-pronged flower attack. Even now, phone calls arranged the influx of house plants to the gym's Tropical Paradise. Donations ranged from figs and philodendrons to coconut palms and calla lilies. Someone was even hauling in a group of live coffee plants, grown from beans and now four feet tall.

"Is Ryder going to be at school tomorrow?"

Toria smiled. Ryder didn't realize what an instant hit he'd become with the teenagers. They loved the way he stood up to Mrs. Sidorsky in the gym. "Call him Mr. O'Callaghan. Or Mr. Ryder."

"I tried calling him Mr. Ryder."

"And I tried calling him Mr. O'Callaghan."

"But he said to call him Ryder."

"Or just O'Callaghan."

She sighed, feeling her shoulders droop. It probably didn't matter. It wasn't as if he was their teacher.

Unfortunately, Mrs. Sidorsky didn't like him. But then Mrs. Sidorsky was like that. She kept special grudges, obviously for a long time.

"Just don't let Mrs. Sidorsky hear you call him that." Another tiny battle to avoid.

"Why not?"

A prod of irritation. *Yes, why not?*

"It affects her blood pressure if people don't do things the way she wants."

"Can't she get medication?"

Protectiveness welled inside her, but she couldn't do it all. "Think of some way to work around it. I'm sure you can come up with a way to make her happy."

"Nothing makes her happy."

"He's here now," four students announced at once.

The black truck pulled up to the curb. Ryder got out and walked around to meet them on the sidewalk.

Peter opened the back door, holding it for the two girls.

"Hey, Ryder. You going to be at school tomorrow?"

"Sure. What time do you start work on the gym?"

Peter passed his packages to Sandra and Leslie who were already buckled in. "Spares start at one. Will you be there? With the ladders?"

Ladders? She didn't want to know.

"You bet," Ryder answered. He opened the front passenger door and watched her, inviting her with his eyes to move toward him.

She'd been avoiding him at the school, trying to keep a physical distance. Now she moved toward the door, unsteady on her crutches. He caught her elbow and helped her as she stepped up into the truck.

When he touched her, she felt protected . . . and vulnerable. Wanting to shrink from his touch—and relishing it, at the same time.

He was unaware of her feelings, she could tell. Nothing like this was happening for him. Once she was settled, he took her crutches and handed them to Paul who passed them to Peter in the back. Then Paul got in beside her, nudging her closer to Ryder. Reaching for seat belts, the boys jostled around and packages tumbled to the floor.

Ryder settled in the driver's seat, his elbow brushing hers. "Who goes home first?" he asked them.

They gave him a reverse route so those who lived farthest out got delivered home first, and the ones who lived closest in, got delivered last. That way they had more time to discuss the grad decorations, university transcripts, and how Mrs. Sidorsky needed medication.

After the last student was dropped off, he drove into the parking lot at Dalhousie Towers.

"They like you," she told him, slipping her purse strap over her shoulder.

"What's not to like?" He grinned at her, looking happier than he had since she'd met him.

Warmth flooded her soul and she relaxed against the seat of the truck. She was glad he was getting a break from his work. And she was glad he was helping her, but—

"You have to try to get along with Mrs. Sidorsky."

"Why?"

I don't know why, she thought, as he opened her door.

After a full day of stumbling along on crutches, she needed a rest. Her body ached and she could hardly string a thought together, much less a reason for pacifying Mrs. Sidorsky.

"Do you want all this stuff to go upstairs?"

"Just the leis. These packages," she said, pointing. He would deliver the rest to the school tomorrow. "Isabelle and I are starting work on them tonight." Isabelle's orange Firebird was already parked on the ring road.

They followed the path to the building, Toria on her crutches, Ryder loaded with packages. She fished her keys from her purse and unlocked the door. Ryder held it open with his foot, waiting for her to go ahead of him. She dropped her keys back in her purse, gripped the crutches and went inside. Then she looked at the elevator, and paused.

"Can you do stairs?"

"Yes," she said, not liking the elevator. "Slowly."

"Better risk the elevator," he said. "You look tired."

"I'm not tired."

"Come on."

They did use the elevator, and it did make it to the third floor. It even landed level with the hallway.

Two Hudson's Bay shopping bags, heaped with crepe and ribbon, sat outside Toria's door. Isabelle stood beside them holding her blue cookie tin with the pumpkins on it. No doubt another famous Isabelle recipe.

"Hi, Isabelle. Been waiting long?" She wondered who let Isabelle into the building.

"Not at all, dear. I just got here."

Toria leaned on the crutches while she found her keys again.

Weariness sapped her concentration. Weariness—and the fact that Ryder was watching her search in her purse for the keys. They fumbled out of her hand and dropped.

Ryder eased his packages onto the hallway floor and retrieved the keys . . . at the same time as Isabelle was tapping on Mrs. Toony's door.

The old lady poked her head out. It was most likely Mrs. Toony who had buzzed Isabelle into the building.

Lifting the lid of her cookie tin, Isabelle said, "Would you like one?" She held the tin up for Mrs. Toony to see. "Coconut and chocolate and marshmallow and caramel."

Mrs. Toony piled three cookies into her hand, mumbled a thanks, and closed her door again.

Ryder moved the packages and Isabelle's shopping bags inside Toria's apartment.

A wisp of longing threaded its way into her mind. She'd kept her distance from him while they'd worked in the gym. It had seemed like the sensible thing to do. And they'd been so busy, both of them, that it had been easy. But now, lacking resolve, she wanted to talk to him.

"Would you like to come in for some coffee?" she asked. "And . . ." watching as he took a stack of cookies out of Isabelle's tin, ". . . and cookies?"

Immediately the longing was replaced with guilt. An old familiar guilt, pressing against her, asking, *Who are you to spend time with him?*

And what was she doing anyway? She'd just ended her engagement and she was lusting after this unavailable guy.

No, not lusting, she told herself. It was simply a reaction to the circumstances.

"I can't," he said. "I've got something I need to do."

And then he was gone.

. . . . .

"But, I don't understand." Isabelle scooped coffee into the filter. "You *want* them to think you're still getting married?"

"Not them," Toria said. "Not the teachers. But . . ." How could she say this?

"Ah, I see. But Ryder."

"Uh . . ." Could Isabelle see right through her?

"You want Ryder to think you're getting married." Isabelle made it sound like a perfectly normal thing to do.

Toria wasn't ready to talk about it. She would probably never be ready to talk about it. "When he found me, with the wedding dress, I told him I was getting married."

Isabelle shrugged. "At the time, you really *did* think you were getting married. So when do we plan the un-shower party?" She filled the coffee reservoir, moving on to another topic.

The un-shower party. The time to give back all the shower gifts for the wedding that was not happening anymore.

"We can plan it," Toria said. "But they won't have time to come. Not until school is out."

"But then they'll all leave on vacation."

"No, they won't. They'll all collapse first, after the year is finished."

"How about right after the Grad Dance?"

"Good idea. The Sunday after the Grad Dance. Sunday afternoon. But we won't tell them. Not yet."

"You should tell them you're not getting married. Tell them soon."

"But Isabelle—"

"And tell Ryder. What would it matter to him? So what if you changed your mind?"

A knock sounded on the door.

Greg? She remembered now, he'd said he was coming.

Bracing for the intrusion, she moved toward the entrance, and stumbled as one crutch caught on the little burgundy carpet.

She opened the door and, sure enough, it was Greg.

"I don't want you here," she said.

"Well, I'm here and we're going to talk." He strode past her, his arm knocking against her shoulder.

She hopped with her crutches, getting her balance. Then, still standing in the entrance, she turned around. "We've talked."

Had Mrs. Toony let him in? Was the old lady listening to this right now? Toria pushed the door shut with the end of one crutch.

"Isabelle?" she heard Greg say. He stood in the middle of the kitchen. "What are you doing here?"

"Cutting out flowers," Isabelle said. "Would you like to help? There're some scissors in that box."

Greg didn't respond to her question. Instead, he looked at the dining room table where Isabelle was unloading the bolts of material for the leis. "What is this?"

"We're making leis."

"Leis?"

"You know," Isabelle told him. "Those flower wreaths you wear around your neck when you go to Hawaii?"

Greg paused for a beat, as though he was trying to catch up. "And you need these because?"

"They're for the Grad Dance. The theme is a Tropical—"

He spun around to face Toria.

"—Paradise," Isabelle finished.

"You're working at the school?" He stood halfway between Toria and Isabelle. "You're supposed to be off." He pulled his shoulders back, standing taller, and possibly trying to intimidate her. "You're supposed to be helping your mother with the wedding." His eyebrows pinched and his mouth tightened.

Was this another reality? She blinked. "I'm not marrying you, Greg."

"So you said." He seemed to forcibly calm himself.

Behind him, Isabelle continued laying out the bolts of cloth. "Would you like some coffee and cookies, Greg? Then you can help us cut out flowers."

Greg closed his eyes. Then, "I left an important meeting to talk to Victoria. I don't have time to cut out flowers." He leaned forward, his hands on the counters on either side of him. "Did your lawyer friend help you?"

"My lawyer friend?"

"The one with the weird name. Pro Something? Your prenuptial agreement?"

"Oh, that."

"You don't need one," Greg said, and he smiled. The smile he used when he'd found a weak point in the customer's argument. "You have no assets, darling. And—" he added, letting the pause drag, "—your mother has no assets."

"My mother?" What did her mother have to do with this?

"In fact, she has less than no assets. Your father left her with quite a substantial debt."

Debt? No. "He— Certainly not. He didn't have any debts."

Greg smirked. "You'd better ask your mother about that." Then he pushed away from the counters, walked past Toria, and left.

Ten minutes later, the coffee was ready. "He showed up this morning," Toria said, "with a courier package in his hand." She blew out a breath and crutched over to the table.

"Yes, the ring." Isabelle reached in the cupboard for mugs. "You've got to make your announcement. Tell the teachers."

"Why? What difference does it make?" She pulled out a chair and dropped into it. "I can tell them later."

"Greg is the only one you've told. He thinks you're just angry." Isabelle poured coffee into the clear mugs with the shamrocks around the rims.

Toria had never expected Greg to get pushy. He *was* pushy, but not with her. Not usually.

"Are you?"

"Am I what?"

"Angry about something? Are you waiting for him to do something so the engagement can be back on?"

What? How could Isabelle think that? Toria stared at her friend. "No. The engagement is over. It never should have happened in the first place." She slumped in her chair and looked at the black coffee. "I knew that, the day after he proposed."

Isabelle added milk to Toria's coffee and pushed the cookie tin toward her. "But you didn't do anything about it."

"No. I couldn't. Not then."

"Your mother?"

Toria let go of a tired breath. "Yes," she said. "It made my mother happy. I couldn't tell her." And it seemed she couldn't tell her now.

"You've got to make your announcement. So somebody starts realizing this wedding is over. Or else Greg will keep showing up here and you'll have to keep doing this little dance with him."

"Ryder." If only she knew what to do about Ryder. She didn't want him to know the engagement was off.

"Ryder?" Isabelle prompted.

"He'll be bored with the grad decorating soon. And

then he'll be back at his work. Then I'll tell the school."

"Why not tell him now?"

"Because."

Because she'd known Greg for six months. He'd been friendly, charming, interesting. And safe.

She'd known Ryder for two days. Barely. And from the moment she'd met him, her heart and her mind had been torn apart in a race to keep up with each other. If she got close to Ryder, she knew she could feel something with him that she didn't want to feel. She didn't know what it was, but it was scary.

A scary, risky feeling.

He thought she was getting married. And that was a good thing for him to think.

Chapter Ten

He'd started out driving to Catherine's, and then somehow his route had changed and he'd ended up in his parents' neighborhood in Valley Ridge.

His father would be home.

They hadn't talked since the second Sunday in May, when they'd all met at the Keg for the obligatory Mother's Day feast. And they'd talked as little as possible.

As he parked out front of the house, his cell rang, playing its familiar William Tell Overture tune. It was beginning to grate on him. He reached for the cell and checked the readout.

A bolt of relief hit him. It wasn't Catherine. It was Jim.

"O'Callaghan."

"Your fiancée is looking for you."

"Don't worry about it."

"Ryder, I—" Jim hesitated. "She told me not to say anything, but . . ."

"Tell me."

"She wants me to keep tabs on you. Let her know where you are."

His brain paused, digesting that. He should have felt distressed, but he didn't. The astonishing thing was, he was not surprised.

"And will you do that?"

"Hell, no. I mean, I don't want to upset her, but—"

"Don't worry about it. I'll upset her myself."

He turned off the phone and dropped it on the seat beside him. She was probably phoning his mother too. He glanced at the house again. Lights all on.

He was here for the second time in a week, when he usually avoided dropping by at all. And tonight his father would be home.

He put the truck back in gear and drove away.

The next morning the sun was gone, and the sky was gray, filled with heavy clouds that rolled along, threatening more rain. Toria plugged the kettle in and reached for the teapot.

Thursday morning already, her first week off work, and she wasn't any closer to Kalispell than when she'd set out on Monday.

Maybe she should postpone her trip? Maybe she should give her mother time to adjust to the idea of . . . no more wedding. The wedding plans had kept Samantha happy. Visiting Aunt Glenda, and getting Aunt Glenda to come to Calgary, that was going to upset her mother. The two sisters had not spoken to each other since January when they'd argued.

The kettle whistled and Toria unplugged it.

With the old sense of hopelessness weighing her down, she took a deep breath, let it out slowly, and focused on the box of tea. A gold box with a green banner, a calm woman dressed in purple and sitting in a garden near a silver teapot made to look like a fountain.

In January, Samantha and Glenda had had their big argument. And in the end, Greg had smoothed it out. But it wasn't over.

Toria sighed, feeling stuck between the two sisters.

She opened the box of tea, took out a tea bag, and then dropped it into the Brown Betty pot. At least, she wouldn't see Ryder this morning. Last night she'd called and left him a message, that she'd meet him at the school at one o'clock.

As she poured the hot water into the teapot, the buzzer sounded.

Good. Isabelle was here. Toria put the lid on the teapot, crutched over to the intercom, pressed the button, and felt relief settle over her. Isabelle was taking her out for breakfast and then they would go to the school.

Counting the flowers they'd made last night, Toria dropped each one into the Hudson's Bay shopping bag. When she heard the knock, she crutched over to the entrance, silently holding the count at seventy-three flowers, and opened the door.

"Mom?"

"Good morning, Victoria," her mother said, as she walked inside holding a silver box in her hands. "Are you *still* using those crutches?"

What kind of a greeting was that? And what was her mother doing here anyway? Her mother rarely visited here. "I'm not supposed to put weight on my ankle," Toria said. "Not until next Tuesday."

"Oh. Well. As long as you can walk down the aisle." Her mother closed the door. "You've got two full weeks so it should be all right."

Toria tensed. "Mom—"

"Otherwise, maybe they can make you a cast or something." Samantha glanced at her watch.

Toria squeezed the handles of her crutches and tried to breathe deeply.

"You can't use those crutches," Samantha said, as she walked through the kitchen toward the table. "It wouldn't look right, and it would spoil the pictures."

The tension changed to annoyance. "Mom—"

"What are these?" Her mother examined the pretend plumeria.

"They're for the leis."

"Leis?"

Now the annoyance was replaced with guilt. Because, as clearly as she knew anything, Toria knew her poor mother would have trouble letting go of her fairy tale wedding.

"You know," Toria explained. "In Hawaii? They—"

"I know what leis are, for Pete's sake. But why . . ."

"We're making them for the Grad Dance decorations."

"Grad Dance?"

"At Aberton. I'm volunteering—helping them—"

"Volunteering? But why?"

Because I've signed off for the year and they already have a replacement for me. "I can't go back to my regular—"

"Oh, I see. This will take your mind off the stress of the wedding."

Stop it! "Mom, I'm not getting married."

Samantha scowled at her, holding the silver box close to her chest and tightening her lips in a thin line. "You still want to postpone?"

"No, not postpone. I'm not marrying Greg. The engagement was a mistake." A huge mistake. A mistake she should have fixed a long time ago.

"Victoria." Her mother fake smiled. "You haven't been yourself lately."

"And Mom?"

Samantha opened her mouth, ready to speak.

"Greg was here," Toria told her, rushing the words. "Last night."

"Oh, good." And now a genuine smile.

"He said Dad left debts."

"He what?" Surprise etched Samantha's face and she clutched tightly to her silver box.

"Is that true?"

Almost immediately, the surprise was replaced by anger, then something that looked like . . . uncertainty?

"Of course not. Why would he say something like that? That was silly of him."

Toria tightened her grip on the crutches and stood up straight. A new strength flowed into her. "You can't spend more money on renovations. You don't have the money."

Her mother opened her mouth, then snapped it shut. Tilting her chin, she said, "So now *you're* going to tell me what I can buy?"

"No. I just meant—"

"It's not your concern. Don't worry about it. We have plenty of money."

"Maybe *you* do." Toria gripped her crutches. "But I don't. I don't have any money." A picture of her car in the ditch played in her mind. "I have to buy a new car."

"Greg can—"

The buzzer sounded and Toria felt relief flow through her. Saved by the bell. Or, in this case, the buzzer.

Her mother frowned.

"It's Isabelle."

"Not that woman. I can't stand her."

What? Who wouldn't like Isabelle? "Why not?"

"She puts ideas in your head."

Toria moved toward the door. "She's driving me to school. We're working on grad decorations together." She reached the intercom and pressed it.

"But what if we need you for a decision?"

"Mom! Listen to me!" She twisted around on her crutches and almost stumbled. "I said I'm *not* getting married."

"You're just upset." Her mother presented another false smile. "And you don't have to yell. It's not ladylike."

"I'm not upset!" But she was. "All right I *am* upset— because you're not listening to me."

Samantha patted her silver box and smiled harder. "Geraldine said it's all right if you don't get her china pattern."

"Well . . ." How could she answer? "Tell Geraldine, thank you!"

"Victoria, don't be like that," her mother said, setting the box on the table as though everything was perfectly fine. "Now, come and look at this."

Praying that Isabelle would hurry, Toria hobbled over to the table.

Samantha opened her box revealing little bits of fruit cake wrapped in clear plastic and doilies, and tied with curling gold ribbon. "We thought you'd like to see the party favors."

Isabelle jammed Toria's crutches into the back of the Firebird and headed for the driver's seat. "Did Ryder return your call?"

The dark sky spit a few drops of rain on the windshield. "He didn't need to. He'll just show up at the school. If he wants to."

"He wants to."

"Why? You seem sure of that."

"I am."

A tiny flare of hope ignited but, just as quickly, guilt extinguished it.

The wheels of the Firebird squealed as Isabelle took the corner a little too sharply, turning left onto Collins Street. "So how come your mother looked so . . ."

"Upset?" Toria suggested.

"Upset is putting it mildly." Isabelle merged into the traffic on Dottridge Avenue.

Speckles of rain gathered on the windshield. Not enough for wipers yet. "She's trying to convince me I've made a mistake—cancelling the wedding." Toria grabbed hold of the armrest while the Firebird's motor roared and Isabelle changed lanes. "She's going ahead as though the wedding is still happening." An understandable approach, since her mother thrived on denial.

"Your Aunt Glenda needs to talk to her." Isabelle shoulder checked and maneuvered to the right, getting ready to exit.

"I know." The water on the windshield feathered into patterns. "As soon as I give Mom some time to adjust to the idea of no wedding, I'll phone Aunt Glenda. I'll have to tell her everything on the phone."

"Will Glenda come?" Isabelle asked, as she turned on the wipers.

"Yes." And hopefully Glenda could coax some reasonableness into Samantha. They were approaching the exit onto Stelmack Boulevard. "But it's going to upset Mom."

The more she thought about it, the more Toria knew she had to do something soon. Before her mother emptied her bank account on useless renovations.

The Firebird rumbled, adjusting to a decreased speed. "What is it with those two?" Isabelle turned onto Stelmack.

"Years of rivalry," Toria said, remembering bits of conversations with her mother. "She thinks Glenda was the favored child."

The wiper blades squeaked over the glass, halfway between the points of needing and not needing wipers. "Because?"

Toria could hear her mother's voice, complaining about her sister Glenda. "Apparently, no matter what Samantha did, Glenda did it better. Better report card. Better friends. Bigger bouquet of flowers for Gramma's birthday." They were almost at Wickens Street. "My mother was the little sister who never could." More rain splashed down, smoothing out the path of the wipers.

Isabelle slowed for the next turn. The engine emitted low, heavy strokes. "So if the big wedding is supposed to impress Glenda, why not invite her?"

Pain and regret twined in Toria's heart. It wasn't about trying to impress Aunt Glenda. Not anymore. "She's not just impressing her sister. She's impressing everyone. Mom loves making impressions."

Signals that told the world, *watch me, see how great I am, you can't keep me down.*

"And—" Toria added, "—there would have been pictures to send." Like waving a red flag. A passing transport fanned a spray of water over the Firebird.

"She would have done that? Sent pictures?" Isabelle curved onto Wickens.

"Of course." That was how her mother operated. "The pictures represent reality the way Samantha Whitney wants it to be. Perfect." Toria looked out the window at the gray world slipping past. In her mother's pretend world, everything and everyone was perfect. "She wants me to be perfect."

"You already are, dear."

No, she wasn't. She was always competing—against some unseen, impossible standard. She was never good enough. Smart enough. Pretty enough. Not for her mother.

And not for Greg, who always seemed to find more ways she could please him. *Quit your job, finance a new car, move the wedding date ahead.*

Way ahead. A year ahead.

A distant flash of lightning brightened the sky for a second. Just a few more blocks and they'd be at Tim Hortons.

And then, a thought came. She'd told Ryder he could help with the waterfall, but he could only *supervise* the building, not *do* the actual building. And he had not tried to change her mind.

But why would he want to? He had no interest in her or in what she did. The only reason he was helping at the school was to give himself something to do while his partner apprenticed. The students were simply a distraction for him. And so was she.

"You might have to leave town for that day."

"What day?"

"The last Saturday of June. Your ex-wedding day?"

She almost laughed. "Oh, I'll be here. I'll be chaperoning at the Grad Dance."

Isabelle glanced at her. "Won't that look odd?"

"Odd?" Teachers chaperoned all the time. "Why?"

Isabelle stared straight ahead. "The teachers might wonder why you're not at your wedding."

Oh, that. "I'll have told them by then." Because Ryder would be gone. He'd work today and maybe tomorrow, but after the weekend, he'd be bored with this project. The rain tapped a steady rhythm over the car as she snugged her raincoat around herself.

Then Isabelle pulled into the parking lot and executed a perfect landing in the small space between a minivan and a black truck.

"Don't worry, dear. Everything will work itself out." She patted Toria's hand. "Now, let's go in and order some breakfast."

Inside Tim Hortons, from a table next to the window, Ryder watched as the pumpkin-colored, supercharged Firebird came to a stop next to his truck.

"That's Toria," he said. His mind relaxed and his senses woke up. Sitting straight, he inhaled, filling his lungs. Not that he was *glad* to see her. It was just *amusing* to see her. Especially with Isabelle, who was getting out of the driver's seat.

Today the old lady wore a bright blue kerchief that partially contained her wild blonde frizz. She'd conceded to the weather conditions by wearing a very ordinary beige trench coat that came to her knees. Under that, about six inches of a tourist-tropical print peeked out—blue, pink, white, orange. More conservative today, she wore plain stockings. Orange ones. And what looked like wooden shoes.

"Do you think that car is safe?" Pro asked.

"It's the driver I'd be worried about," Ryder answered.

Isabelle walked around to Toria's door. She was already getting out, holding onto the door for support. The wind blew her hair over her eyes for a second and then she tilted her head, letting her hair sift away from her face.

Ryder felt a warmth in his chest and his head. Blinking, he touched his forehead. Cool, no sign of a fever. Just this odd sensation . . .

"I'd better be going," Pro said. He drained the last of his coffee.

Ryder looked at Pro. "Aunt Tizzy?"

"Yes." Pro got to his feet, picking up his coat from the bench.

"How's Aunt Tizzy's project coming along?"

"It looks promising," Pro said, as he shrugged into his raincoat.

Ryder waited a beat, thinking Pro would say more. And then, "You're not going to tell me what it is."

"It's too complicated to explain." Pro grinned. "Want to go out for a beer tonight?"

"Can't. I'm visiting my parents."

Pro nodded, as though Ryder visiting his parents was a normal thing to do. Tactful of Pro not to mention that.

"I've got to go," Pro repeated. "Say hello to Toria for me."

"Sure."

Pro exited the door on the opposite side of the restaurant. Ryder looked out the window again watching as

Isabelle yanked Toria's crutches out of the backseat. She passed them to Toria who took them with one hand while she tried to loop the strap of her purse over her shoulder. Her navy trench coat was buttoned to her neck and the rain danced over her hair.

He'd drive her to the school, he decided. Because there was more room in his truck for the crutches.

They were at the restaurant door now, Isabelle holding it open, letting Toria go ahead. Toria stopped just inside the door when she saw him. Isabelle bumped into her, Toria smiled, and so did he.

It felt like freshness and light had walked in on a stormy day.

Or something like that. It was an odd feeling, anyway. Maybe he was still hungry. Maybe he needed to eat more. He got to his feet and moved Pro's empty dishes to make room for Toria and Isabelle.

Reaching the table first, Isabelle slipped out of her raincoat and plopped it on the bench that Pro had just vacated. She sat and rummaged through her huge, pink, canvas bag.

Toria arrived at the table and stood beside him, leaning on her crutches. Without thinking, Ryder lifted her purse strap over her head and set the purse on the table. Then he stacked her crutches in one hand, and helped her out of her dripping coat with the other.

"Thanks," she said, looking flustered.

And pretty. Her damp hair curled around her face again, the way it had when they'd been caught in the rain on Monday.

A sense of wonder, of unreality, floated around him. He stared at the crutches and the raincoat he was holding. Was that only three days ago?

He felt like he'd known her forever.

After shaking out the coat, he folded it in half and

tossed it and the crutches on the bench behind them. Then he waited for her to slide in on his side of the table.

"What would you like to eat, dear?" Isabelle asked, still searching in her bag.

Ryder sat down and heard Toria say something about orange juice and bagels, and he noticed he was breathing with a renewed kind of energy.

Toria propped her purse at the end of the table by the window. "Was that Pro?"

Pro? Of course. She would have seen Pro . . . would have wondered why he'd rushed off.

"Yeah," Ryder answered, looking at the door where Pro had made his hasty exit. "He said to say hello. He had to leave—has something to do before he goes to his office."

"Oh," she said. "Must have been important." She was rubbing her arms like she was cold. She wore long sleeves today, a cream-colored turtleneck, some soft fabric. And jeans.

"It was," Ryder said, looking at the way the turtleneck smoothed over her throat. "His crazy Aunt Tizzy."

"Pardon?" Isabelle asked, looking up from her search.

"He has something to do for his crazy Aunt Tizzy— before he goes to work. He wanted to have breakfast with me first."

"That was nice of him," Isabelle said, as she foraged in her bag.

"To have breakfast with me?"

"To help his aunt," Isabelle clarified.

"Yeah," Ryder said, feeling a little dazed. He watched as Isabelle deposited a hair brush, a mirror—a large one, and a paperback novel on the table. He moved the ketchup aside.

"Have you met her?" Toria asked. "His aunt?"

"Not yet," Ryder answered, watching the collection on the table grow. Isabelle added an orange pad of paper, a letter opener and one of those Magic 8-balls. "But I probably will someday." And then a can of apple juice, two elastics, a pair of black gloves and finally a purple embroidered wallet.

"I knew I had it," Isabelle crowed, holding the wallet with both hands. She set it on the table and began to repack her bag.

"Pro talks about her a lot," Ryder said, speaking to Toria but still watching Isabelle. "She sounds like she's off her rocker but she's the one who raised Pro—his parents died when he was young. His Aunt Tizzy took care of him—he'd do anything for her."

"Nice," Toria said, approval in her voice.

And something that sounded . . . wistful, like *she* wanted a crazy aunt. Or just an aunt, crazy or not.

"He helps her a lot?" she asked, still rubbing her hands over her arms.

"She usually never asks for anything." Ryder had an urge, a stupid urge, to put his arm around Toria's shoulders to warm her up. "But now she has some big, important project and needs his help. So, he's helping."

Isabelle left the table with her wallet in hand. At the same time, Ryder's cell rang, playing its programmed tune. He checked the readout.

Catherine.

Again.

He could get fitted for the tux today—except he'd promised the Star Committee he'd get their stars strung before noon. Before Mrs. Sid tried to put a stop to that idea. So, no time for a tux fitting. He turned off the phone.

"Work?"

"Wedding stuff."

"Oh."

"How are your wedding plans going?"

"Fine," she said. "How are *your* wedding plans going?"

"Fine."

"The grad decorations," she said, pausing, playing with the strap of her purse. "I don't want you to think you have to—"

He touched her hand, his fingers skimming hers. "I don't have to." Beneath his fingertips, her hand felt like ice. An urge, almost irresistible, made him want to wrap his hand over hers.

He took his hand away. "I hate *having* to do anything," he said. He—and no one else—was in charge. "So don't worry. I don't do what I don't *want* to do."

Except, he'd have to deal with Catherine and her phone calls.

Eventually.

Chapter Eleven

So much for her plan to stay away from Ryder.

The rain had stopped. Clouds skidded across the sky. Toria followed Isabelle and Ryder out of the restaurant, wishing she could risk putting weight on her ankle. But if she did that too soon, she'd be back at square one and need the crutches for longer.

Part of her was sorry she'd committed to the grad decorations. She should have been talking to Aunt Glenda by now, convincing her reluctant aunt to pay a visit. But that, of course, was not the biggest problem. Working on grad decorations meant she was spending more time with Ryder, and the more time she spent with him, the more she—

"I'll take you to the school."

"But—"

"Your crutches will fit better in my truck."

"Okay." Her mind raced. "You can have the crutches. I'll ride with—"

"Oh, good," Isabelle said, as she opened the driver's door of the Firebird. "You go with Ryder." She dropped her big pink canvas bag on the front seat and knelt beside it. "I forgot my calendar at home so I have to go there first." She reached into the backseat. "I'll meet you at the school," she said, her voice muffled.

Toria drew in a deep breath. There had to be a way out

of this. Standing tall, she faced Ryder. "Are you sure you want to come to the school this early?"

"Are you trying to get rid of me?" He'd already opened the door for her.

"It's just that—none of the students will be in the gym—before the one o'clock spare."

Isabelle handed Toria one of the bags of plumeria they'd made last night.

"Don't," he said, grinning.

"Don't what?" She clutched the shopping bag of brightly colored flowers, pressing the handle of it against the handle of her crutches.

"Don't worry about how I use my time," he answered. "I want to be there." He made it sound like she was doing him a favor. "I have some lumber I need to get to the gym."

"For the waterfall?"

"Yeah."

Unwanted, an image of Mrs. Sidorsky popped into her head. They didn't need any more arguments. "You have to be nice to Mrs. Sidorsky, okay?"

"She's not nice to me."

"She doesn't mean—"

"She's bossy and likes to have her own way."

Isabelle was back, carrying two more shopping bags. "Do you know anybody like that?" she asked Ryder, as she passed him one of the bags, this one full of aluminum foil stars.

Ryder accepted the stars and frowned at Isabelle. "Are you saying *I'm* bossy and like to have my own way?"

"It's something to think about," Isabelle said with a shrug, giving him the second bag of flowers. "I'll see you later." She hopped into her Firebird, revved the motor and backed neatly out of her stall. Three seconds later she was gone in a cloud of blue exhaust.

They were silent for a few seconds, watching the car disappear. "She needs to get someone to look at the rings on that engine," Ryder said, mostly to himself.

Toria hadn't recognized Ryder's truck when they'd parked beside it. Now she glanced in the empty truck bed. "Where's the lumber?"

"Different truck," he said. "Why are you worried about Mrs. Sid?"

"I don't like arguments."

"Arguments can be good."

"She means well, you know."

"I mean well, too," he said.

Toria spent the next hour on the stage in the gym. Ryder balanced on the school's ladder, tossing strings over the curtain rods, while she worried at the base of the ladder and handed him stars. Two students, Brenda and Donna, had somehow escaped class—she didn't want to know—and they stood in the center of the gym, instructing Ryder on heights for the starscape.

"I don't like this ladder. It shakes," Toria told him.

"The ladder's fine."

"I can see why Mrs. Sidorsky didn't want them climbing on this thing. It's dangerous."

"As long as Mrs. Sid doesn't climb on it, it's safe."

She sighed, feeling the futility of this conversation. It was pointless, she realized, trying to mend the rift between Ryder and his former teacher.

"Last one," she said, handing him the last silver star.

"Oh, Ryder! It looks uber cool!" Brenda shouted, twirling. Then she stood still. "I mean, Mr. Ryder."

Ryder dipped his head and grimaced at her.

"I mean, it looks great. It really does." She clasped her hands and glowed at him.

Donna, the quieter one, smiled, looking pleased with the project. Her project. She hurried over to the lighting panel. "Lights out," she called.

Toria, on her way down the stage stairs, had almost made it to the bottom step when the gym pitched to blackness. She stopped moving.

And felt Ryder's arm come around her waist. "Hold on, tiger. I've got you." He gathered her crutches away from her, tightened his hold and lifted her down the last step. They were on level floor.

But he kept holding her. Then, effortlessly, he swung her around, so she faced the stage.

A whirl of sensation spun over her, feelings she could not name. She clamped a hand on his arm. "I'm all right. Give me my crutches. I can—"

"Look at the stage."

She stared into the blackness and felt his arm, pressing her to his side. Felt hard muscles and warm body and that familiar spruce smell. And then Donna turned the lights up.

Blue light illuminated the stage, highlighting two hundred and fifty silver and gold stars suspended at various heights, gently turning and shimmering in unseen air currents.

The magic washed over her like a wave. And at the same time, heat coming from Ryder's body pressed against hers and took her away from reality, to another realm where responsibilities didn't exist, where she could follow what her heart wanted, where she could be who she—

The gym doors opened and someone clicked on the main lights.

"Hey! Ryder!" Mr. Harvey, the school janitor, bellowed from the doorway. "You order some stuff?"

"I did." Ryder released her, returned her crutches and then headed to the door.

. . . . .

Toria came back to earth, lined up her crutches and fitted them under her arms.

Mr. Harvey left and a man wearing taupe-colored overalls and heavy work boots poked his head inside the door. He located Ryder, held up an index finger for a second, like he was testing the air, and then disappeared again.

Ryder, at the door by now, followed him outside.

Crutching her way across the gym, Toria dodged between potted plants, bags of fabric flowers, and islands of paving stones. By the time she reached the entrance, Mr. Harvey was back, propping open both doors.

"How's the ankle, Miss Toria?"

"Fine," she answered automatically.

Ryder came through the doorway, carrying a coiled orange extension cord. Then the man with the taupe-colored overalls and work boots reappeared along with another man in a similar uniform. The two workers lugged a heavy-looking orange machine about the size of a big wash tub.

"It's a compressor," Ryder said.

"What do we need a compressor for?"

"My nail gun."

Gun? A sense of foreboding stole over her. She tightened her grip on the crutches. Mrs. Sidorsky wasn't going to approve.

Ryder's workers hauled in three more loads. Two ladders, rolls of plastic, cans of *expanding foam*—at least, that's what she thought he'd called them. Two saw horses, the nail gun, a box of staples, a box of nails, four hammers, a circular saw, a huge pile of lumber and a tray of Starbucks Frappuccinos.

"How much is this going to cost?" Mrs. Sidorsky

wanted to know. Mrs. Sidorsky had arrived with the third load and now she hovered near Toria's shoulder.

"We're within budget," Toria answered, remembering what Ryder had said—and wondering.

One of the workers handed Ryder a sheet of paper and a pen. He signed and then accepted the rest of the tray of coffee drinks from Brenda. Three glasses remained.

"The stars look better than I thought they would," Mrs. Sidorsky admitted. And then, "Why aren't you in class?" she shouted, as she noticed Brenda and Donna holding their drinks. The two teenagers quickly slipped out of the gym.

In a moment Ryder was there, handing Mrs. Sidorsky a Frappuccino. Toria felt a sudden sense of calm, and she relaxed. He was making a peace offering.

But then he said, "Don't they need you at the principal's office?"

Ryder liked working with high school students. They learned quickly, they had creative ideas, and some of them were even good persuaders—bringing the school caretakers on side as they worked out the problems with the water pumps. In fact, the caretakers seemed pleased to be included in the project.

"Does this angle look good, Ryder?"

"It's perfect," he said.

Budge had thanked him privately for doing this *community* work. Apparently some of Ryder's best helpers were frequent flyers at the principal's office.

Four boys sat on the floor amidst paper and pencils and protractors. Mr. Benjamin, one of the caretakers, looked over the shoulder of one of the boys. And, oddly enough, one of the math teachers stationed himself outside the perimeter of the group. As he watched the calculations taking place, he squinted and scratched his head.

Ryder checked the latest additions to their drawing. And that same awareness of peace and purpose invaded his thoughts again. He grinned, knowing he was where he needed to be right now.

He liked these kids. He'd already arranged summer jobs for two of them. And if they wanted to work on Saturdays during the university year, he could arrange that too.

Working here felt . . . fulfilling. Almost as satisfying as watching a house take shape. And it didn't have anything to do with Toria, he told himself. Again.

He watched her dealing with the students, shuffling along on her crutches, going from group to group, sometimes mediating disagreements, mostly letting them solve their own problems, only interfering when Mrs. Sid tried to veto something.

Toria spent a lot of time doing that—appeasing Mrs. Sid. Right at this moment Toria was urging Mrs. Sid away from the Waterfall Committee—on the pretext of showing her the plumeria.

Plumeria. He shook his head. Who knew that's what leis were made of?

His cell started playing the William Tell Overture. "O'Callaghan."

"Catherine called." Jim's voice. Right to the point.

"And?"

"I told her you're taking time off to let me get some experience being in charge," he said. "And I told her I had no idea where you are. And I don't."

"Good. West Hillhurst?"

Jim updated him on the West Hillhurst project. And on the two crews working in Royal Oak. "We're right on schedule," he finished, a touch of pride slipping into the report. Then he added, "And I have no idea why two of my crew disappeared for an hour this morning. But they came back with invoices initialed by you so I'm assuming they were where they were supposed to be."

"They were. It's for my personal account."

"Right."

Toria sat with Mrs. Sidorsky in the Leis Section, and for something to do she threaded the colorful flowers onto a string while the older teacher complained.

"Back when I first started teaching," Mrs. Sidorsky was saying, "we didn't waste a lot of time on grad decorations. We spent that time teaching the students."

Toria's enthusiasm drooped and she almost squashed a flower. She hated it when Mrs. Sidorsky went into this rant. They had this same conversation at least once a day.

Well, not conversation, she thought. More like— soliloquy.

"Your father believed in teaching," Mrs. Sidorsky said. "He wouldn't let them get out of a single class."

No. He would not have. Not a single class, Toria thought, as panic flickered around her, hemming her in.

"He was an excellent history teacher. Have I told you that?"

Only about a hundred times. And Toria was sick of hearing it. Over and over. Her hands stopped working and her chest tightened.

"I'm sure he wanted you to carry on in his footsteps," Mrs. Sidorsky said, never taking her eyes off the gym as she waited for something to go wrong. "Why did you quit teaching history anyway?"

Toria dropped her needle. Her hands were shaking. Her arms and her legs were shaking. Did her voice work?

"I still teach history," she said, hearing the tight words.

Mrs. Sidorsky didn't notice, just steamrolled ahead. "One class of history," she said, with what sounded like disdain. "Your father wanted—"

"Hello, Mrs. Sidorsky." Isabelle joined them and pulled up a chair.

Toria inhaled and focused on the crushed fabric flowers in her hands. It would be all right. Isabelle was here. Isabelle to the rescue.

"Hello, Mrs. Jones," Mrs. Sidorsky said, sounding tired, and sounding like she didn't want to talk to Isabelle. Mrs. Sidorsky never called Isabelle, Isabelle. It was always *Mrs. Jones.*

Toria could feel her heart racing. But it was slowing now, returning to normal as quickly as it had stopped being normal. She needed to get over this. To forget this. This simple memory that refused to go away.

"Mr. Burrows wondered if you could help him at the office with the Refreshment Committee's order for coffee and soft drinks," Isabelle asked Mrs. Sidorsky.

"Didn't he already do that?"

"Maybe he needs to do it again." Isabelle looked completely sincere. "You know how unfocussed he can be. He needs someone with your eye for detail."

Mrs. Sidorsky preened at the compliment, then got up and walked away.

"What was that all about?" Isabelle asked.

"What was what about?"

Isabelle smiled, offering sympathy. "Was she talking about your father, dear?"

Yes, that same flashback. "I guess I still feel responsible." She tried to restore the damaged flowers, smoothing them with her fingers.

"You're not that powerful, dear. You have to give people credit for their own choices."

I know. The concept made sense, but Responsibility still boomed in her mind. The pain of Responsibility refused to leave her.

"What did she say?" Isabelle asked, casual and nonchalant, as she picked up a lei string.

Even though it was difficult, talking about it was the only thing to do. Toria knew that. All around her, the activity in the gym went on. But it felt like she and Isabelle were in a bubble, in some kind of twilight zone.

That same strength nudged her. The strength she'd felt this morning when she'd talked to her mother about the renovations.

She could do this. She could get past this. "Mrs. Sidorsky was saying what a great history teacher he was."

Isabelle worked a pink plumeria onto her needle. "So I've heard," she said, watching the flower. "But he was never my teacher so I wouldn't know." Slipping the flower down the string, she said, "Do you know why he taught history?"

"He liked to travel."

The words tripped off her tongue. "He figured he could work on his PhD and travel at the same time." Keep talking, an inner voice urged her. "He loved going to Spain and Germany and doing his research."

"And dragging you along."

Not dragging. "I enjoyed it." Sometimes, though not always. And there it was again. The defense of her father.

Isabelle added another pink plumeria. "He never finished his doctorate, did he?"

"No, he never finished. They always needed more money." *Her mother* always needed more money.

"Is that why he didn't finish? Because of the money?" A third flower slipped along Isabelle's string.

"You don't make a lot on a teacher's salary," Toria answered, realizing she was talking about him and her world was not falling apart. "But then . . ."

She picked up her lei, pulled off the broken flowers and searched for the needle end of the string.

"Then . . . ?" Isabelle encouraged her.

He hadn't gone back. It was like he'd thrown his dream away. "Then," she took a deep breath, "then he started supplementing his income with some projects he did with Greg."

Isabelle looked up from her work. "With Greg?" She puzzled her eyebrows. "Is that where all that money came from?"

"It wasn't that much money."

"Enough to go to Paris last summer."

"My mother wanted a vacation." Her mother always wanted a vacation. To anywhere. As long as she could be traveling somewhere new, somewhere different.

"And all those trips to Reno?"

"That was *my father* wanting a vacation."

"Gambling?"

No, not gambling. Toria tried to fit a flower on her needle. He did like the casinos, but he wasn't gambling. Not really. "It was a diversion. A rest. He wouldn't lose money gambling."

Isabelle continued to work on her string of plumeria, adding one pink flower after another. "What kind of projects?" she asked.

"Projects?"

"The ones he did with Greg."

She'd never known what they did together. Only that her father had been excited when he was working with Greg. "I don't know," she said. "Real estate investments, I suppose. Since that's what Greg does."

"You haven't told me about the honeymoon," Catherine's mother said.

"I'm thinking Hawaii," Catherine answered, as she dropped a stack of brochures on the table. She poured tea for her mother.

Catherine sat in her parents' living room talking with her mother about the wedding details. Tonight, her father, Herbert George Forsythe of Duncan Pansmith, had joined them.

Theoretically. He sat in his easy chair, across the room, reading the newspaper and updating his cell phone.

"That sounds nice," her mother commented. She sipped her tea from a Wedgwood china cup. "Does Ryder like the idea?"

He would if he stopped to think about it. "He can barely get time off work for the wedding," Catherine answered, without answering. "He says we'll do something once it starts to snow. Or once this building frenzy is over." Catherine filled her own teacup. "He works *all* the time."

"Why are you marrying him if you never see him?" her father asked without looking away from his cell phone.

Catherine humphed. "I suppose *you* spend a lot of time at home, Daddy?"

"I'm here," he answered, then set the cell phone on the arm of the chair and picked up the newspaper again.

"Yes, you are," Catherine's mother said, leafing through the Hawaii brochures. She sipped more tea. "Did he get his tux fitted yet, sweetheart?"

"No, not yet," Catherine reported, with a sigh. She didn't say that he wasn't returning her calls. This was the first time that had happened.

"Fara and Emmaline have their dresses now. They look smashing. You'll be very proud of your sisters." Another sip of tea. "And their husbands have been fitted for their tuxedos."

"Don't worry, mother. I'll make him go to the fitting."

Her mother opened another brochure. The one on Hawaiian volcanoes. "You don't want to be a nag, sweetheart."

Oh, wonderful, it was advice time. She'd better focus. Getting upset around her mother was never a good idea.

"You need to hire a wedding planner."

Catherine closed her eyes for a second and clenched her teeth. Sometimes her mother could be so dense. "I don't need a planner. I know what I'm doing. I—"

"For him. For Ryder."

"How will that—"

"He'll listen to someone else," her mother stated, like she was giving her directions for a recipe. "Men are like that. Somehow, it makes them think it's their own idea."

The newspaper rustled in the corner of the room. Catherine glanced at her father. His attention focused on the business section.

She centered herself. It wouldn't hurt to see where this was going. "You think I should hire a wedding planner for Ryder?"

"I know just the person."

Her mother would. "Who?"

"Her name is Geraldine Lorimer."

"Lorimer?" It seemed her father *was* listening after all. "I know that name."

"You do?" they said together.

"Lorimer," he repeated, tapping his fingers on the cell phone. "But not Geraldine," he said, looking in the middle distance. "The first name starts with a G though."

"How do you know her?" Catherine asked.

"Him. The man's name is Lorimer. Name came up in a real estate fraud," Herbert Forsythe of Duncan Pansmith continued. "Some so-called Creative Financing. Don't think they charged him though. Not enough evidence. But the fellow took a beating in the market. Had to dump a lot of property."

Catherine's mother rolled her eyes. "Well, that was a man. Geraldine is a woman and she's an excellent planner.

I've used her for some parties. And your sister had her for her baby shower."

"Mother, I don't need—"

"Give her a call," her mother said. "She can deal with Ryder."

Chapter Twelve

Leaning on her crutches, Toria surveyed the evolving chaos.

Thursday was almost over and the day had evaporated. After classes ended, many of the students had stayed to work on their various committees. Pizza had mysteriously shown up at half past six. And, eventually, the gym had cleared a few minutes before nine.

It was unfortunate that Mrs. Sidorsky didn't like Ryder, because the students did. Several of the boys who'd had no previous interest in the grad preparations had come out of the woodwork to help.

She laughed at her little pun.

During the afternoon, the students had sat on the floor drawing plans. Then they had constructed the framing for the waterfall.

Ryder had been patient. She'd thought he'd take over, but he hadn't. He let them work at their own pace, accepting the give-and-take of ideas and answering their questions.

Now the skeleton of the structure stood ready. Tomorrow they would *sheet* it and then the foam would be applied so they could mold it into a cascade of rocks.

In these past two days, they'd advanced the decorations to the point where she knew they'd meet their schedule, the last Saturday of June—their graduation celebration—her ex-wedding day.

A spark of anxiety popped into her head. Her mother had phoned her cell seven times today. But there hadn't been time to take those calls. Now it was nine-thirty and she needed to find Isabelle and go home. She'd have to deal with her mother tomorrow.

"Ready?" Ryder materialized by her side.

"Yes. Do you know where Isabelle went?"

"She's gone. She told me to take you home."

"She did? I—I don't want to be any trouble. Don't you have to—"

"I don't have to do anything. My partner gave me a report. All is well."

"So he's your partner now?"

"Almost. I'm getting used to the idea." Ryder grinned. An absolutely charming grin. "Let's go."

On the way he told her about *his* students and the next steps for the waterfall. He also told her how they had outwitted Mrs. Sidorsky, again. When they arrived at the apartment building, the ring road stood silent and deserted.

Thank goodness. No sign of her mother. And no sign of Greg.

Ryder held the door for her as she slipped out of the truck.

She slung her purse over her shoulder and accepted the crutches from him.

"Thanks," she said. For the ride, and the crutches, and for . . . just being him. They stood for a moment by the truck. Awkward. Maybe she should tell him *not* to come by in the morning? In case he was planning to.

But she didn't. She just said, "Thanks." Again. Then she adjusted the crutches and started up the sidewalk.

He kept pace with her.

"You're coming up?" Did she want him to?

No. She didn't.

"I want to make sure you get in all right."

He was thinking about Greg, the same as she was. They rode up the unenthusiastic elevator, which stopped three inches above the level of the hallway. Then the door almost didn't open.

"I'm going to phone someone about this thing," Ryder said, shoving the door back.

"I could have taken the stairs." She crutched her way to her door.

"You could have."

"I'm not tired." Stopping in front of the door, she fished her keys out of her purse.

"It's okay. You can be tired." He wrapped a hand around her wrist and, with his other hand, he took the keys from her.

Her mind jolted—her wrist echoed from the touch of his hand.

"I'll make some coffee," she said, recovering her composure. "The Program Committee gave me their draft of the Celebration Program." She was babbling. "I need to check it before I give it to the printers." And then, before her brain could stop her, she added, "Would you like some coffee?"

He hesitated. "Not right now." He unlocked the door for her, handed her the keys—this time without touching her—just dropping them into her palm.

Then he gave a wave to Mrs. Toony's peephole, and he left.

He pulled up in front of the house in Valley Ridge. Ten o'clock. Later than he'd planned, but it didn't seem to matter. All the lights were on.

Almost as if he were expected. He dismissed the thought. Completely crazy to be expected here.

For some reason, he'd wanted to join Toria for coffee.

But it felt as if he were walking on quicksand with a very thin crust on top.

And for some reason, he felt like his life was about to change, but—for better or worse?

For better or worse? The wedding vows. Looming like an exam he didn't want to write. Why didn't he feel ready?

Jim's new partnership agreement. That's what it was. It was distracting him. Other than dealing with the partnership, he was completely ready.

Wasn't he?

His hesitation confused him. In his mind he knew what he wanted, but his gut told him to wait. When had his life got so complicated?

He stepped out of the truck and inhaled the clear night air. He could smell fire pit smoke, and he heard some older kids laughing at the end of the block. A slight breeze chilled his skin, announcing another change in the weather. Hopefully, it didn't mean more rain.

"How are you, honey?" His mother greeted him at the door and he followed her into the kitchen. "Would you like some hot chocolate? I just made a pot."

The smell of chocolate settled over the kitchen. A platter of little muffins sat on the table next to a stack of cards. Thank you cards, white with loopy gold writing. There was also a travel brochure for—he checked—Hawaii?

His parents were going to Hawaii? They never went anywhere.

"Sure," he answered. "That would be great."

She went to the cupboard and took out a mug. Her sewing machine sat open on the dining room table, spilling out some gauzy pink fabric.

"Have you ever thought of getting a maid?"

His mother shrugged, as she filled a mug. "I'd just be in her way. I like to spread out."

He picked up the travel brochure for Hawaii. "What's this? You guys going to Hawaii?"

"Oh. That. Catherine dropped it off. She said you were taking your honeymoon there."

"We are?" They hadn't talked about it. When would he have time? He pushed the thought aside.

He still had to phone her about rescheduling the tux fitting. That was supposed to be yesterday. Now another day had gone by. Another day closer to the wedding. Everything was moving along on its inevitable path.

Except him. Ever since his trip to the cabin.

No, before that. He'd gone to the cabin because the poodle had been the last straw and he'd needed to regroup. To get away and think, Pro had said. To put it all in perspective, Pro had said.

But Ryder still didn't seem to have the right perspective. In fact, things seemed to be getting worse.

He was lucky he'd met Toria and he had the high school job to keep him sane. "Toria liked the cookies. She said to say thank you."

"She's very welcome." His mother handed him the drink and then sat down at her sewing machine. "How's her ankle?"

"She's still on crutches." Another four days, and then she could try to put weight on her foot. He tasted the hot chocolate. Rich and satisfying. "I gave Jim total charge of the sites today. And yesterday."

"Mmm hmm." His mother concentrated on her sewing.

Something about the wedding was bothering him but he couldn't say what. Everything inched along that inevitable path, and he was starting to resent the inevitability. It was as if he'd suddenly been flung out of orbit and his world didn't make sense anymore.

"Mom? Do you think I'm doing the right thing?"

"What right thing, honey?" She adjusted the pink fabric

on the machine. "Getting a partner for that business of yours?"

Well that, too. "Yeah."

"Jim seems like a competent young man. Not as experienced as you, of course, but he knows about accounting. And he's been a framer before."

"Yeah." Just say it. "Do you think—"

His mother waited, listening, her eyes on the sewing in front of her.

"The wedding. Do you think it's happening . . . too fast?"

Her scissors clattered to the floor and she bent to pick them up. And then instead of answering his question, she asked, "Do you think it's happening quickly?"

"I don't know."

His mind flashed on the past three days . . . the students working on the waterfall, Toria watching as three students discussed the Refreshments Area, Jim sounding more certain each time he called in with a report, Toria leading Mrs. Sidorsky away from the Music Committee, the elevator jolting to a stop, Pro's cabin with the fire ring behind it—

"Do you like her?"

"Who?"

His mother paused. "Catherine. Your fiancée."

"Oh. Right. Of course I do. Why would you ask me that?"

His mother nudged the fabric under the needle of her sewing machine. "She's just . . . different from you. Nothing specific."

Different? Was she?

They had all the same goals. The house in Royal Oak—

No, not *house*. The *estate home* in Royal Oak. That was the goal—estate home. Impressive home. Something his father would be forced to admire.

But, the decorating. Ryder paused, tripping over the thought.

What about the decorating? The way it would change from a house to a home . . . He and Catherine weren't quite on the same page for that.

More like they were in different books. Not that it mattered. They had other things in common. Like—

He drew a blank. She liked the theater, especially dressing up for it. And he didn't mind going. She liked the opera, too. And he didn't mind going to that either. Except for that time it conflicted with skiing.

Catherine didn't like skiing. Last year, she'd spent all that money on ski outfits, and then ended up staying in the lodge for most of their week in Banff.

But she did like the house they were building. With its arches and gables and facades. She wanted all the trappings and he—and he—

His throat felt tight and suddenly it was hard to swallow the hot chocolate. He felt trapped.

Then there was the poodle. When he was ready to get a dog, it would be a Golden Retriever. Or a Lab.

"Mom?"

"Yes?" She glanced up from her sewing for a second, then looked down again and adjusted a pin, realigning it.

"What if I didn't get married? I mean, right now? Would that be a big problem? I know all the invitations . . . and everything."

"Not a problem," she said as she worked at her sewing machine. "The important thing is you're ready."

"I am ready. To get married. I just wondered what you would think if . . ." *If what?*

"I know, honey. You take your time."

Time. Right. He had time. Two and a half *weeks* of time.

He heard a door close, heard footsteps on the stairs coming up from the rumpus room, and then his father stepped into the kitchen.

Ryder's mind jerked and all thoughts of postponing anything fled. He knew what he wanted—his estate home, his sophisticated wife, his place in the universe.

"Hi, Ryder."

His dad looked at the sewing machine with the fluffy pink, and Ryder could hear what the next words out of the man's mouth would be. *How long will this be out here? How long will this be taking up space?*

But his father didn't say that. Instead, he . . . smiled?

Funny to see him smile.

"For Jilly and Joanne?" Donald Michael O'Callaghan asked.

"Yes," his mother answered. "They both want to be princesses and Kathleen doesn't have time to sew."

His father nodded, still smiling. Then he walked over to the pot of hot chocolate and poured himself a cup.

Ryder watched and tried to understand, but something was out of sync.

Was his father mellowing out? Were his grandchildren doing this to him? Had those two little girls put a spell on Donald O'Callaghan?

"I hear you're looking at a partner," his dad said.

"Yes. Jim Bondeau."

"I've heard of him. Used to work for Foster. Does good work."

The words buzzed, sounding strange. Ryder blinked.

Was that encouragement? Hard to tell. It was like a glitch in the matrix. "How come you're up so late?"

His father raised his eyebrows. "Late?"

"It's ten-thirty. On a weekday. You're usually at the office at five o'clock in the morning."

"Not tomorrow," Donald O'Callaghan said, helping himself to one of the little muffins on the platter. "Tomorrow's Friday."

"So?"

"So, I don't work Fridays anymore." His dad shrugged, looking down at the pink fluff rippling along under the needle of the sewing machine. "Switched to a four-day work week."

"You did?"

"Yep."

"When did that happen?"

"About two years ago."

Toria hovered on the edges of dreams. Another restless night of trying to sleep and fight off the images. Of Greg with a huge diamond ring, clamping it around her wrist. Of her mother in her big empty house. Of Mrs. Sidorsky falling down the waterfall. Of Ryder in the cabin, sleeping next to her, his warm body pressed against hers—

She awoke with a start.

Out of bounds, she told herself. He's getting married. And even if he wasn't, he was not the right person for her. Not right at all. He made her *feel* too much.

She hated this raw, exposed, vulnerable emotion. Pulling the pillow over her head, she tried to shut out the world.

And then she heard someone knocking at her door.

Or was that part of the dream?

She groaned, rolled over and peeked out one eye. Looking past the tipped over teacup, she spied the alarm clock.

Seven o'clock? The sun had been up for an hour and a half, but only a dim, cloudy light seeped into the bedroom from behind the curtains. Isabelle was supposed to come at eight. Why was she here this early?

Because it wasn't Isabelle, a warning voice told her. It was Greg. And she was not answering that door. She was going to have to speak to Mrs. Toony about letting people in.

The knock came again. Several light taps, and then a voice. A female voice. Not Greg. And not Isabelle, either.

Her mother.

With a dreary burden settling over her, Toria forced herself to get out of bed. Might as well get this over with. She grabbed her robe and her crutches, and stumbled down the hall. The knocking continued, persistent.

She stood in front of the door, braced herself, and then opened it.

Samantha Whitney waited in the hallway.

"Oh, good." Her mother pushed past her. "I'm glad I caught you," she said, with her fake smile firmly in place.

"Good morning," Toria said.

It *was* a good morning. And it was going to be a good life. For her. She was moving on, learning. She didn't have to be the person her mother wanted her to be.

"Is there something wrong with your cell phone? I tried calling you yesterday. Several times." Displeasure laced her mother's careful tones.

Toria winced as guilt clouded her thoughts. This was not going to be easy. "We're very busy at the school."

"Geraldine and I are very busy too. We need to finalize the—"

"Mom, I'm not marrying Greg." The words were out, uttered in a reflex.

Her mother paused for a beat. And then, "Of course you are."

Resolution welled in Toria's soul and her heart started to beat faster. "You need to talk to Aunt Glenda."

"Glenda? What does she have to do with any of this?"

"She's your sister. You need to get over your argument with her."

Her mother paused, narrowing her eyes. "Have you

been talking to her? Is *that* why you're being so difficult?" Her lips compressed to a tight line. "She puts ideas in your head."

"You need to talk to Aunt Glenda," Toria repeated, but her resolution was fading.

"Certainly not. She's jealous of me."

"Then I'll talk to her," Toria said, trying to hold on to those last wisps of determination.

"You can't. You have no business—" And then her mother drew herself up, jutted her chin and huffed an indignant breath. "You're going to tell her I'm having some financial difficulties, aren't you?"

Samantha Whitney always had financial difficulties, from as early as Toria could remember. But that was not what they needed to talk about.

"Well, they're temporary," her mother insisted. "And my finances are none of Glenda's business."

Toria sighed. Temporary or not, her mother needed to stop her irrational competition. "You need her, Mom."

"I most certainly do not."

"Aunt Glenda can help you."

"*You* can help me. Marry Greg and get these stupid ideas out of your head. This is what your father wanted."

Doubt chased resolve. Toria took a step back, wobbling on her crutches. "You can't know that."

"Why do you think he spent a fortune on that dress?"

How had this conversation deteriorated so quickly? Toria felt like a fallen leaf, being brushed away by a passing hurricane. "He bought it because you were in Paris and he thought I'd like it." A tiny pause. "Someday."

"He knew you'd fall in love with Greg once you met. And you did. You've just got cold feet now and you're behaving like a baby, getting worked up about a china pattern, for Pete's sake."

"I am not marrying him." Toria knew the words

sounded unconvincing, even to her own ears.

Then the buzzer sounded, blasting like an intruder.

Oh, no. Not Greg. She cringed, and then she glanced at the clock on the stove. Half past seven. Isabelle? Please, let it be Isabelle.

"Victoria, how can you talk like that? You know you love Greg. You know how much it meant to your father to see you together. He was so happy when the two of you finally met last Christmas."

"I'm not marrying Greg." She flung out the words, knowing they had no effect. Moving one crutch slightly, she edged toward the intercom.

"You are," her mother said, blocking her way.

The intercom blared once more and Toria tried to reach it.

"Don't answer that! I need to talk to you!"

The words hit her like a slap across the face and she froze, remembering all the times she had done what her mother wanted. And not what she, Toria, wanted. She reached past her mother and pressed the intercom button.

Samantha Whitney clenched her jaw and her eyes flared. "Tell me this nonsense is over. Right now."

Toria's mind whirled, remembering days of her childhood, hiding from her mother's anger. Her father would step in, when he was there. But often as not, that only made things worse. Even as a child, Toria had tried to mediate between her parents. But usually she'd just give in to whatever her mother wanted.

It didn't have to be like this.

And now her mother leaned against the apartment door, as though she would block whoever tried to interrupt her. "Greg called me last night and do you know what he said?"

A new line of attack. Toria knew that, and she didn't want to talk about Greg. She needed to change the subject.

"You have to stop spending so much money on renovations."

"On *my* suite," her mother emphasized, as if it made a difference. Then she stood up straight. "You can't back out now. You have to marry Greg."

"I'm not marrying Greg," Toria said, pressing the intercom button one more time for good measure.

"You have to. This is all your fault." Samantha Whitney drew herself up and folded her arms. "If you hadn't argued with your father, he'd still be here."

Toria felt a black horror slam into her and her world went still. She stiffened, her hands grew cold and she squeezed the crutches.

Her mother was right. It *was* her fault.

Her fault.

"You will marry Greg. We will all live in our home in Varsity Estates. It's going to be beautiful—my own little suite." Her mother glowed, smiling for real. "And," she added, clasping her palms together and dropping them against her heart, "Greg will take over the mortgage."

Mortgage?

The word clashed in her brain like someone singing the wrong words to a song. "There is no mortgage."

"Oh, but there is." Her mother tilted her head, lifting a brow. "Now."

"You mean you took out a mortgage on the house?" How could her mother do that? Didn't she know—

"I didn't." Her mother straightened, pursing her lips. "Your father did."

"She says Dad intended for me to marry Greg, all along. Even before I met Greg. She says that's why he bought the wedding dress."

Looking at the darkening sky, Toria sat in the passenger

seat of Isabelle's Firebird. How come there had to be so much rain now? Sure the spring was a drought, but why so much rain now?

She glanced at Isabelle. "And I can't believe he took out a mortgage on the house. Why would he do that? Especially when he was making all that extra money with Greg?"

"Who knows?" Isabelle said, as she came to a stop at the traffic light. "And anyway, just because you have a wedding dress doesn't mean you have to get married."

Chapter Thirteen

Ryder sat on the floor watching his students lift a plywood sheet up onto the structure and then begin to nail it in place.

Eight-thirty. Classes wouldn't start for another half hour and already the gym was filled with groups of students working on their committees.

He'd wanted to pick up Toria this morning, but they hadn't made any plans. He'd gone to her apartment, but she wasn't there.

A sense of longing wafted over him and he slumped. She wasn't here either.

No, wait a minute. She was. She was walking in right now . . . with Mrs. Sid at her elbow. A ray of sunshine with a thundercloud. He got to his feet.

She saw him immediately, but then quickly looked down, like she was trying to give Mrs. Sid her full attention. He started to step toward her, but he forced himself to stop, and think.

He was here to do a job. To build a waterfall. Well, to *supervise* the building of a waterfall. If he could just build it and leave that would be—

Not any better. Because then he'd have to go back to the job site and face the partnership problems. He sat down again. The students were lifting another sheet of plywood, nudging it into position.

He tried to watch them, but he kept turning back to

where Toria stood leaning on her crutches near the entrance to the gym, still talking to Mrs. Sid.

An awareness filled his senses. A feeling. Something he couldn't name. Something he'd never felt before.

It was nothing. Just the muddle of his life. The letting-go of control at work. The trusting that Jim could handle it. And it was the constant details for the house he was building. *His* house.

And, it was, of course, his approaching wedding. It hovered there, like an unpaid invoice waiting to be dealt with.

His parents had not talked about it. His mother had been elusive, telling him to take his time. And his father?

His father had said nothing. Nothing at all. They'd talked about his possible partnership with Jim Bondeau and the business in general. But not about the wedding. Not a single word. As if it didn't matter.

Ryder glanced at Toria again. She looked tired. Had Lorimer visited her last night? Had they resolved their argument? If she hadn't been getting married to that Lorimer jerk, he would have—

Shock reflected off the thought. He would have what?

Why was he even *thinking* like this? He pressed the heels of his hands into his temples. He had a wedding to complete, a deadline looming. No way was his father going to be able to say—

Say what? That he hadn't been able to finish what he started? That he didn't have any follow-through?

And what did his father have to do with it anyway? He'd quit doing what his father wanted a long time ago. And the arguments had stopped.

Somewhere along the line, the arguments had stopped. And he couldn't remember why they'd had them in the first place.

Toria was still talking to Mrs. Sid. She hadn't even taken

off her raincoat. And now a student approached them. Donna—the one who was in charge of the stage. Toria started to turn and then she stumbled with her crutches, falling.

He leapt to his feet, but then he saw Donna had caught her . . . steadied her. Brenda was there now, bringing her a chair so she could sit, and Donna was helping her out of her coat. Mrs. Sid threw her hands up in the air, and left the gym.

And then Toria looked his way. And smiled.

A shot of desire charged through him, followed by a flood of confusion. He wasn't attracted to women like Toria. She was spinny and ditzy and unorganized and—and—

And totally in charge of this gym and this grad project. Without seeming to be in charge. She gave complete control to her students and yet, without her here, nothing would get done. Before she'd shown up on Wednesday, nothing *was* getting done.

How the hell . . .

He squeezed his head again. Why had he ever thought she was a bimbo? Being around Toria was unsettling. And soothing at the same time. He liked her, even when she told him what he couldn't do. And yet—

Focus, O'Callaghan. What he needed was a problem to focus on. Maybe Jim needed him. Maybe he should call and see if—

No, Jim would call him. That was the plan.

The other plan was to get this waterfall sheeted. Waiting for these kids to do it was frustrating and he wanted to take over.

But Toria wouldn't let him.

Work progressed throughout the morning and the lunch hour and now it was just past one. Ryder watched as

Brett and Brandon lifted another sheet, and then Megan tacked it. He could have done it in two minutes with the nail gun. But, he conceded, they needed to learn. And they needed the satisfaction of doing it themselves.

"What kind of corsage should I buy, Ryder?"

"Corsage?" Ryder was sitting on the floor again, watching them work.

"Y' know," Brett elaborated, as he positioned the plywood. "You're supposed to get them this little bunch of flowers they wear on their shoulder."

"Or their wrist," Megan said, looking up from pounding nails.

"Well, what would you want, Meg?" Brett asked her.

"Depends on the guy."

"Like, give me a hint."

"Roses, I guess."

"What kind?"

"The color matters." Brandon joined the discussion. He leaned across the structure, measuring. "Color is important. Each color means something."

"It does?" Brett nudged the plywood into place.

"Yellow means friendship," Brandon said, closing his tape measure.

"I like pink," Megan said, slipping her hammer into her utility belt. "What's pink mean?"

"Let me check." Brandon pulled a chart out of his pocket. He stared at it a moment. "*Damn.* Pink can mean lots of things, depending on the shade of pink."

"We need someone from Home Ec over here. Those people know their pinks," Megan said.

"How about Derrick?" Brett asked. "He'd know. Right?"

All three of them had stopped working as they stood around Brandon and his chart. Ryder listened, curious. He hadn't gone to his Grad. He'd never bought a girl a corsage.

"Just because he's gay doesn't mean he knows," Megan said. "What's the chart say?"

"Deep pink is gratitude and respect," Brandon read. "Light pink is sympathy."

"Like a funeral?" Brett grimaced.

"Maybe," Brandon said. "Or maybe you have sympathy for her being your date."

Brett elbowed him. "Read more."

"Light pink can also mean," Brandon paused, and looked up, "*I think you're special.*"

"I think we're doomed," Brett said.

"Orange is desire, or new beginnings," Brandon read, sounding hopeful.

"I like desire," Brett said, nodding his head.

"How about red?" Megan asked.

"Love, respect, courage."

"How about white?" she asked.

"White means humility," Brandon read. "Or, *I apologize.*"

"Uck," they all said.

Brandon looked again. "But red *and* white is unity . . . or mending bridges."

"I'd go with red and white," Brett said, looking off into the distance.

"You need to apologize?" Brandon asked.

"No, not freakin' apologize. But if I needed to, like, mend bridges, y' know?"

They stopped talking for a moment, as if they were weighing options. As if the choice of a corsage was harder than building the waterfall.

And maybe it was.

"How about we just ask *them* what color they want?" Brett said.

"Yeah." Brandon closed the chart. "We could do that."

. . . . .

"They don't look like they're working," Mrs. Sidorsky said.

"They're having a discussion. Planning. It's part of the process," Toria answered. "How many chairs are we putting in the Refreshment Area?" Her cell was vibrating. She risked a glance.

Greg, this time.

"Who is it?" Mrs. Sidorsky wanted to know.

"Greg," Toria said, without thinking.

"Oh!"

"Oh what?"

"You'd better take it. He's your fiancé."

"I—"

"You go ahead. Answer. I'll go over and count chairs."

Toria braced herself. The phone continued to vibrate. Mrs. Sidorsky waited, smiling. What to do?

There was nothing to do but answer it. "Hello?"

"Hello, darling."

"Hello," Toria repeated, watching Mrs. Sidorsky, who was *not* going over to count chairs.

"I wanted to let you know your mother and my mother will be at your apartment on Saturday." He paused. "Tomorrow," he added, as if she had lost track of the days.

Wishing Mrs. Sidorsky would leave, Toria said, "Saturday." And she also wished she had not answered the phone. Except she'd had to, or risk having Mrs. Sidorsky find out the wedding was cancelled. And then Mrs. Sidorsky would tell everyone, and Ryder would know.

It shouldn't matter if he did know because *he* really was getting married. But, somehow, Toria felt safer with Ryder thinking she was engaged. It was like she was doubly protected from this—this inconvenient infatuation of hers.

"I know you're under a lot of strain," Greg's voice said.

His appease-the-client voice. "You need to forget about your father."

Her mind buzzed. Of course, she needed to forget about her father, but Greg kept reminding her, and her mother kept reminding her. They would never let it go. And then, like a book opening to the right page, the beginnings of a plan formed in her mind.

"On Saturday," she said, agreeing. "What time?"

"Does one o'clock work for you?" he asked, like it was a business appointment. To him, it probably was. He was letting Samantha and Geraldine smooth out a minor problem for him, so he could deal with more important things.

"One o'clock is fine. Are you coming?"

"I'm leaving for Edmonton. I'm on my way to the airport now."

That made sense. Perfect sense. She'd been slipped into the slot of taxi travel. How come she'd never noticed how little time they spent together?

"I'll drop by Monday night when I get back, darling," he said, still in his appeasement voice. "Play nice with the parents." He disconnected.

Toria turned off her phone and stared at it.

"Is everything all right?" Mrs. Sidorsky wanted to know.

Toria looked up. She could see the wheels turning, the gossip forming. *Trouble in paradise.* She'd have to fake this.

"He's going to Edmonton for the weekend," she said, trying to sound disappointed.

"Oh." A small note of sympathy. "Well, don't you worry. It will make it all the nicer when he comes back."

A few minutes later, Isabelle appeared, carrying two heaping bags of plumeria. "Hello, Mrs. Sidorsky," she said. "Mr. Burrows was wondering if you could help him with his opening comments."

Mrs. Sid scurried off and Toria wondered if Isabelle and Mr. Burrows had some kind of system where they traded off on the lady.

"What was that all about?"

"It was nothing, Isabelle. Don't worry about me."

"You just looked . . ."

"That was Greg."

"Why did you pick up?"

"I happened to say it was Greg and Mrs. Sid expected me to . . . you know." Ryder would be bored soon, and he'd leave and then she'd announce the cancelled wedding, but until then—

"Now you're calling her that."

"Calling her what?"

"Mrs. Sid."

"Oops."

Right after they'd solved the corsage problem, Brett, Brandon and Megan had to return to classes. Ryder studied their progress. They'd have to work quickly to get the waterfall finished by tonight.

And then Toria was there. He could sense her standing behind him. The noise in the gym had masked the sound of her approach on her crutches, but he knew she was there so he turned around.

She looked shy, like she always did when they first started talking. A sense of warmth, of goodness, of all is right with the world washed over him. He wanted to reach out and touch her—

What a crazy way to think . . .

"You've got a lot done."

"They've got a lot done. I could have finished this thing yesterday."

"You have to let them do it."

"They have to be in classes, Toria. Just let me do it." He knew she wouldn't, but she was fun to annoy.

"You supervise."

"I don't have anyone to supervise. They're all making flower wreaths."

"Leis."

"Listen," he said, touching her shoulder. Awareness brushed him and he took his hand away. "We need to finish the sheeting today. The expanding foam needs to be applied before we leave tonight."

"I know. And here he is now."

"Who?"

"Your new student."

A tall, young man with baggy clothes draped over his thin body ambled toward them.

"Hi, David."

"Hi, Miss Toria. Thanks for getting me time off."

"I'm glad you can help us. This is Mr. Ryder. He'll show you what to do."

After she introduced them, she left. Ryder wanted her to stay, and he almost said so. But the rest of the students needed her.

The boy stared at the frame of the waterfall, studying it.

"What did she mean, time off?" Ryder asked.

"I'm in the Apprenticeship Program," David said, turning away from the structure. "But Miss Toria thought I'd like to work in the gym for a day."

"Apprenticeship program?"

"I get to work as an apprentice auto service technician in between semesters. So when I graduate I have some hours toward a trade." David looked around the gym. "And I make some money at the same time as I learn." He waved to the group of boys testing the rigging for the balloon drop. Then he turned back to Ryder. "Besides, Mrs.

Sidorsky didn't want me in her English class."

Good ol' Mrs. Sid. Inspiring students again. "Done any woodworking?"

"Some. Helped my dad build a gazebo."

"How's it going?" said a familiar voice.

Ryder turned around. "Pro?"

Pro stood there, dressed in his lawyer uniform. Navy suit, white shirt, red tie with thin blue diagonals. Odd, Ryder thought, seeing the man here, in a high school gymnasium. Especially one full of activity like this one.

"This is David," Ryder said. And, "This is Pro."

Pro shook hands with David. David eyed the suit.

"He's in the Apprenticeship Program," Ryder said.

"I've heard of that," Pro answered. "You collect hours toward a journeyman ticket and go to school at the same time."

"That's right," David said.

"What are you working on here?" Pro studied the framing.

"I'm helping Mr. Ryder build a waterfall."

"Call me Ryder."

"A waterfall?"

"They want to build a waterfall," Ryder said.

"Of course."

"It's a Tropical Paradise," David explained.

Pro glanced around the gym, which overflowed with plants, paving stones and garlands of fabric flowers.

"Want to meet me for a beer after work?" Pro asked him.

"Don't know," Ryder answered. "We have to get the foam applied before we leave tonight."

"Of course," Pro said. "The foam."

"And then Isabelle has me taking some stuff to Toria's apartment." He motioned for David to pick up the other side of a sheet of plywood.

"I still have to go over that prenup with her. We can meet there."

"We can?" They were lifting the plywood into place, lining it up.

Pro walked around the frame of the waterfall and stood near the end of the pool they'd built this morning. He nodded, considering the structure. "Aunt Tizzy wants me to help make these flower things."

"Leis."

"That's it."

"Isabelle knows your Aunt Tizzy?"

"Yes," Pro said. "As a matter of fact, they know each other quite well."

Typical of Isabelle—to recruit volunteers for her project. Funny that she knew Pro's Aunt Tizzy.

At any rate, it sounded like a good plan and he didn't have anything else to do. Except get that stupid tux fitting over with. But that could wait until Monday. Today he needed to get the waterfall to the painting stage.

"Where are you doing your apprenticeship?" Pro asked David.

David was eyeing the suit again. "At Carron Motors. Right now, I'm a garage serviceman. I do mostly oil changes."

"How do you like that?"

"It's easy," David said, with a touch of attitude. "Drain out the old. Put in the new. Change the filter. Anything with a grease fitting gets lubricated. Drive shaft U-joints, tie rod ends, ball joints, other steering components."

Pro nodded. He stood at ease with his hands behind his back. "And you enjoy doing that?"

"Oh, I like it," David said, not quite sounding that way.

Pro was nodding again, encouraging the boy to talk more.

"When I take out the drain plug, depending on how

quick I am, I get hot oil all over my hand. Sometimes, when I'm not careful, hot oil splashes in my face. When I remove the filter, hot oil usually runs down my arm. Oil changes are fun."

"So you're not finding it a challenge right now."

The boy smiled. "The challenge is dealing with the customers." He whacked some nails into place.

Pro changed his stance, slipped his hands in his pockets, and waited for the boy to continue.

"The ones who want you to tell them why their engine is leaking oil and to check their tire pressures and their brakes *while you're at it.* They pay for an oil change but they want a complete vehicle inspection." He reached for another handful of nails.

"Mmm hmm," Pro nodded. "I see."

"Even if there's nothing wrong with their car and all they really need is an oil change, they still manage to dream up more things for you to do."

"Such as?"

"Adjust their seat." Whack. "Polish their steering wheel." Another whack. "Empty their ash tray." David was turning out to be talkative. "One guy had me program his radio."

Pro nodded. "I'd say you're being underutilized."

David turned out to be a natural. He needed little instruction and hardly any supervision.

"What do you think?" Ryder asked, looking back at the waterfall frame.

"I can't believe you're actually doing this," Toria said.

He watched those strange green eyes and thought of Kananaskis lakes again. "You don't have a lot of faith in me, do you?"

"I didn't mean that," she said, blushing for some

reason. "I knew you could build a waterfall. I just didn't know you could . . ."

He waited. What was going through that un-bimbo head of hers?

She watched as David showed one of the other students how to square the plywood. "I didn't know you could work so well with the students. Bring out their initiative."

Initiative? *He* was bringing out initiative?

"Some of these students have never been enthusiastic about school."

He shrugged. "Never thought of that."

Isabelle appeared next to Toria. She did that a lot— turning up out of the blue.

"Pro is coming over tonight," Isabelle told them.

Ryder noticed the confusion flicker across Toria's expression. Like him, she probably hadn't realized that Isabelle knew Pro and his Aunt Tizzy.

"To your apartment," Isabelle continued.

Toria frowned. Obviously, Isabelle hadn't filled her in.

"It's Friday night," Isabelle said. "No one has to be at work tomorrow. I thought we could get a lot done."

"I suppose," Toria answered, sounding bewildered.

"I'm bringing the pizza," Ryder added. He didn't want her to nix the idea. "You've got to eat."

She looked like she was coming up with an objection, but Isabelle was talking again, distracting her.

"Are you worried about them missing school?" Isabelle asked.

"They're not missing school." Toria turned around on her crutches, and scanned the room. "They're all here, aren't they?"

"You know what I mean," Isabelle said. "Mrs. Sidorsky keeps saying they're missing classes."

"Oh, they may be missing classes, but this is school.

Look around you," Toria said. "What do you see?"

Isabelle surveyed the gym. "I see them creating a Tropical Paradise?"

"And, you see teamwork, cooperation, problem solving. What more could you want them to learn?"

Toria collapsed in the passenger seat, exhausted after the long day. Ryder eased through the traffic, not looking tired at all. Friday night had arrived and the stretched-out school day had ended.

In two and a half days, the Tropical Paradise had evolved faster than she'd imagined. But then, the students always amazed her with their energy.

Ryder pulled up to a stoplight. They waited in an easy silence, comfortable in their own thoughts.

The four boys in charge of the water pumps had sketched out the plans for the water flow and assembled the pool at the base of the waterfall. They'd needed some help from the caretakers and a lot of advice from Ryder but they'd done it.

Then they'd created the Rock Committee. Two dozen students each brought in their rock—their large borrowed rock from the Bow River. Today the group had begun painting the rocks bright colors for the rainbow waterfall.

The waterfall foam would set over the weekend. On Monday they would finish shaping it, and then waterproof and paint it.

They had two weeks until the Grad Dance. Two weeks of before school time and noon hour time and after school time. And borrowed time from missed classes.

Ryder drove into the entrance at Dalhousie Towers and parked. Then he walked around to the passenger door. "How's your ankle?" he asked as he held out her crutches.

"Doesn't hurt a bit. I think I could put weight on it now."

"Dr. Delanghe said Monday at the earliest. Better wait till Tuesday."

He was worried about her ankle? She accepted the crutches.

He leaned into the backseat and came out holding two large Pop's Pizzas and a six pack of beer. Tall-necked brown bottles—something from a local brewery with a picture of two pine trees and a mountain peak on the label.

"I wonder how Isabelle got Pro to volunteer?" he said, reaching back for the three bags of plumeria.

Like he was mulling it over in his mind, Toria thought. "She probably wanted to make sure you would come."

Oops.

"I would have come anyway."

They took the elevator and it delivered them to the third floor without incident.

Chapter Fourteen

Three teacups and saucers sat stacked next to the sink in the kitchen. Toast crumbs dusted the counter. A tub of margarine sat on top of the crumbs, opened, with a knife placed crossways on the container as though Toria had left in a hurry this morning.

Ryder looped the three new bags of plumeria over the chair backs in the dining area. The table already overflowed with the imitation flowers. Then he made space for the pizzas on the counter and put the beer in the fridge.

He found her in the living room, staring at the flashing light on her answering machine.

All of the wedding gifts—the shower gifts—had been moved off the makeshift bookshelves and piled in the center of the living room floor. On the garage-sale-style coffee table, a pad of paper and a pen waited.

She was inventorying the gifts.

As usual, a sense of scattered bedlam pervaded the apartment. But there was a pattern here that seemed to work for her.

"Are you going to check your messages?"

"It'll just be my mother."

She said it like that explained everything. He was going to say something, but he didn't have anything nice to say about her mother so he didn't. And then, looking around at the jumble of confusion, "You're competent, you know. In your own way."

She smiled, that slow smile of hers. "And you're encouraging," she answered. "In your own way."

Touché, he thought. And then he wondered, "But not competent?"

"Your competence has never been in question. But yes, you are very competent."

That made him feel good. He wasn't sure why.

"Has your competence ever been in question?" He knew it had been. By him. And he bet Mrs. Sidorsky always questioned Toria's competence. Budge seemed happy with what she did though.

With both crutches in one hand, she leaned down and picked up the package of beige and navy sheets, still partially wrapped in the striped yellow wrapping paper. "My father never agreed with the way I run my classroom."

Her father. She hadn't said much about her father since she'd told him the guy was waiting for her in Kalispell. "What is it with your father?"

Her hand jerked as she placed the sheets on top of the pile. Several of the gifts wobbled, spilling to the floor.

"I—"

He waited.

"I don't want to talk about it."

"Why not?"

"I wonder where Isabelle is. She should be here by now."

Toria looked pale. She was doing it again, the way she had when they'd had breakfast at the cabin. And when he'd first come to her apartment on Tuesday night. She was avoiding the topic of her father. She gave up trying to stack the packages and tried to get her crutches lined up again.

There was something bothering her, about her father. And Ryder wanted to know what it was. "What's he doing in Kalispell? Is he coming to your wedding?"

She dropped one of the crutches. It fell against the

stack of presents sending more of them toppling. "Who said he's in Kalispell?"

"You did. When I found you on the side of the road."

"I—I just said that."

"So? Where is he?"

She let go of her other crutch, letting it fall with a bang on the floor and she covered her eyes with her hands. "He's dead." Her voice sounded small and her shoulders were shaking. "I killed him."

And then she started to cry.

His reaction had been automatic. He'd gathered her up in his arms and taken her to the couch. The little love seat. Now he sat there, holding her and rocking her while she cried.

She told him the story . . . of the argument with her father, a simple argument about classroom styles, where she'd refused to back down. Of his anger . . . and the anger turning into a heart attack. Of the ambulance coming to her parents' house in Varsity, and her father not surviving the trip to the hospital.

And of her mother—her *goddamn* mother—blaming her.

"I've cried all over your shirt."

"I'm glad." She felt so small in his arms, so defenseless. He knew she wasn't defenseless, but right now she needed someone. And he was glad he was here.

"You are?"

"You haven't cried about this before, have you?"

"No. I guess I haven't."

He knew she'd been holding those feelings inside and he gently tightened his arms around her. "It's not your fault. The heart attack."

"The argument was my fault."

"So you had an argument," he said. "People argue. It's not going to kill them."

"It did this time."

He sighed, a quick release of air. That hadn't come out right. "Sorry," he said. "But it still wasn't your fault."

She rubbed the palms of her hands over her eyes, wiping over the tears.

He loosened his grip on her, letting her move in his arms. "Your father was going to have a heart attack anyway."

She lifted her head and looked at him. That sad expression still in her eyes. Those amazing green eyes.

"You can't tiptoe around people forever, Toria."

"I know." She sniffled. "That's what Isabelle says."

He put his hand on the back of her head and pulled her against his chest. She didn't resist. He brushed his chin over her hair. "What did Isabelle say?"

"That he was a heart attack waiting to happen. She used to be a coronary care nurse."

Isabelle? She seemed too crazy to be a nurse. But there were probably a lot of things about Isabelle he didn't know. "Speaking of Isabelle . . ."

"Yes." Toria lifted her head again. "Where are they?"

"Held up, I guess. But they'll be here. Pro wants to go over your prenup with you."

Toria frowned.

He could understand. She probably didn't like working on prenups any more than he did. Hopefully, she would forget about the prenup for tonight. Then he asked, "Hungry?"

Finally, she smiled. "Starved."

"Then let's eat. They can eat when they get here."

He slipped her off his lap and onto the love seat. Then he got both pizzas, a bunch of paper towels, the beer and a bottle opener, and brought it all to the little coffee table.

He watched as she lifted the lids on the red and green cardboard pizza boxes. One of them was vegetarian with tomatoes, mushrooms, peppers and zucchini. The other, pepperoni and bacon. Both smothered in cheese, apparently three different kinds.

He opened two bottles of beer—Highgate Ancient Old Ale from the brewery near Canmore—and handed her one, clinking the top of her bottle with his. They ate in silence for a few minutes. She finished a slice of the vegetarian and drank half a bottle of the beer. She looked exhausted and emptied out.

And a little stronger. She'd get over this. She had stamina, and brains, tucked away in that pretty head of hers.

"Why did you have it with you?"

"What?" She reached for a second slice of the vegetarian.

"The wedding dress."

"I don't know." She lifted the pizza out of the box, twining the dripping cheese over one finger. "I was going to show it to Aunt Glenda." She licked the cheese off her finger. "And, it just seemed . . . important. That dress."

Her eyes had that faraway look again as she nibbled on this slice of pizza—she'd devoured the first one. She set the half-finished piece on a paper towel on the coffee table and dabbed her finger on her lips, catching some cheese.

"He bought it for you."

She didn't answer right away. She was staring across the room at the toppled stack of gifts. "Yes, he did. I hadn't even met Greg at the time."

"Out of the blue your father bought you a wedding dress?"

"Yes. My parents were on vacation in Paris, and they saw it. He wanted me to have it, so he bought it."

"Had he met Greg?"

"Yes."

A tinge of horror rippled into his thoughts. Followed by anger, and a need to protect her. "Do you think he wanted—I mean, do you think he was planning . . ."

"I don't know. I keep wondering about that."

"Is that why you're marrying him? Because your father wanted you to?"

"I'm just going to drink this," she said as she picked up the half-full bottle of beer.

It seemed as if there was only so much she could talk about in one night. He watched her take several long swallows of the beer, gulping.

She finished it.

"My mother suggested that I let them put a cast on my ankle," she said, setting the empty bottle on the coffee table and changing the subject. "So I can walk down the aisle without crutches."

And if she didn't want to talk about it anymore tonight, he wasn't going to push her.

"You won't need the crutches by then." He thought a moment, calculating the date—calculating how much time he had left. "In two weeks."

"I might." She reached for the bottle opener and a second beer.

"What's the problem with walking with crutches?"

"Pictures."

He laughed. "Maybe she thinks you'll trip." And he noticed she was having trouble getting the cap off the beer.

"I won't trip."

He wasn't going to help her. If she wanted to drink it, she'd have to open it herself. "It's a long dress," he said.

"That's right, you've seen it." The cap popped off, flipping up into the air and pinging into the brass colander beside the stack of gifts. She took a long drink.

"You don't drink much, do you?"

"Not usually. But this tastes good with the pizza." She

picked up her slice of pizza from the coffee table, took another bite and set it down again.

He took a second slice from the pepperoni box. But he just sipped his beer. If she was going to get drunk, he'd better make sure he didn't.

After she finished that slice of pizza and the second beer, she said, "We need dessert. I've got some strawberries." And she stood up.

So did he. "I'll get it."

"No. You sit down. I'm fine."

She was probably a little drunk, but he'd watch out for her. "You're drinking. You'll tip over."

She tested her ankle.

And he felt a touch of anxiety. "Don't walk on it. Not yet." He grabbed her crutches and handed them to her.

Thankfully, she accepted them. Otherwise he'd have picked her up. Now she was aiming toward the fridge. He followed her, half-hoping she'd stumble so he could catch her.

Wrong.

She wasn't swaying or anything. Maybe having the beer with the food would be all right. She got to the fridge and opened the door.

"Oh good," she said, pulling out a clear container with a blue lid. "We have some left. Isabelle brought these this morning." Toria picked up another clear container with an orange lid. This one was grapes. He took them out of her hands.

"I've got them," he said. "Go and sit down."

When she was safely back on the couch—the love seat—he stacked her crutches at the end of it and sat beside her again.

She opened the containers. "We each get two strawberries and a bunch of grapes," she said. "And they'll go good with the beer."

"Do they?"

"I don't know. I just made that up."

They both laughed, and then he leaned over and kissed her. Just a light touch, his lips on hers.

He pulled back, about two inches, watching her.

She didn't move. She sat very still, staring at his lips.

He leaned forward again, and kissed her again, nibbling, lingering over the light kiss. And then a sense of disorientation flashed through him and he realized what he was doing. "That didn't happen."

"Yes," she said, looking like she was waking up from a dream. "It did."

"No. That was a mistake. That didn't happen."

"You're getting married," she said, wonderment in her voice.

"I'm—"

I'm not.

Whoa. When had he decided that?

He hadn't. And even if he had decided, it would make sense to tell Catherine first. And it didn't matter that he wasn't getting married because she *was* getting married. To that Lorimer jerk.

And she was drinking . . .

And she didn't know how. And—and, he was taking advantage of her.

"I've got to go."

"Yes," she said. "You do."

He left Toria to explain why he was gone. She would, in her own tactful way, come up with some story. She wouldn't tell them he'd kissed her. Or that she'd kissed him back.

Because she had.

He wouldn't think about that. Not yet. One thing at a

time. Something about his wedding had been bothering him for quite a while and he knew what it was now.

He was not in love with Catherine. He never had been. She'd been his ace in the hole in the status war he'd waged with his father.

And that war had fizzled out.

The sun had gone down behind the mountains a few minutes ago. Not a flashy sunset, not the kind that predicted good weather the next day. Just an ordinary sunset with pinks and blues radiating across the western sky. With the long days leading up to the summer solstice, it would be light for another half hour, maybe three-quarters of an hour.

Ryder pulled up in front of Catherine's apartment and parked the truck. He hopped out, feeling lighter and more in charge than he had in days.

Scanning the number pad, he found her name and buzzed her unit.

"Who is it?"

"Ryder."

The entrance door buzzed open.

When he got to her door, he knocked and waited, and then knocked again.

She opened the door, wearing a flowing, silky robe. Something with orange and red geometric angles. Her hair looked like she'd just combed it, and her lipstick looked fresh.

"It's about time." She stepped aside to let him in.

"Yes, it is," he said.

"Don't get all cocky. You know you messed up. Big time. My mother says—"

"No," he said, tapping his index finger on her nose.

"No, what?"

He walked past her and into her living room. She already had the drapes pulled closed, even though it was still light outside. "Please. Don't tell me what your mother said."

Had he really voiced his thoughts? Finally?

Yes, he had. And it felt good—really good—to know what he was feeling. In fact, he had to say it again to make sure. "I'm tired of hearing what your mother says."

"You'd better get used to it." Catherine came around from behind him and stood in front of him. "If you expect to be part of my family, you'll have to learn to tow the line."

He laughed. And then he reached for her, hugged her and swung her around.

"Be careful," she shrieked. "If you break my grandmother's lamp—that's an antique, you know. My mother would kill you."

He set her down.

She straightened her robe.

"You always know just what to say to make me happy," he said. How come he hadn't seen this before?

He thought a moment . . . and he knew. It was because he'd seen what he'd wanted to see. Sophisticated, elegant, in charge. And able to do battle with his father. And anyone else for that matter.

"What's wrong with you?" She stared at him with her arms folded. "You've been drinking, haven't you?"

"I had a beer."

"Just one?" She tilted her head and raised her eyebrows, expecting a confession. Or an apology. Or both.

"Yeah."

"With Pro." She was nodding her head.

"Not exactly."

"And that's supposed to mean?" She stopped nodding and her freshly made-up lips tightened.

"That means Pro was supposed to meet me and he didn't."

She blinked, seemed to give up on expecting a confession, or an apology, and lifted her chin, tossing back her smooth hair. "That reminds me. We have to talk about Pro."

"We do?" He couldn't help smiling, he felt so good. For the first time in weeks, his head was clear.

"I called him," Catherine said, as though she were gritting her teeth, "and he wasn't nice to me."

"You called Pro?"

"I was looking for you. And he knew where you were and he wouldn't tell me."

"Why would he?"

"I don't like Pro," she answered, ignoring the question. "I think you need to find some friends that we both like."

"You do?" Ryder nodded his head, listening. Listening to it all.

"Yes. Mother says it's important for us to have similar friends."

Mother again. It was like he was marrying her mother. *Had been.* "And what if we don't?"

"Ryder, this isn't funny. Stop grinning like that. You missed the last shower party my mother held. And you missed the last two appointments for your tux fitting. And you were supposed to be at dinner tonight."

"I was?"

"We were supposed to have dinner. Tonight. At my parents' house."

"I didn't know that."

"Of course you didn't. You haven't been answering your phone. You're being selfish. My mother says—"

"Catherine, do you love me?"

"Love you?" She seemed surprised by the question. "Not at the moment. Not if you're going to act like this." She shook her hair back, away from her face, like she was trying to clear her thoughts. And then she faced her grandmother's antique lamp. "What does love have to do with it?"

She seemed out of her element, in a conversation she couldn't control.

"And what about you?" She turned back to him. "Do you love me? Because if you really loved me, you wouldn't be so selfish."

He waited a beat. Had she said it all? Was she finished?

"I don't see any point in us getting married if you're going to be so selfish," she said, with a quieter voice, as she tried a new approach.

"Right," he said. "Neither do I."

She twisted up her eyebrows. "What's *wrong* with you?"

"Catherine, I think I'm in love."

"Then you'd better start acting like it. And the first thing I want you to do is get a different Best Man."

"A different Best Man," he repeated. Was he really hearing this? He put his hands on her shoulders and held her in front of him. And looked at her. He hadn't ever really just looked at her.

"I don't like Pro and I don't want him in the wedding party." She stared up at him, determination in her eyes. She was serious.

"I don't think I've ever appreciated you for who you are," he said, still holding her by her shoulders.

He'd come so close. So close. It was scary.

"Nice words," she said, shrugging out of his hold. She took two paces away from him and then turned around. "But I want to make something perfectly clear. Right now. If you think you're marrying me and keeping up with this constant work schedule of yours, you can think again."

Lightness filled his senses. Power and possibility flowed into him. "Oh?" he said.

She held up her index finger, pointing it at his face. "You can sign that partnership agreement with Jimmy Bondeau."

Yes. "Yes." He knew, now, with complete certainty. He could not marry this woman.

She drew herself up tall, a Sergeant Major disciplining a lower ranking man. "And you can start winding down your time on the job site."

"Yes," he said. Might as well hear the whole sorry thing.

"And you can enroll in night classes and finish that degree you started."

"Really?" He laughed.

"Yes," Catherine said, flatly. "My mother thinks it's important for you to finish your degree."

"Catherine, you know what?"

"What?" she snapped. "And don't think you can sweet talk me into—"

"You're going to make someone a great wife." He paused and looked at her face.

She frowned.

"But it's not going to be me."

The weather waited. The air smelled like rain, but the cloudy sky didn't send any more rain. It waited.

He'd tried to find Toria but she'd gone into hiding.

At last, it was Monday morning and she'd be at the school. She had to be. He turned off Collins Street and aimed the truck onto Dottridge Avenue.

On Saturday morning, he'd called Pro to find out if he'd shown up at Toria's apartment, finally, on Friday night. And Pro had said they hadn't because Aunt Tizzy had other plans at the last minute.

Then Ryder had called his mother. Just a quick call, telling her the wedding was cancelled. And his mother had taken it in stride.

After that his cell kept ringing. The readout said Catherine some times, and other times it was the number for her parents. He would have turned it off, but he left it on in case Toria tried to call him.

But she hadn't.

He shoulder checked, changed lanes and exited onto Stelmack Boulevard.

She hadn't answered her phone all weekend. And even on Saturday night when he buzzed Mrs. Toony to let him in and he'd gone up and knocked on her door, it was Mrs. Toony's door that had opened. "She's not here," Mrs. Toony had said. "Left on Friday night. Had the taxi driver come up and get her suitcase."

Her suitcase?

He'd tried to focus on other things. He'd phoned Jim and walked around the sites with him, trying to listen to what Jim was saying. He didn't hear much of it, except to realize that Jim's confidence had grown by leaps and bounds since Ryder had stepped out of the way. And that was another thing he'd come to realize. Part of the reason he'd been resistant to taking Jim on as a partner was because Catherine had been lobbying so hard for it.

Jim had everything on schedule. There were no problems to divert Ryder's attention. His mind kept returning to one thing, to a strange, out-of-place moment in time. A time when he was alone with Toria in a quiet cabin. She snuck into his thoughts everywhere. All he thought about was her.

To hold her again. That had felt so good. Like that's all there was to do in the world.

He was at Wickens Street. He'd head over to Tim Hortons for a quick breakfast and then he'd be at the school. First thing.

Maybe he should apologize, though he wouldn't mean it. No way in hell could he ever be sorry he'd kissed her.

And, he remembered, still feeling the taste of her lips, she'd kissed him back. Maybe it had been the beer, or maybe it had been the circumstances, or maybe it had been a combination. But she had kissed him back.

Why was she marrying Lorimer? Did she *want* to marry Lorimer?

Feeling a deep pain settle in his chest, Ryder pulled into the Tim Hortons parking lot. After he'd had something to eat, he'd find her.

Twenty minutes later, he parked his truck in front of the school. And *damned* if that wasn't her mother.

"You?" Toria's mother said, as she approached him on the sidewalk. "What are *you* doing here?"

Another woman accompanied Mrs. Whitney. One who looked a lot like her, only slightly older. "How do you do," she said, extending her hand. "I'm Glenda. Toria's aunt. You must be Ryder."

"Yes. I am." He shook hands with her. The aunt seemed glad to see him, even if the mother did not.

"Is Toria here?" Glenda asked.

"I hope she is." Because he needed to see her.

"Of course, she'll be at the school," Mrs. Whitney said, yanking her purse strap, lugging the heavy purse onto her shoulder. "She practically lives here."

When he walked into the gym, Toria was standing in the middle of it, facing away from him. Without her crutches.

It wasn't even nine o'clock and the gym was full of students, clustered in groups. Toria was the sun at their center.

Two students were talking to her. The ones he'd helped with the starscape, Donna and Brenda. Toria wore blue jeans, a jean jacket and runners. And a red shirt. He could see the collar of it, peeking up over the blue jean jacket.

Mrs. Sid would probably have something to say about proper attire for school.

Donna said, "Okay, we'll check with you later," then she and Brenda disappeared. Toria bent her head, reading some notes she was holding.

He stood behind her, smelling the flowery scent of her hair. Then he leaned down by her ear. "You're rushing this, aren't you?"

She startled, and then she slowly turned around. "It doesn't hurt," she said, not meeting his eyes. She pretended to read the papers in her hands.

"You look tired. You should sit down."

"I'm fi—" She cut herself off. And she sighed. "I mean, I'm not tired."

"I should tell you—"

"Don't," she said, still watching her notes. "It was my fault. I'm not used to drinking. It was a mistake. Can we forget—"

"Not that." It wasn't her fault, and it wasn't a mistake. He knew that as well as he knew anything.

She looked up at him then. Right into his eyes. And she looked frazzled, and hunted and afraid.

"Your mother is checking in at the office."

Toria clutched the papers in her hand and dropped her arms. Closing her eyes, she slumped.

That's what he'd thought. She didn't want to see her mother. But maybe— "Your aunt is with her," he said.

"She is?" Now Toria lit up. The aunt was a good thing.

"Can we talk?" he asked her.

"I don't think we should."

Never mind *should*, he thought. And then Mrs. Sid descended on them.

"I can't believe you're letting the students play with all this water! In the gym!"

Terrific. "It's a waterfall, Mrs. Sid. It has . . . water?"

"But I thought you'd make *artificial* water. And this pool— The flooring can't—"

"It's safe. The caretakers have checked it. Don't worry about—"

"There you are." A woman's voice. "I need to speak to you, this minute."

A bolt of irritation shot through him. Toria's mother had found her.

"Who are you?" Mrs. Sid asked, ignoring the water crisis and staking her attention on Mrs. Whitney. "We don't have time for parents in the gym. The students are missing enough classroom time as it is."

"I want to speak to my daughter," Samantha Whitney insisted. "Now."

"Is your daughter assigned to the gym for this period?"

"She's right here!"

Toria wasn't saying anything. She stood next to him, looking at the notes in her hands, frozen.

"You can't interrupt the students now." Mrs. Sid bulldozed over Mrs. Whitney. "They have so much to do. Especially now that they've taken on this ridiculous waterfall project."

"Ridiculous?" Ryder could hardly believe the woman. He glanced at the boys standing behind the waterfall. Brett and Brandon quickly hid the water pistols they'd brought in last Friday.

"This pool cannot be here. I never agreed to this!"

"Mrs. Sid," he said. "Are you allowed to tell parents they can't see their children?"

"Don't you tell me what I'm allowed to—oh!"

Mrs. Sid jumped forward as a stream of water caught her in the back. Toria's mother jerked to the right, trying to avoid the same stream. Then another stream swept over them from the other direction.

Mrs. Whitney's expression changed from anger to disbelief. "Is this how you discipline your students? What kind of school is—oh!"

A third stream of water, and a fourth, and a fifth.

Ryder laughed. He couldn't help himself. Mrs. Sid's mouth gaped open as she stared at the foam-covered waterfall with the pool at its base. A second later, she charged toward the structure, screaming at the boys.

Then she tripped over a hammer and splashed down into the water.

Chapter Fifteen

Toria sat in Mr. Burrow's office thinking about Ryder. Her mind replayed Friday night—the pizza, the beer, the strawberries. Their kiss.

When he'd kissed her, she'd felt as if the other half of her soul had clicked into place.

She'd felt afraid and confused. And wonderful. All in the blink of a moment. But even after a whole weekend had passed, she still didn't know what to do about it. About the fact that she'd fallen in love with a man who was getting married in two weeks.

She'd thought about it all weekend while she'd hidden out at Isabelle's condo. They'd strung leis and talked and drank tea. And Toria had managed to avoid her mother and Geraldine. And Ryder.

"Stupid. Arrogant. Smart-alecky." Mrs. Sidorsky mumbled next to her.

Toria couldn't help smiling, even though disaster swirled around her. How could he let them have water pistols? Encourage them like that? Let them douse Mrs. Sidorsky of all people?

And how could he kiss her? He was getting married. This was not what Ryder would do.

At least she'd escaped her mother. Aunt Glenda, bless her, had taken her sister over to Tim Hortons to calm her down. They had been caught in the crossfire, but they weren't very wet.

Unlike Mrs. Sidorsky.

The overweight Mrs. Sidorsky, with her usually tidy dark brown bun of hair, sat in the chair next to her, dripping wet, while they waited for Mr. Burrows to return to his office.

"You and your fancy notions about what students need."

"They're not my notions. Everyone is trying to incorporate teamwork and problem solving—"

"Teamwork! I'll say. They acted as a team, all right. A team of hooligans."

It had been impossible to tell who had opened fire. And none of the students were talking. Their solidarity was admirable.

Unfortunately, the decorating had come to a halt and Mr. Burrows had sent everyone back to classes. Now he was out in the hall, talking to Ryder.

"You always want to let them think for themselves."

"What's wrong with that?"

"They need to be told what to think."

"Mrs. Sidorsky. You don't mean that."

Drops of water tapped onto the carpet under Mrs. Sidorsky's chair. Toria tried to block out the sound as a sense of futility coupled with desperation seeped into her mind. She shivered, even though she hadn't got wet at all.

It didn't need to be like this. There had to be a way to protect her students from Mrs. Sidorsky's interference . . . and also teach them to temper their enthusiasm. To find safer ways to express it.

She'd tried to prevent the conflict that threatened to take over the gym every time Mrs. Sidorsky walked into it. But—like Ryder had said on Friday night—she couldn't tiptoe around people forever. She'd tried to. And, obviously, she'd failed.

Maybe that was a good thing. Maybe this needed to

happen. Because the strain of trying to keep the peace was wearing her down.

The carpet under Mrs. Sidorsky's chair had turned a muddy brown.

"You always say, let them be and they will learn. Well, you're wrong. You have to *force* them to learn or they'll never learn anything."

"Mrs. Sid, listen to what you're saying."

"Don't call me Mrs. Sid!"

Oops.

A tired-looking Mr. Burrows finally trudged into his office.

"I want them expelled," Mrs. Sidorsky said, before Mr. Burrows had even reached his desk.

He pulled his chair out and collapsed into it. Then he gathered pen and paper, like he always did when he wanted to think. "Who?"

"It was a joke," Toria said. "They've been playing with water and—"

"All of them. I want them all expelled. Everyone on that waterfall committee."

"They didn't mean any harm—"

"And Ryder O'Callaghan. I want him out of here. Now."

Mrs. Sidorsky vibrated in her chair. Water from her hair bun dripped onto the rounded white collar of her blouse.

Mr. Burrows, looking grim, floundered in the middle of the argument. He arranged his pad of paper directly in front of himself and clutched his pen, holding it in midair. Then he took a deep breath, let it out, and said, "We can't have this kind of behavior, Toria."

"Expelled!" Mrs. Sidorsky's voice rose a notch and she gripped the arms of her chair.

"They'll graduate in two weeks. They've *already* graduated. You can't expel—"

"I want the Grad Dance cancelled. They can't get away with this. They don't respect me."

Respect? The word clanged in Toria's brain, out of context.

"Respect?" She got to her feet and turned to face Mrs. Sidorsky. "And *you* don't respect them," she said, with a strength of voice she was surprised to hear.

"What?"

"They are treating you the way you treat them."

"They—I—" Mrs. Sidorsky sniffled, and hiccoughed, and rushing the words, she ended with, "You're just their favorite." Then she started to cry.

Mr. Burrows dropped his pen on the desk, shook his head, and stood up. "You two work it out," he said, and he left the office.

Mrs. Sidorsky ventilated for about fifteen minutes, alternating between sobbing and shouting. And finally the strength of her rage drained away. She sat there wringing out her cardigan.

"I don't know what's right anymore," she said, twisting out the drops. "It used to be so simple. We stood at the front of the room and told them what they needed to learn."

Toria had found a box of tissues on Mr. Burrow's desk and she handed another one to Mrs. Sid.

"All this nonsense about cooperation. Leadership." Mrs. Sidorsky blew her nose. A loud honk. "I'd like to catch the leader of that attack."

"It was good leadership," Toria added, without thinking. And then she cringed as she realized she was speaking out loud.

"Yes, it was," Mrs. Sidorsky said, nodding her head. She squinted and stared at the ball of tissue in her hands. "A whole gym full of students," she mused. "The jocks, the preppies, the goths, the skaters."

Mrs. Sidorsky knew the designations?

"And what do they call them? Those with the . . ."

"The hip-hops."

"Yes," Mrs. Sidorsky nodded. "It's hard to keep up."

But—apparently—Mrs. Sidorsky was keeping up.

"All cooperating." Mrs. Sidorsky shook her head, like she'd observed a strange phenomenon.

"Pretty amazing," Toria said, agreeing.

"They *have* accomplished a lot," Mrs. Sidorsky admitted. "I never would have thought it possible. Not when they started so late. They only really started last Wednesday."

Last Wednesday. Once they had been allowed to go with their own theme.

Mrs. Sidorsky lobbed her ball of tissue into the waste basket. "And Ryder," she humphed.

Toria braced herself. What had he been thinking? Water pistols? She smiled, because it was what Ryder would do. He must have been a challenging student for Mrs. Sid.

"I expected him to take over," Mrs. Sidorsky said. "To do it his way."

Toria had expected him to take over as well.

"But he's been teaching them. Standing back and letting them do it. He's changed," Mrs. Sidorsky said, reluctantly.

Hopefully we all change, Toria thought. She felt the change inside herself. This could have been such a disaster, and maybe it still was. But, she didn't feel as worried about it as she might have.

As she would have, if this had happened a month ago. Or even a week ago.

A week ago, she'd been upset about a china pattern. Today, Mrs. Sidorsky wanted to expel students. She wanted to cancel the whole Grad. Of course, she couldn't do that, but she might be able to stop the waterfall . . .

And Toria cared—but not so much that her heart hurt. What would happen, would happen.

"Maybe I need to change." Mrs. Sidorksy shook out the damp cardigan and held it up. "But what am I going to do about this?"

She didn't mean the sweater.

"I can't just pretend it didn't happen." She crumpled the cardigan in her lap. "I don't know what to do."

Sometimes, Toria thought, it's when we reach the point where we can admit we don't know, that we finally figure out the answer.

"I have an idea," she said. Then she took out her cell and speed dialed Isabelle's number.

Ryder sat on the floor beside the waterfall. Mrs. Sid had gone home to change her clothes, and Budge had let the students return to the gym.

The atmosphere remained leaden. But each committee and each student knew what they had to do. They worked, and they would continue to work, until the decision came down that they couldn't.

Maybe he'd gone a little far with the water pistols. He hadn't expected her to get so wet. Or so angry.

And Toria was caught in the middle.

The final shaping of the hardened foam progressed with the help of two new students who'd joined the waterfall group. Anna and Kyle excelled in art, and occasionally worked on pottery. Now they were challenged with something much larger.

"She's been accepted into the Silver Springs College of Art and Design," Brett said, glancing at Anna. "She's a natural."

"So what kind of corsage are you getting her?"

Brett grimaced and looked at Ryder. "I haven't asked

her yet. Not sure how."

Ryder paused. "I think you just have to do it," he said. "However it turns out. Waiting always makes it seem worse than it is."

Like with Toria. How did he ask her if she was sure about marrying Lorimer. And—

He smiled to himself. How did he ask her if he could kiss her again?

A quarter past eleven. Toria and Mrs. Sid still had not returned. Toria's mother and Aunt Glenda had also not returned. And, come to think of it, Isabelle wasn't here either.

"O'Callaghan?"

A voice he recognized. Ryder turned around.

Greg Lorimer, dressed in an expensive pinstriped navy suit, wandered over to the waterfall.

"Lorimer," Ryder said, by way of greeting. *Jerk*, he thought.

"What are you doing here?"

"I'm a volunteer," Ryder told him. "What are you doing here?"

"I'm looking for Victoria. Her mother told me I could find her here. Do you know where she is?"

"No."

"Samantha said she'd be here." Lorimer frowned. "I'll wait." He reached in his suit jacket, pulled out his cell phone and started scanning it, ignoring Ryder.

And then, from behind him, another voice he recognized. "Ryder?"

Catherine.

Surprise hit him, closely followed by resignation. This is what she'd do. She would refuse to believe he was serious about cancelling her wedding.

Terrific.

"Are you a friend of Victoria's?" Lorimer asked her, looking up from his cell phone.

"Victoria? No. I'm Ryder's fiancée. And you are?"

"Greg," he said, preening.

The ass was preening. And Catherine was giving him her megawatt, make-the-customer-happy smile.

"Greg Lorimer," Lorimer said, extending his hand.

"Catherine Forsythe." She shook his hand. And then, "Lorimer," she repeated, frowning, like she knew the name and was searching for it.

"I know that name," she said.

"Ah, you've heard of me." He pocketed the cell phone. "I'm in Real Estate."

"That's it," she answered, smiling. "It was a Real Estate fraud."

Lorimer's face fell like an unstable wall crashing into the dirt.

"Fraud?" Ryder said, turning to the man. The man Toria was supposed to be marrying.

"A misunderstanding."

"My father sat in on the trial," Catherine continued, oblivious to the distress she was causing Lorimer.

He looked more than distressed. He looked . . . nervous. Like he was about to be found out. He straightened his shoulders. "And your father is?"

"Herbert Forsythe. Of Duncan Pansmith."

Catherine always added that designation to her father's name. Titles were important to her.

"But they never had enough to convict," she added, as though they were talking about someone else.

"He can't talk about the case," Lorimer said, trying to rouse some indignation while he backpedaled.

"Of course he can. It's in the public domain," Catherine informed him.

It was a rare day when anyone could tell Catherine anything. She kept talking about it, like other people would talk about the weather. "When my mother mentioned a wedding planner," she said, "by the name of Geraldine Lorimer, my father remembered the name."

As Lorimer squirmed, Ryder eyed him.

"It's none of your business, O'Callaghan."

Suddenly Isabelle was there, standing next to him. Today she was dressed completely in orange—blouse, full skirt, stockings, sandals. She even had an orange bow in her frizzy blonde hair and dangling tiny orange pumpkin earrings.

"That's why his heart blew up," she said.

"Somebody's heart blew up?" Catherine scrunched her nose as she took the image literally.

"Hello, Isabelle," Lorimer said. Disdain etched the words. "And you don't know what you're talking about. As usual."

"I do." Isabelle bounced on the balls of her feet, the pumpkin earrings swinging. "Know what I'm talking about." And then, "People tell me things."

"I'm sure they do," Lorimer said, his voice sounding weary.

"His heart would have blown up anyway," Isabelle said, explaining. "He was a coronary waiting to happen, but that stress didn't help."

"Yes," Lorimer admitted. "The stress of his argument with Victoria."

"No, the stress of his investments gone bad. That mortgage sham he had with you where he lost everything." Isabelle paused, and her earrings kept swaying. "Including his house."

Lorimer paled and stood even straighter. "He had a heart attack," he said, slowly, like Isabelle might be hard of hearing. "He had a heart attack because Victoria got in an argument with him."

"He was ready for a triple bypass," Isabelle answered, equally slowly. "He didn't want to book it. Not until he had Toria married and he owned his house again."

Lorimer's jaw clenched. "He didn't lose the house," he said, his voice singsonging.

"You hold the mortgage."

"Because Victoria's father needed more money. For some debts." Lorimer sounded tired, like he'd said this before. "I helped him by taking over the mortgage." He adjusted his suit jacket, straightening the lapels. "Of course, once we're married, it will be *our* house."

Stunned, Ryder took a step back. He wanted to pinch himself. Was he actually hearing this absurd discussion, while he stood next to an unfinished waterfall in a high school gymnasium? And while his ex-fiancée tapped her toe beside him as she tried to rein in her impatience?

And did Toria know about this?

Because he couldn't wait to tell her. Anything to make her reconsider her decision to marry this jerk.

"Ryder?" Catherine touched his arm. "I thought we could have lunch? Are you ready to go?"

The demanding person he'd spoken to on Friday was gone, replaced with the smiling, charming woman who was attempting to get what she wanted . . . in a different way.

"How did you know I was here?"

"My mother called your mother."

Movement by the gym door alerted him to Toria's arrival. That, and the fact that he seemed to be able to sense when she was around. Mr. Harvey, the head caretaker, accompanied her, pulling a cart loaded with what looked like terry cloth towels.

Mr. Harvey was late if he thought there was still water on the floor. They'd cleaned that up a long time ago. There hadn't been much water anyway.

Then, a ripple of chatter, and someone whooped, "Miss Toria's back!" She came farther into the gym with Mr. Harvey at her side. But—

Oh no. Mrs. Sid had returned. She'd changed out of her wet clothes and, for once, she wasn't wearing her prim and proper skirt and blouse. But he'd never seen her dressed like this—in track pants and running shoes. And an overcoat.

A large overcoat.

She waited by the door. Gradually, the students noticed her, the chatter stopped and silence slammed over the gym.

What was going on?

"Ryder, can we leave now?" Catherine tugged on his sleeve.

Leave? Now? No way.

All at once, Mrs. Sid lunged and advanced into the gym, heading toward him. And the waterfall.

Brett and Brandon and Megan and Anna and Kyle formed a line in front of the structure. Protecting it from her.

They waited . . . and the whole gym waited with them.

Mrs. Sid reached the waterfall. "It's payback time!" she yelled, drawing out a two-barreled super-charged Max D Super Soaker, and opening fire.

Chapter Sixteen

Sitting on overturned milk crates in the supply closet of the art room, Toria and Isabelle regrouped. This was not hiding. This was regrouping, Isabelle had said. But it was more like . . .

Breathing. This was breathing room. From her mother and Greg, and their plans for her life. And breathing room from—

Her heart tightened. Her soul ached. This was breathing room from her feelings for Ryder. "I can't go back in there."

She hadn't known if he would come to the school today. He'd been calling all weekend, never leaving messages, just phoning. Trying to get her to answer her cell.

But she couldn't answer.

The kiss had been her fault. She took full responsibility. She should not have been alone with him in her apartment—not the way she felt about him.

Except, on Friday night, she hadn't really known how she felt about him.

If only she had answered his call on the weekend, she could have got the awkward conversation over with. He would have given her some reason why he could no longer work on the waterfall—

No. He wouldn't have done that. He wouldn't have tiptoed around the issue. Not Ryder. He wouldn't just slip away.

He would *announce* he was leaving.

Oh, what must he think of her? He thought she was getting married. He thought this was her idea of commitment. He thought—

But, a little voice intruded, *he's* getting married. What about him? Surely he played some part in this. Didn't he?

The thought jangled. This was not something Ryder would do. He was getting married in two weeks. He would not kiss another woman.

Except, the little voice persisted, he had. Shouldn't she be angry about that? Shouldn't she at least let him share some of the responsibility?

No, not her. Her middle name was Responsibility and she would shoulder it all. Her own actions, her mother's, her father's.

Anyone's.

The voices argued in her head. And finally, she shook herself back to reality, to the supply closet where Isabelle waited patiently for her to come out of her reverie.

Toria had rehearsed a dozen different excuses for why she'd let him kiss her. Blaming it on the beer was the one she'd given him, knowing it was an excuse.

Knowing there was no excuse.

"I can't go back in there. I can't, Isabelle. It breaks my heart to see him." The thoughts refused to settle. "I don't know how I did this."

"What did you do?" Isabelle asked.

"I fell in love."

A pause. The sound of Isabelle's quick intake of breath. The swish of her orange skirt as she gathered it around her milk crate seat. "That's not so bad, dear."

Of course it was. It was the worst thing that could have happened. "He's engaged to be married, Isabelle."

"But he's not married yet."

"He will be in two weeks." How could she do this to herself?

"You need to get away and think," Isabelle said, like nothing drastic at all was happening.

Overwhelming vulnerability pressed on her from all sides. She'd never wanted to fall in love. She'd wanted to marry someone safe, like Greg.

But she hadn't been able to do it.

"At least I know, absolutely, that I could never marry Greg. Even if that's what my father wanted."

Isabelle adjusted her long skirt again. "Dead men don't care."

The words clunked into place and Toria lifted her head to look at Isabelle.

"Well, even if he were alive," Isabelle said, with a shrug, "he wouldn't care. He'd want you to be happy." Isabelle leaned forward on her crate, took Toria's hand and squeezed it. "And so does your mother—want you to be happy. If she stopped to think about it. She's just used to . . ."

"Me always doing what she wants."

Isabelle nodded, her pumpkin earrings nodding with her. "And now you can do what *you* want."

Isabelle had a way of making everything sound so simple. Toria looked at her friend. "But I don't know what that is." She wanted Ryder, but she couldn't have him. There was nothing more to want. "I don't know what I want."

"Well, if you did know, what would it be?"

Trust Isabelle to put it that way. Toria laughed to herself, and listened to her inner voice. "It would be to go somewhere quiet. And think." And get over this. And move on.

"That's a good idea." Isabelle nodded. "Greg is here. Did you see him in the gym?"

"Yes."

"And your mother will be back at any moment."

Her mother would be on a face-saving mission. Trying to resurrect the doomed wedding. "I know." Toria let go of a long breath.

"And, of course, Ryder is there."

Isabelle hadn't asked about Ryder. Not all weekend.

And Isabelle hadn't explained about Friday night. Hadn't explained why she and Pro and Pro's Aunt Tizzy hadn't come to the apartment. Isabelle had been evasive, saying something about last minute changes of plans.

So now what?

Her mother clung to her wedding fantasy. Greg still expected it to happen. A mortgage hovered in the mix.

And Ryder was getting married.

That's why it had seemed . . . safe, to be around him.

If she could be the person she wanted to be, she'd walk back into the gym and kiss Ryder. Right there. Right in front of everyone.

The man who was getting married.

He wouldn't let her, of course, but that was what she wanted to do. She wanted impossible things.

She sighed wearily. She could face her mother. And even Greg. She'd already done that, several times. But they didn't believe her. They wouldn't believe her until the wedding day arrived—and she didn't.

But Ryder? Could she face him?

Could she stand seeing him again, knowing he was not a possibility in her life?

Why had she found him now? Why had fate introduced them, only to have them never be together?

"Okay, that's a good idea," Isabelle said.

"What is?"

"To get away. To somewhere quiet. And think. Take a little time to put things in perspective."

Déjà vu. Isabelle had used those same words a week ago. "That didn't work last time," Toria said, remembering the aborted trip to Kalispell.

"Yes, it did," Isabelle said, like everything in her—Isabelle's—life was going according to plan. "You decided not to marry Greg."

That was true. "But I can't go to Kalispell now. Aunt Glenda's already here."

At least, the sisters were talking again.

"Go to Pro's cabin." Isabelle gathered a section of her skirt, making little pleats with her fingers.

"*Pro's cabin?*" Sometimes Isabelle conjured up the strangest ideas.

"The cabin where you met Ryder? Can you find it again?"

"Yes, but—"

"Go there. Give yourself some time alone."

"But . . . I'd have to phone Pro. Ask him for the key."

"You don't have to talk to Pro," Isabelle said. "I have a key."

Toria's mind flickered. It felt like she was in a different conversation than the one Isabelle was in. "You have a key to Pro's cabin? How?" On Friday night? When Isabelle was with Pro and Aunt Tizzy?

"Never mind that, dear. Just go. Take my Firebird. You can drive a standard, can't you?"

Toria felt her head nodding, automatically, as Isabelle bounded over details.

"Your suitcase is still in it from the weekend. Just go."

"But . . . Mrs. Sidorsky. Do you think Mrs. Sidorsky will be all right?"

"We have Mrs. Sidorsky on side now. Don't worry about her."

They hadn't stood a chance. Ryder had caught the first blast and everyone on the waterfall committee dripped water. Even Lorimer and Catherine got wet.

But Mrs. Sid was laughing. Never in his whole time at Aberton had he heard her laugh.

Kyle attempted a shot at Mrs. Sid but missed and got Catherine instead. And then when Lorimer tried to be gallant and rescue Catherine, they emptied their water pistols into him.

Ryder didn't think they were trying very hard to hit Mrs. Sid. They just wanted her to think there was a water fight going on.

And that she was winning.

Someone near the gym doors shouted, "Hey! The principal's coming!" And every student in the place grabbed one of Mr. Harvey's towels and mopped up. By the time Budge walked through the doors, the floor was dry.

Silence crowded the gym. The students stood facing the principal, each with a wet towel hidden behind their back. Brett and Brandon kicked the water pistols behind the waterfall.

"Everything all right, Mrs. Sidorsky?"

She'd stashed her gun under her coat again. Some hair from her bun had come loose, but she stood ramrod straight, in her prim and proper way. "Everything's fine, Mr. Burrows."

He stayed by the entrance, surveying the gym. It seemed as if he was trying for a stern expression, but he wasn't getting it quite right. After several long moments, he left, closing the door behind him.

A gym full of war whoops sounded as towels were tossed into the air.

"It was never like this when I went to high school," Catherine said, looking puzzled.

Lorimer flapped his wet suit jacket. "Not for me, either," he said.

· · · · ·

Toria inched onto Wickens Street, careful with the accelerator so she wouldn't rev the engine as she tried to slip away undetected. Not an easy feat in a bright orange classic Firebird.

Two students leaving for lunch saw her as they dashed down the back stairs. They gave her a thumbs up. She waved back.

Heading for Pro's cabin was a good idea. She was *not* running away. Not this time. This time it was like climbing out of a dark hole and crawling into the light. This time was different. A week ago, she was escaping from Greg and her mother. And the china. Now she was giving herself some space.

And maybe that translated to running away from Ryder.

He'd wanted to talk to her about Friday night. And it was her fault, not his. Normally he wouldn't have kissed her. It was the beer, and the circumstances. Ryder would not have—

But, he did.

Stop. She focused on the road as her mind threatened to collapse on itself. Ryder was a blip on the radar of her life. Ryder was a wakeup call. Ryder was an example of how good life could be.

And Ryder was getting married. To someone else.

She needed some time to sort it out, to make peace with it. And she still needed to talk to her mother about the mortgage. There had to be a mistake. Her father would not have risked their security. But right now she couldn't deal with that. She couldn't deal with one more of her mother's ploys. Not now.

When she turned onto Stelmack Boulevard, her cell started ringing and the readout said *Greg.*

She answered. "It's over, Greg. Stop calling me." She

ended the call, dropped the phone on the seat beside her and felt energized. And free.

Don't be so sure of yourself. Her mother's words—the constant message—played in her mind.

She brushed the thought aside. She could do this. She could get on with her life. She'd take a break now, and then she'd come back, refreshed from a few days at the cabin. She'd deal with her mother then. She'd figure out her mother's mortgage. Then.

Now she'd go straight to the cabin. The old brass key dangled on the Firebird's key chain, offering a safe haven only a couple of hours away. An image popped into her head. A row of eleven jars of peaches, lined up on the shelf above the counter.

She couldn't survive on Aunt Tizzy's peaches. She'd pick up bread, cheese, some fruit and some eggs on her way out of town. There was coffee at the cabin. Her suitcase was in the trunk. She didn't need anything else. As she shifted gears, her cell started ringing again. This time the readout said *Mom.*

Foreboding washed over her and her stomach tightened. She'd better answer, or her mother would worry.

"Hello?"

"Victoria? Where are you?"

"What is it, Mom?"

"Victoria," her mother started, seeming hesitant. And then the words came out all at once. "Victoria, if you don't marry Greg, I'll lose the house."

A chill fell over her and she almost drifted into the next lane of traffic. Not a good idea, answering her cell while she was driving.

Trying to concentrate on the road, she said, "Mom, it's a mistake. There can't be a mortgage. Dad would never have—"

"He had to. It's a big mortgage. Over half the value of

the house. I can't make the payments. Greg is waiving the payments."

"But—"

"Greg holds the mortgage . . ." Her mother paused, losing steam.

Toria pressed the phone to her ear, gripping the steering wheel with her other hand. Emptiness and Responsibility circled through her mind.

"I can't talk now, Mom. I have to drive." She ended the call.

A sick feeling threaded its way inside her as she remembered her mother's single-minded focus on the renovations, her strength of purpose in executing this wedding. If there was a mortgage, then there were no savings. And no savings meant her mother was—destitute.

Toria approached the intersection for Dottridge Avenue. Turn right and head for the mountains. Turn left and—

That was the way to her apartment.

The decision crashed into place. She turned left onto Dottridge Avenue, making the detour to Collins Street and Dalhousie Towers.

Catherine Margaret Forsythe stood next to Ryder in the middle of the gym. Apparently, these students were decorating for their upcoming Grad Dance. And Ryder, for some reason, had decided to help them. Throughout the room, the buzz of conversation mixed with the sounds of hammering, the clank of tables and chairs being moved, and occasional bursts of laughter. Assorted flowering plants filled the air with their perfume, mixing with the smell of freshly sawed wood. Groups of students busied themselves with everything from setting up chairs and hanging murals to arranging paving stones and . . . painting rocks?

What a mess.

But it wasn't her problem. She was here to deal with Ryder. He'd always struck her as levelheaded. Difficult to manage, yes, but not impossible. Now he was going through some kind of crisis. He hadn't meant a thing he'd said on Friday night. Trying to cancel the wedding was his way of coping.

He'd visited his father, recently, by the looks of things. And where his father was concerned, it was hard for Ryder to make decisions.

Unlike her. She made decisions all day long. The BD Builders home buyers relied on her. She told them what matched and what increased resale value. She rescued them from their own stupidity. All the time. Because she knew what worked and they didn't. They needed her.

And so did Ryder.

Determination filled her as she welcomed this new challenge. She'd get Ryder on board with the wedding planner, and then she'd manage the other distractions in his life so he could concentrate on his wedding.

First, he needed to settle the partnership deal with Jimmy Bondeau.

A trace of irritation popped into her head. The stupid man wasn't returning her calls. She'd have to deal with him.

But right now, Ryder needed to sign the partnership agreement, get a schedule worked out and register for his remaining courses at the University. That would keep his father happy.

But do you think Ryder could figure that out on his own?

No. Not him. He was here, volunteering at a high school when he had a wedding to prepare for.

Men.

"You need some lunch, Ryder. We'll leave now. Would you like to go to Kipling's or La Petite Maison?"

"I don't have time to eat."

He knelt on the floor and studied some drawings. A boy dressed in a black T-shirt, black jeans and black runners shifted the drawings as he explained something. A girl with long, shiny brown hair and bib overalls sat cross-legged next to them. She was arguing with the boy about colors. Ryder penciled something on one of the drawings and then stood up.

Catherine touched his arm. "There's someone I want you to meet. She's a wedding planner. She'll—"

"Isabelle?"

Catherine looked over her shoulder and saw the old, frizzy-haired lady dressed in the horrible orange outfit. The woman had disappeared right after the water fight and now she was peeking in the gym door. She took one look at Ryder, and quickly left again. But he'd seen her, and now he was heading straight toward her.

What was that all about?

Catherine humphed and followed. This was annoying, but maybe she would have to do something with these people. Ryder wanted to be involved here and she could help him. After all, decorating was her job.

"If these decorations are that important to you, I can help." She rushed to keep up with him and almost collided with a potted fig tree.

"Yes," he said. "You can."

His eyes glowed with purpose. She'd never seen him looking so—emotional? "It's your father, isn't it?"

"I've got to catch her."

"If you would finish your degree, he would—"

"I don't need a degree." He stopped walking and looked at her, like he was finally seeing her. "But I've got three years done. I suppose I could finish it." He pulled his cell from his belt and walked away from her. "I have to make a call."

"If you signed that partnership agreement with Jimmy," she said, hurrying to keep up, "you'd have more time."

"I am."

"What?"

"I'm taking him on as a partner."

What? "That's—" That's not what she'd expected. She'd been prepared for more arguments but this problem had somehow solved itself. "That's wonderful," she said. "Then you can finish your degree. Your father will be so pleased."

"My father doesn't care," Ryder said, as he exited the gym. "Do you have a number for a florist?"

A florist? *Oh good.* She followed him out of the gym, flipping through her cell directory. "There's one near here." She gave him the number.

He punched it in as he walked. "Isabelle! I see you!"

Standing next to a bulletin board, the old lady was talking to a young girl in a painting smock. The sadly neglected bulletin board displayed a banner, *Diplomacy starts with You,* along with some football team photos and some straggling essays. The hallway smelled like chalk dust and textbooks.

This Isabelle woman didn't seem to be going anywhere for the moment, so Ryder came to a halt. Catherine put away her cell and pondered her next move.

"Do me a favor?" Ryder held his cell in his hand, in the middle of making his call to the florist.

"Of course."

"Help them with the rock colors. So it looks like a rainbow waterfall."

A rainbow waterfall? It had to be Ryder's father, clouding his judgment. Ryder didn't care about waterfalls, or rainbows.

But maybe painting a waterfall would be fun? A change of pace from picking out tiles and paint chips and trim. "I can do that," she said. "Then we can talk about the wedding planner?"

"Wedding planner," Ryder repeated, sounding distracted. "Get her to come to the gym." He had the phone to his ear, waiting for the call to go through. "She can help with the rocks," and then speaking into the phone, "I need some roses sent to the gym at Aberton High School. Right away." He rushed past her, heading toward the old lady in the orange outfit.

Roses. The image settled in her mind. Warmth flooded over her, and she felt herself smiling. He was easier to manage than she'd thought. Or, she was better at managing him than she'd thought. She inhaled, thinking of the roses.

She liked roses. Maybe she'd forgive him.

But first she'd call Geraldine to join her here, and then she'd find out who was in charge of the painting.

He caught up with Isabelle again. This time, one of the library volunteers had distracted her but as soon as she saw him, she headed down the hall.

Terrific.

"Don't go anywhere, Isabelle. I'll follow you—and I need to make this call."

"Yes, sir. Roses. How many?"

Isabelle paused, looked back at him, and then moved into a workroom. He followed her. No students in here, only tables littered with paint cans, unglazed clay pots and stacks of colored paper.

"A dozen," he said. "Make that two dozen."

"Color?"

"A dozen red. A dozen white. Mix them up." Unity, he thought. And mending bridges.

"And the card?"

Right. The card. He thought a moment. "Way to go, Mrs. Sid."

"S. I. D.?"

"Right. Don't bother signing it. She'll know who they're from." He gave his credit card info and the school address, and turned off the phone.

Isabelle sat on a high stool by one of the tables, tapping a stack of paper into place. And then it hit him.

It hadn't bothered him when Catherine had brought up his degree—his non-degree. Not one bit. He didn't need it. He was all right without the piece of paper. But, he shrugged, he had three years done, he could finish the fourth, if he wanted to.

The degree and the partnership agreement lined up in his mind. Maybe he'd been dragging his feet because of Catherine's pressure. Was that it?

He'd think about it later. The loose ends in his life were solving themselves, getting neatly tied off. Except for one.

"You know where she is," he said. "Tell me."

"Why should I?" Isabelle sat up straight on her stool, holding her chin high.

"Because I'm in love with her, that's why."

"Well," Isabelle said, a big grin on her face. "It's about time you figured that out."

As Toria raced up the stairs, careful of her recently recovered ankle, her cell started ringing.

Greg. Again. She paused on the landing of the third floor and answered the phone. "What!"

"We need to talk."

"I don't want to talk." She pulled the door that led into the hall. "Why is there a mortgage? I don't want to marry you!"

"Victoria, you're distraught. You don't know what you're saying. You can't just throw this away."

Did he mean the house? She hurried to her apartment. "Throw what away?"

"Us," he said, simply.

She reached her apartment and jammed the key in the lock, still holding the phone to her ear. "Greg, do you love me?"

"Of course I do, darling. How could you doubt that?"

The apartment door opened. She was inside, slamming the door behind her and leaning against it.

But then the buzzer in front of her sounded, making her jump. She stared at the little beige box next to the kitchen wall.

"Let me in," Greg said, on the phone, his voice soothing. Not really soothing. Pseudo soothing. Fake. The buzzer sounded again.

Was he in the lobby? "You're at my apartment?"

"We need to talk, darling."

Damn. How did he get here so fast? He must have left the school right after she had.

Just talk to him about the mortgage, the voice inside her head argued. They needed to talk about the mortgage. Her mother needed her.

"Victoria?"

The buzzer sounded again.

Her hand hovered above the button on the intercom.

"Buzz me in, darling."

He could help her mother. She could help her mother. Her whole body tensed. She could marry him, and . . .

And get on with her staid, boring, unloving life.

"I'm not letting you in," she told the phone.

She heard a distant buzzer, over the phone connection, coming from the lobby.

"Your neighbor already has."

No!

"I don't want you making a scene," Greg continued in his unbelievably calm voice. "I'm going to knock once and I expect you to open the door."

She spun around, stared at her door and turned the dead bolt. What if—Was he—"Greg? Are you marrying me because of the mortgage?"

"Of course not."

"But Mom said—"

"Yes, I hold the mortgage. It's just a technicality. I would have told you, but I didn't want you to worry. Don't even think about—" Greg stopped talking. And then, "What the—"

Toria could hear him swearing into the phone.

"Victoria?" His tone had changed.

"I'm here," she said.

"The damn elevator is stuck. The door won't open."

Saved! She turned off her cell, ran into her bedroom and grabbed the wedding dress. Then she peeked out her door, heard Greg shouting from the elevator, and took the stairs.

Chapter Seventeen

Standing in the cabin's little bedroom, she twirled around in a circle.

She wore the ivory couture gown, the Emilie Celeste original, with its French lace capped sleeves, its embroidered bodice with the delicate Swarovski Crystal detail, and the full skirt of satin and organza. Her father had wanted her to have it. Her mother had loved it on sight. And so, without even a boyfriend on the horizon, they had brought the dress home from Paris.

Her mother had promised a professional seamstress for the alterations, but they didn't need any. The dress fit her perfectly.

What they'd done was outrageous, now that she thought about it. They'd picked out her wedding dress without any input from her. She should have felt offended.

But she hadn't. Instead, she'd fallen in love with the soft, flowing, romantic style of the princess dress called *the Madeleine*. She'd thanked them for it, hung it in her closet and gone about her life, thinking that someday she would meet him, her prince.

As she walked into the kitchen, she listened to the swish of satin and organza. The sun, now low in the sky, streamed through the leaded panes of glass. To allow more light into the tiny room, she bunched the yellow checked, lace-trimmed curtains to the ends of the rod. And then she concentrated on making a sandwich.

Her bag of groceries sat on the counter next to the propane stove. The shelves above the counter displayed a selection of china bowls. She chose a white one and turned it over. Wedgwood, England 1759, Countryware.

If she ever chose a pattern of her own, it could be this one.

She opened the carton of eggs, took out two, and cracked them into the bowl. Then she retrieved a fork from the tumble of cutlery in the blue plastic box and mixed the eggs, being careful not to splash on her dress. She could have looked for an apron, but an apron over a wedding dress just didn't seem right.

Taking a deep breath, she considered the last few days. It had all happened so quickly. She'd fallen in love. This is what it was like. This feeling of connection and completeness. And ache.

Nothing could come of it but, somehow, the peace of having found it—found what love is—spread into her being. The wonder of how good life could be bloomed in her mind. And the guilt she'd felt about her father lessened, and faded.

She could let go of her father. And her mother. She could live her life, not borrowing *their* dreams and goals.

She flicked the lighter on the propane stove, set the frying pan on the burner and added a dollop of butter.

She'd tricked herself into thinking Ryder was safe. Safe, because he was getting married. She'd taken pains to make sure he thought *she* was getting married. So she'd been doubly safe. But it hadn't worked.

She'd fallen in love. *How had that happened?*

She tipped the scrambled eggs into the hot pan. The yellow mixture rippled with bubbles as the liquid swirled.

Letting the eggs cook, she pulled the loaf of French bread from its paper wrapper, sliced two pieces and placed them on a tin plate. Then she picked up the dill pickle jar and gripped the lid, straining until it popped.

Life would go on. If Greg really held the mortgage, then maybe it was for the best. Her mother could let go of the house that had chained her to Calgary, and finally return to her family in Kalispell and make peace.

Toria spread butter over the slices of bread and cut a pickle into thin strips. The eggs were almost done. Pushing them aside with the spatula, she put the buttered bread face down in the pan to warm.

Her mother would be all right. Her mother was strong and capable.

And Greg? Toria felt no regret about leaving him in the elevator. Well, she smiled, maybe a tinge of regret. But someone would have heard him and called the building super. And the elevator would finally get fixed.

She assembled her egg and pickle sandwich on the tin plate. Tin plates and china. Strange. Pro and his Aunt Tizzy had an interesting cabin.

Taking her sandwich, she stepped outside, feeling the breeze in her hair and the ripple of the light wind as it sifted over the wedding dress.

She followed the brick path to the patio behind the cabin, then continued down the dirt path that led to the fire ring. As she walked between the trees, it was like she was walking down the aisle carrying her tin plate, instead of a bouquet.

The natural grasses next to the path feathered against her dress. Sitting down on one of the six wooden benches that surrounded the fire pit, she set the plate on her lap and took a bite of the sandwich.

A tiny chickadee landed on top of the fire pit's stack of wood, paused for a second and then disappeared down the slope, following the path that led to the lake below.

Toria took a second bite of the sandwich and felt her appetite returning as she tasted the tang of the dill pickles with the warm eggs. Some bread crumbs dropped onto the organza-covered satin. She brushed them away, letting her hand pause a moment on the smooth fabric. Then she rested her palm on the rough wood of the bench. The smell of the fresh washed air, after the recent rains, mingled with the scent of the dry wood stacked in the fire pit.

She'd light the fire later tonight.

A magpie landed on the bench opposite her. He tilted his head, bowing. His long tail feathers looked like a tuxedo coat.

She rose to her feet and curtsied to him. He bent his head again, and then he lifted up into the sky. She could hear him talking to the other magpies, hear them flitting in the trees all around the cabin. Far off a pair of crows argued. Beside her, a squirrel scampered up a lodgepole pine.

She sat on the bench again and finished her sandwich supper. Then she stood, shook the crumbs from her skirt and twirled around, closing her eyes and savoring the sound of the rustling satin. Letting herself feel it for one moment longer.

It was time to go inside and get changed. The light was dimming. She could barely see the lake at the bottom of the hill. It had been turquoise in the daytime. Now it shone silver, reflecting the moonlight.

She'd hung on to the threads of her old life for long enough—afraid to disappoint her mother, afraid to disappoint her father. But somewhere between her father's death and the rushed wedding plans, she'd realized it was not the life she wanted.

She would not disappoint herself.

She'd come here to forget Ryder. That's what she'd told Isabelle. But thoughts of him pushed through the restraints of her mind. She couldn't stop thinking about him. She remembered his eyes when he challenged her, his laughter when he stopped being serious, his battle with Mrs. Sid. His never letting anyone push him around.

Her complete opposite. And yet, he had never pushed her. He'd accepted her.

And he'd kissed her.

The birds chattered overhead, a twig fell to the ground, the wind sighed through the trees, and one thing became more certain.

Ryder O'Callaghan was going to be hard to forget.

The sun had set half an hour ago. The days were growing longer. He'd caught a glimpse of the moon as he'd left the highway. The first quarter, clearly visible on the cloudless night.

Two weeks into June and most of the details of his life had fallen into place.

He parked next to Isabelle's Firebird in the graveled area at the head of the path to the cabin. The crooked old sign, *Road's Inn*, had fallen on the ground. Probably during last week's storm. He'd fix it, later.

The night was almost still. A slight breeze stirred in the trees, making its own music. For the hundredth time, he felt the doubt enter his mind. Taking a deep conscious breath, he realized how much he needed to talk to her—needed to convince her to take a chance on him.

High in the western sky, the waxing moon lit the way as he walked down the curving path to Pro's cabin. He smelled the wood fire. She'd already lit the stove.

As he paused in front of the porch, uncertainty beat at him. In the next few moments, he had to say the right thing. But what was the right thing?

As he opened the door and stepped inside the cabin, a flash of panic grabbed him. The cold stove stood empty. No one was here. But the lantern was burning on the table.

She had to be nearby. *At the fire pit?*

He rushed out the door and, a moment later, he saw her. The tension left his body and he realized he'd been bracing.

She stood in front of the blazing fire wearing the same jeans and jean jacket she'd worn earlier today at the high school. And she held something, bunched in her arms. Something big and white.

And fluffy.

Her wedding dress? What was she doing?

In the next instant, she fanned out the dress and settled it over the flames. A puff of smoke billowed up—the dress almost smothered the fire—and then a fierce bright burning escaped out of the smoke.

Calmness hit him like a bolt and he felt his shoulders drop, felt himself grinning like an idiot. She'd definitely cancelled her wedding.

He moved closer, coming behind her, resisting the urge to reach out and touch her. "Kind of drastic, don't you think?"

She spun around. "You're here."

He wanted to pull her into his arms, but he clamped down on the impulse and forced himself to wait. "Most people just return it to the store."

"The store is in Paris. And why did you kiss me?"

No dancing around the issue. Fine with him. "That wasn't a kiss."

"Yes, it—"

He touched his finger to her chin, lifting it. Then he leaned down and touched his lips to hers. A light touch, a feather touch, an asking.

She stood still, like she was holding her breath.

He kissed her again, longer this time, deeper, feeling her arms come around him, feeling her body sway into his, feeling his arms gathering her up. Finally, he raised his head, still holding her, like she might disappear if he let her go.

"*That* was a kiss," he said.

The fire crackled behind her. "But—"

"I'm not getting married."

"You're not?"

"And you're not either." At least, he thought, not to Lorimer.

A tiny smile hinted at the edges of her lips. "How did you know?"

He looked over her shoulder, at the fire, sparking and crackling. "You're burning your wedding dress?"

She smiled then. That beautiful smile he loved to see. "No one wanted to believe I'd cancelled," she said. "And . . . I needed to get rid of it anyway."

"Because?"

"Because of what it represented," she said. "It was their dream. My parents' dream. Not mine."

Borrowed dreams, he thought. Someone else telling you what your life should be. He'd been caught in the same trap.

Joy cascaded over him. Joy so strong he didn't think he'd ever felt joy before. His arms looped around her as he stood there, holding her. "I'm glad you burned it."

"Yeah?" She looked up at him, a question in her eyes.

"We'll get a new one," he said.

"We'll—uh—"

"We'll take our time. When you're ready, we'll talk about it."

A shudder went through him as the realization hit him and he hugged her tighter. She could have married someone else. He could have lost her.

And then he knew it couldn't have happened. "You haven't been marrying him, not since the night I found you out here."

"Not since then," she confirmed. "You were right." She

brushed her hands over his chest. "I was running away."

Lucky for him. "Are you running away now?"

"No," she said. "I'm regrouping."

He kissed her again. A light quick kiss. "I like kissing you. I could get used to it."

She kissed him back, pulling his head down, claiming his lips, holding onto him. After several long moments, she released him. "How did you know I was here?"

He smiled, and he felt like laughing. "Do you need to ask?" He touched his forehead to hers.

"Isabelle?"

"Aunt Tizzy," he said.

"Aunt Tizzy? I need to meet her."

"You already have."

She frowned. "I have?"

"Aunt Tizzy," he paused, "is Pro's Aunt . . . Izzy."

She looked confused.

"Aunt Isabelle. Aunt Tizzy," he said. "They're one and the same."

"You mean . . ."

"Yeah. She set up this whole thing, with some help from Pro. Except you weren't supposed to end up in the ditch that night. You were just supposed to find the cabin."

Toria's face lit up.

"She knew you wouldn't be happy marrying Lorimer. And Pro had figured out I wasn't in love with Catherine." He tightened his arm around her . . . touched her chin. "I'm in love with you." He kissed her again.

"And I'm in love with you," she answered.

The moon shone, the stars winked and the music in the pines sang over the cabin and the surrounding hills. The fire burned, erasing every last shred of satin and borrowed dreams. And sitting next to the fire, with her in his lap, Ryder held on to Toria and she held on to him, for a long, long time.

If you enjoyed spending time with Ryder and Toria
in ON THE WAY TO A WEDDING
would you please consider leaving a short review on
Amazon?

Next in the *Something Old, Something New* series is
Logan's story—

Wedding Bell Blues

The lady goes to the highest bidder!

Alone and new to the city, with all her possessions in a single suitcase, Krista MacKenzie stumbles into a gentleman's function—given a little shove from an earthbound fairy godmother disguised as her new best friend.

Logan Nicholas, CEO of Peregrine Oil & Gas, thinks that auctioning off escorts—even if only for dinner and a drink—is a poor idea for the fundraiser. He'll make a donation for the cause, but he does not intend to bid. Not until he sees the stunning brunette come across the stage. Suddenly his competitive spirit takes over and he's desperate to win her.

But what happens when the clock strikes midnight? Technically, he's still got a girlfriend—who's pushing him to set a date. He's not ready for a wedding, and he's sure not ready for the irrational feelings he's having for this lady of the night.

About the Author

I've been telling stories since I was a child. Then, it was stories about fairies and mermaids, told to my sisters when we were supposed to be sleeping. As a teenager, I wrote long diary entries and I wrote short pieces of fiction—that no one but me ever read.

Don't get me wrong, I was not a total recluse. I did lots of "real world" things too. I became a nurse, I spent time with friends, I traveled a lot. And I always wrote.

Sometimes after a difficult day at work, I would re-create the day in a story that had a better ending. That's still what I do—I create stories with happy, hopeful endings.

"Suzanne Stengl has a lovely voice with a subtle hint of humor."
—*A.M. Westerling, author of A Knight for Love*

"Suzanne Stengl's descriptions and characters are really memorable."
—*Amy Jo Fleming, author of Death at Bandit Creek*

Find more books by Suzanne Stengl at
www.SuzanneStengl.com

Made in the USA
Columbia, SC
14 July 2023